My Brother's Keeper
(The Veronian Archives)

BY DANIEL L WELCH

MY BROTHER'S KEEPER

DEDICATION

To reality television.
Because of it, I read and write a lot more.

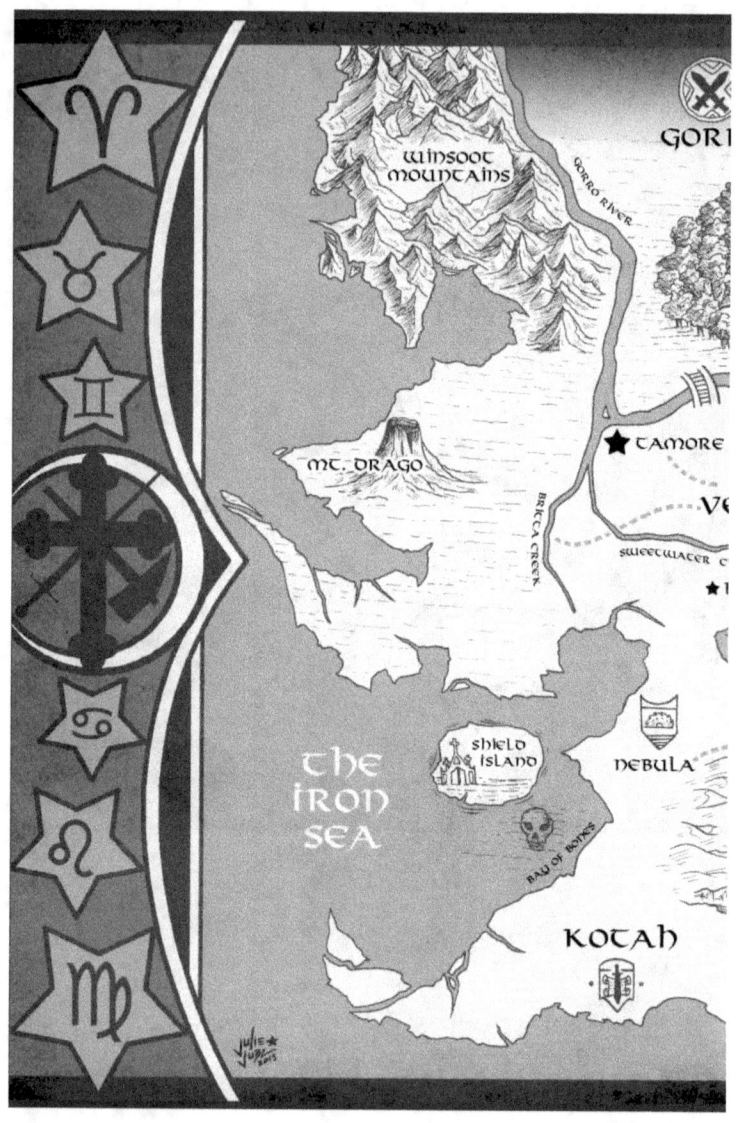

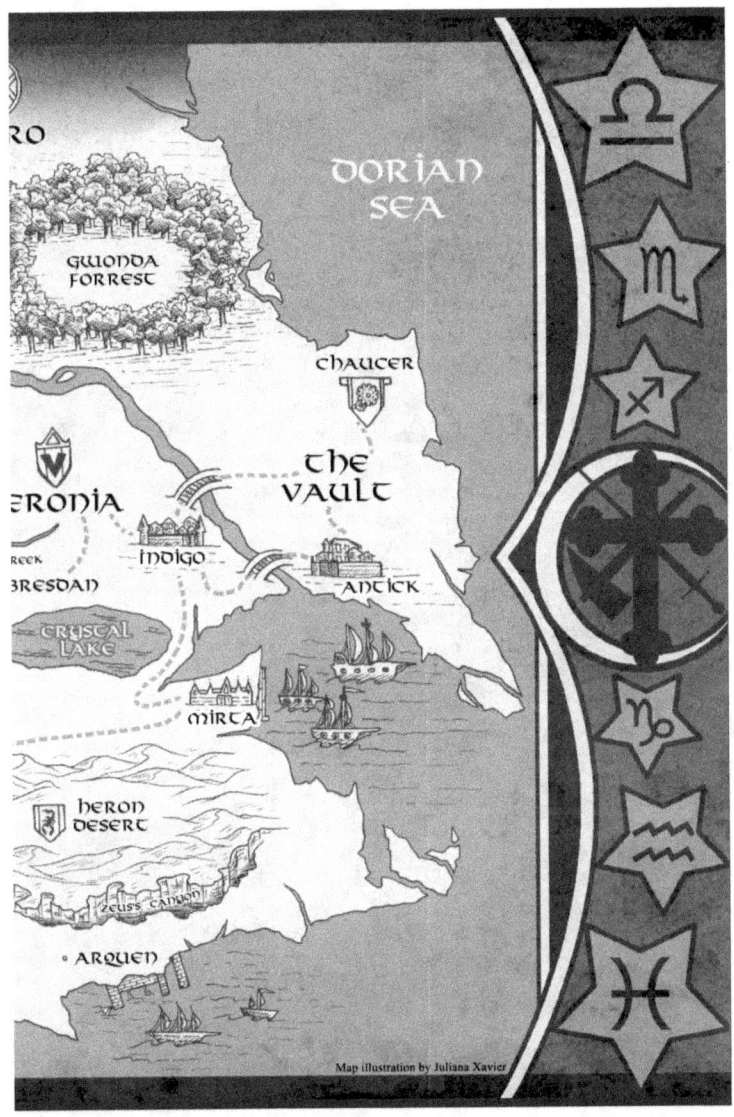

Map illustration by Juliana Xavier

CONTENTS

ACKNOWLEDGMENTS

I'd like to personally thank the following people for their contributions to my inspiration, knowledge, and other help in creating this book:

Pun, for putting up with my passion for reading and writing, even though you read only for instructional purposes.

My editor, Michelle Josette, for her eagle-eyed attention to detail and steadfast encouragement.

Juliana Xavier, for all the artwork you've done for the series and your determination to get it just right.

My family, who I don't tell nearly enough how much I love them, how much they mean to me, or the lengths I'm prepared to go for them.

And to the readers. That's you there holding this book. Thank you.

CHAPTER

1

"I'll be fine—stop worrying about me. I'm just going to do a little reconnaissance. Shouldn't take more than a few hours."

Kano fastened the last of the stubborn buttons on his ash-grey cloak, a gift from Killian to each of the Zodans. The twelve stars and their signs embroidered in gold ran vertically down the front, the zodiac wheel on the back. "I'm tired of playing catch-up with the Prothica, and we have to find Nicolai."

He'd had his reservations about Killian, the Heron

nobleman turned ally, who'd invited the Zodans to his humble abode. It was the closest alliance they had near Zeus's Canyon, and they needed to regroup after spending so much time in the desert.

After the Tribesmen, Ansuk, and Trechon rode north to the Gwonda Forest, Kano, Ambrose, Liz, Brielle, and a handful of minor namers had spent the last few weeks at Killian's sprawling villa, situated on Heron's northern region. It turned out that Killian was much more connected than Kano had given him credit for. The noblemen answered only to Pharaoh, Tompea, and his vizier, Ra. Neither of which had the urge to send their minions snooping around Killian's estate lest they be struck down by the starborn's wrath and their souls bound to the sorcerer's will for eternity. At least that was the Heron belief. To them, the starborn were magi best left to their own accord, and the quicker they left the desert the better.

Liz's auburn hair cascaded down the shoulders of her matching grey cloak. Borin and his twin brother had given Liz their worst, but she'd managed to put the latter in the dirt, and Borin out of commission at least for a while. Despite Ansuke's healing, Liz looked gaunt and pale. Kano imagined it would take her another two weeks to nourish back to health, but they could afford to dally in Heron no longer and they both knew it.

"If you aren't back by noon, we're heading north to find the Tribesmen," Liz said, peering out the second-story balcony to conceal her concern. Below, Brielle and Ambrose soaked up the morning sun, splashing around in one of Killian's marble-lined swimming pools.

Kano reached up to lean his stubby arms against the balcony rail next to her. A lavish garden surrounded the pool, where a breeze carried the scent of honeysuckles. A gust of wind swept the perennial paradise through his lungs one last time and tussled Liz's hair. He fought the urge to reach out and hold her hand. It wasn't easy.

"Listen Liz," he said, craning his head to look up at her. "If anything happens to either of us, I just want you to know. I want you to know that—"

"Save it Kano," she replied. His heart chilled in his chest, and he felt even smaller than before. With a glint in her eyes, her gentle hand reached out to cup his face. Using her thumb she traced his scarred cheek. "I know what you want to say, I'm just not ready to hear it yet."

For a time, the two of them stood there looking at one another. When her eyes began to dry, Kano's lit up as he named his star. There one second, gone the next, leaving Liz alone with her anxious imagination.

She turned back to the balcony, clutching it with both hands, peering out into the cloudless sky. "I love you too."

***

It didn't take long for Kano to spot the bone-armored

Vrattas at the rear of the tribal war band. The Netches looked almost bored as they sat around, fiddling with weapons and gear. The Antucha-whahs busied themselves with song. One of the strangest dance routines Kano had ever seen, and likely able to interrupt his sleep for the rest of his life as they mimed cutting throats and painted their faces with animal blood. Chief Ansuke and his son Trechon sat atop their mounts, both canvassing the area for the starborn they sensed nearby.

Kano was a familiar sight to most of the Tribesmen. Many had taken to calling him the Black Raven behind his back, on account of his coming and going without leaving a trace, and always bearing news. Most of the Netches ignored his half presence altogether as he padded through the Chamood clearing, the hem of his cloak tracing the ground. Others cocked their heads in wonder of the new bright pink scar that lined his cheek from mouth to ear. A constant reminder of Hadrian's death and Borin's sharp metal stars.

"Glad I caught you two before you left," Kano said. "I stopped by Mirta and Bresdan on the way but didn't sense a thing. I imagine Nicolai will likely be in the middle of Tamore's action."

"Nice dress," Ansuke mused, adjusting a bone and feather armband around his bicep. "We'll find out soon enough. Have Liz and the others started riding north yet?"

"I'm sure Liz had them mounted up and riding as soon as I 'ported to Mirta."

Amidst the tribal gathering of painted faces, a domestic scene of sorts began heating up. Kano couldn't hear much of the commotion from where he stood— short as he was, even he couldn't miss the blond-headed paleskin giving the verbal judo to an Antucha-whah warrior, as Chief Dretchel himself fought to separate the two.

"What's that all about, and who's the blonde?" Kano asked on his tip-toes.

"That would be Page, the sister of Leo Rosewood. And that's Chief Dretchel's son Nico she has by the throat." Ansuke chuckled. "She's up in arms about not being allowed to join the war band headed for Tamore. It's well known that women stay behind."

"Well known, but she hardheaded, just like her brother," Trechon added.

With a few choice words, Page detached herself from Chief Dretchel's restraint. She hurried off fuming, cheeks flushed red as her painted lips. She tossed her braided locks over the shoulder of her buckskin blouse and carved a path towards the Vrattas.

"Women aren't warriors?" Page hissed. She turned her scorn to Ansuke. "You expect me to sit in this forest gathering berries while my brother needs help too?"

Ansuke's brow furrowed and he let out a defeated sigh. "You know it's tribal tradition for women to only take up arms during an invasion. Even I am not above tradition." The chief adjusted his saber-toothed helm.

Page planted her heels and crossed her arms over

her chest. "You would rather have me ride to Tamore on my own, like a vagabond?"

"That's not what he meant," Trechon replied.

"Kano, allow me to introduce you to Lady Rosewood," Ansuke said.

Page turned to Kano. "You can't honestly expect me to be oblivious to everything around me. I know who and what he is. The namer of Sadalsuud, are you not?"

Kano's mouth hung open, but he regained his wits quick enough to salvage the poor first impression. "Pleased to meet you—Lady Page, isn't it?"

Ignoring him, she turned back to Ansuke. "If you won't let me come with you, I'll make it to Tamore on my own." Page stormed off before the chief could reiterate his disdain.

The Antucha-whahs resumed their singing and dancing. Tribal elders continued applying war paint to each of the warriors. Each of the kwatina-wielding Tribesmen sat cross-legged while their faces were painted on. Those who had already been painted danced in circles around them, chanting in their native language.

"Follow her, Trechon," Ansuke ordered. "Make sure she doesn't get herself killed. Take as many or as few men as you must and keep her alive." Trechon nodded and rode off after her.

Ansuke turned to Kano. "So what's your plan?" he asked.

"I'll take a peek at Tamore real fast and see if I can't find Nicolai," Kano responded, watching them go. "With any luck I can gather a little intelligence that might assist your army before you get to Tamore. Should be back well before you guys make it to the Netche Bridge, then I'll 'port back to Heron to get Liz and the others. We should be back to Tamore in a few days."

Ansuke leaned over, placing his hand on Kano's shoulder. Beneath the chief's saber-toothed helm, his eyes came aglow and Kano's limbs started to tingle from the chief's healing touch. "Find me if you need another charge. And be careful, friend."

***

In Tamore, a lone rider trotted carefully forward, mindfully avoiding a gauntlet of caltrops and sinkholes as he went. Leo couldn't think of any diplomatic offer the Kimans might present to avoid sacking the last of Veronia's resistance. The envoy was a farce and they all knew it.

"How many swords you reckon?" Wade asked, spitting a mouthful of tobacco down the inner wall. A half mile outside their outer wall, the Reds flexed their muscle, spreading their ranks out far and wide.

"Ten thousand would be my guess," Juan answered, all business. "A conservative one at that."

"Very conservative," Natalie added. She sat atop

the ten-foot inner wall, feet dangling over the edge. "Closer to fifteen thousand I'd say. I guess we should feel flattered outnumbered thirty-sum to one."

"More water," Edger bellowed below where dozens of men scurried about with sloshing buckets. The inner wall that Leo and the others stood upon was built to last. The outer was less impressive but a formidable obstacle nonetheless. Edger staged barrels full of tar between the walls to greet the Kimans with a burning batch. He had the walls soaked with water to prevent them from catching flame.

Bruce scowled over the wall. "Shall we leave him waiting till he figures it out, or tell him to go piss off?"

"Might I make a suggestion?" Abigail asked. "We've got dozens of children within our walls. If it comes to blows, so be it, but perhaps they'll show mercy to our children and elderly."

Leo didn't like the way she mentioned mercy, as if getting their asses kicked was a foregone conclusion. Perhaps it was and he just hadn't come to terms with it yet. He pulled his gauntleted forearm out of the shield straps and slung it over his back. His breastplate, courtesy of the Drago Smiths, was polished to a shine. At its center a miniature shield, the Veronian V, etched within. Leo loathed the way it gleamed and couldn't wait to scuff it up a bit.

He stole a glance at Marie. She rocked heel to heel, nervously regarding the Red Army ranks. A white-knuckle grip on her bow, the safety of her two children no doubt at the forefront of her mind. "Juan, go see what you can do."

"Right," he replied, clanking off.

The lot of them had their eyes sewn to Juan's back as the two wooden gates were rolled aside to let him pass. Nestin, the mayor of Tamore, adjusted his collar but had nothing to share. For better or death, he, like the others, had cast their lot with Leo and there was no turning back now.

The lone envoy had more grey hair than brown and wore a red tunic over light armor and chainmail but carried no weapons, far as Juan could tell. The rider eased carefully out of his mount and tied the reins to a spiked barrier. "Well met, Juan. We had a running wager on who Leo would send to speak for him. You just won me two crowns so we're off to a great start." Juan didn't share the envoy's delight. "Name's Saul Harrington. If I look uncomfortable in this shit, it's because I am. I'm no soldier. I serve as King Xalvador's foreman in Chaucer. Be that as it may, I don't want to take an arrow in the ass either."

"Fair enough," Juan replied unable to replicate Saul's enthusiasm. "Have we met before?"

"I don't think I've had the pleasure. Granted, I wish it were under different circumstances. I was well acquainted with your father. Lord take his bones," Saul added. "For what it's worth, it's a colder world without him. I'm told he and your mother were poisoned, perhaps they felt no pain. My sincerest condolences,

Juan."

Juan shifted uncomfortably. He'd heard nothing of their poisoning before, just that they were found dead in their chambers when the Reds sacked the Capitol. "We've all lost more than I care to admit. I can't imagine either side coming out on top the way things are now. Just a giant shit sandwich and we've all got to take our bites."

"Indeed. I remember your father saying the same thing during the Norse invasion. My how things have changed."

"So where do we stand?" Juan asked. "I can't imagine you donned all that plate mail to reminisce with me about my father."

"Right you are. The Kiman Empire's demands are simple, Juan." Saul stepped forward and Juan held his ground. "Bend your knees."

Bending the knee didn't seem like an unreasonable request given the circumstances. The Red Army had them surrounded, outnumbered, and if push came to shove, it would only take a couple days at most to tear down the walls and put all of Tamore to the sword.

Try as he might, Juan couldn't hold the stare. "You know we can't."

"Oh but you can," Saul added. "You want to already, I can see it in your eyes. Whether you do it on your own accord or by the sword, it's up to you. Look around you, Juan. Have a care for the lives of those behind your walls. This is a battle you cannot win."

Just then, Juan had an urge to put his foot on Saul's neck until his eyes popped out of their sockets. Leo would have already done so, which is why Juan was sent in the first place. "I've heard your demands, now hear ours."

Saul's lips parted into a mocking smile. "Doesn't appear that Tamore is in any position to make demands from where I stand, but I suppose I'll hear them out. A kindness to your father, if you will."

"We've got women, children, and elderly within our walls that mean no harm to either side. Provide them sanctuary, or at least let them come out and leave unmolested."

"Hmm..." Saul's hand cupped his chin in amused reflection. "How about this. Keep your women, children, and the elderly. Send Leo—his blood will suffice for now. Do that, and your women and children may leave unmolested. Surely one man's life isn't worth a whole village."

The notion struck a nerve in Juan. He stepped forward, towering over Saul. "Are you drunk? You know damn good and well this isn't just about Leo. He'd surely bend the knee if that were the case. This is a collision of kingdoms and religion. Even if Leo dies today, you'll be back tomorrow, and the next day, until there's nothing left of Veronia. Force-feeding us your blasphemous Book of Light. That cannot be."

If Saul were even the slightest bit uncomfortable by Juan's towering presence, he didn't show it. "There's nothing left of Veronia now." Saul's wild grin spread as he gave some, stepping back to spread his arms. "Take a look around you, Juan. All of that red you see is here to stay. Veronia is nothing but rubble and muck."

Juan targeted the bastard with his malevolent eyes then pointed a knife hand into the space between them. "Are you going to let our women and children out or not?" he demanded.

Leo and the others shifted in anticipation atop the inner wall, the movement catching Saul's eye. "Not without Leo leading them out. We're going in circles now. It's his neck and your knees, or all of you will die together. Not one of you shall be buried. Your bodies will be left to the crows and whatever mangy animals have a taste for rotting flesh. Clear enough?"

"To hell with your demands," Juan spat. "Stay as far back from the fight as you can, but I'll still find you. And when I do you shall speak no more. On that I swear an oath." Juan's knife hand had turned into a shaking fist and Saul took his cue to leave.

Juan sneered at Saul's back as the envoy climbed atop his mount then spurred the horse back around so he could stare down at Juan. "Oh and one more thing. His smile was treacherous. "Your parents died terrified, holding one another in a corner of their own chambers accompanied by a set of Heron vipers. The fire took them shortly after. Such a terrible loss. I sure do miss those snakes."

By the time Juan lunged for Saul, the envoy had

already dug his heels into his mount; it galloped off across the field. Juan's hate-filled contempt boiled over. He could almost feel his parents' blood crying out to him, pointing their fingers towards their murderer. And Juan would be their blade of vengeance.

***

"Again!" Abaddon shouted, kicking one of the candles out of the pentagram. "No one leaves this blasted island till I get what we came for." Jewel watched Abaddon stomp up the dais and into the Guardian Chapel. The Kiman soldiers had withdrawn to the dock on the west side of the island where they drank wine and made as little noise as possible to avoid agitating Abaddon any further.

Berinon slithered off from behind his Book of Light to replace the broken candles and Lyle crouched within the pentagram just as frustrated but much less animated than Abaddon. Jewel had no idea what the Kotian had been trying to summon throughout the night, but as the sun began to rise, the three failed attempts appeared to be taking a visible toll on the conjurer. Lyle plopped down and rested the weight of the orb on his knee.

Gusts of wind blew sand into Jewel's sleep-deprived vision. He angled his face away from the wind and forced his heavy lids back open, massaging with manacled hands the weariness from his baggy eyes.

Another chain clinked and rattled as a figure stirred to life beside him. Jewel looked to his right where Bishop Michael, or Nicolai as Abaddon had called him, rose from a deep sleep. After seeing the sorcery that Nicolai possessed nearly besting Abaddon and Lyle by himself, it was no surprise that Nicolai would be more heavily restrained.

After the previous night's battle, Abaddon and Lyle worked fast to take advantage of Nicolai's unconscious state by binding his hands and feet in heavy iron chains, and throwing him into what appeared to be a man-sized birdcage.

"Argh," Nicolai moaned, stirring to life. His hands reached to his head but were stopped well short as the chain tightened. He opened his eyes and took in his new surroundings.

"So that's what death looks like, huh?" Jewel mocked, although he didn't find the jest any more comical than Nicolai did.

Nicolai tugged at his chains. "The nerve of those two idiots," he muttered.

He didn't have to mention their names. Abaddon and Lyle were the same ones who'd ordered Jewel bound as well, however Jewel couldn't help but feel a little slighted to see the lack of effort they'd put into his own restraints. Simple manacled wrists and feet with one chain running through iron rings on each set so that he could be controlled by the tug of the chain.

The cage was only tall enough for Nicolai to rise to

a crouch and when he did, he clamped his hands on the bars of his cage. "Blast!" he seethed.

"What is it?" Jewel asked. Some questions you wish you could take back.

With both hands still clutching the bars, Nicolai's head sank to his chest. "Dragonglass."

Jewel had always been a quick study. He cocked his head, examining Nicolai's cage. He hadn't noticed before, just suspected the cage was iron. An iron cage would be strong enough to bind any man, but not a sorcery so it seemed. The dragonglass must be resistant to Nicolai's sorcery.

Whereas Nicolai showed clergy-level restraint before, he curbed his anger with a few choice four-letter words in quick succession. When he'd finished, Nicolai absent-handedly began rubbing the finger where his ring used to be. He leaned his back to the cage and quickly regained his composure. Jewel watched Nicolai staring through the bars at the pentagram where Lyle and Berinon were discussing the proper placement of the candles. Nicolai shook his head. "We're in trouble now."

It was overcast, but Jewel suspected it was nearing midday. Dark clouds rolled towards the island from the west, threatening what looked like heavy rain. Par for the course as far as Jewel could tell. If you're going to be chained outdoors, why would you expect anything less than inclement weather?

Jewel took a cautionary look around before

scooting closer to Nicolai's cage. Only Agnen, the Gorronian general turned Kiman commander, appeared to be within earshot. His meaty hands held the end of Jewel's chain. Agnen sat elbows on knees and looked somewhere between sleep and terminal boredom.

"You've got some explaining to do, brother." Jewel gestured towards Nicolai's star-patterned hands. "How about you start with those tattoos."

Nicolai brushed debris from his sleeveless robe and ran a dirtied hand through his ivory-colored hair. "I'm starborn," he said after a moment's reflection. "A magi if the term suits you. Same as Abaddon and Lyle there, however we possess different celestial abilities if you will. It's a long story, Jewel."

"You're a sorcerer." The word felt odd as it rolled out of Jewel's mouth.

"We've been called many things during our long history. Until recently, the starborn have left as little a footprint as possible. We've got one purpose really, and that's to protect people from what the Watchers left behind when they were bound in middle earth." He peered at Lyle's pentagram. "I fear Abaddon is about to change that though."

"Long history? The Watchers haven't walked the earth in thousands of years." When Nicolai didn't answer, Jewel shook his head and raised his shackled writs, frowning over them. "And what's this celestial power you speak of?"

"The Mozzaroth isn't easily explained, brother, and

even harder to understand in one sitting."

Jewel pressed on. "Well it looks like we've got time. Try me."

"There are twelve major starborn. Each of which are capable of harnessing celestial energy which translates into power and ability that is derived from the twelve major constellations—or zodiacs as many people call them now."

"And just what are those unique abilities?" Jewel hadn't forgotten the light in Nicolai's eyes as he waged war against Lyle and Abaddon. Their sorcery was blinding, their power divine. Jewel's heart quickened at the memory.

Nicolai's cold stare made Jewel uneasy. "I'm the namer of Spica, the Virgo star of wisdom. Lyle over there for example." Nicolai gestured to the Kotian starborn. "Lyle is the namer of Pollux, the Gemini star of conjuring. Abaddon possesses the most dangerous ability of us all. He's the namer of Antares, the Scorpio star of shape-shifting."

"Shape-shifting, huh?" Jewel thought aloud. "Animals and people alike?"

"Indeed." Nicolai turned sour at the thought. "Imagine your most trusted friends and family. Go on now," Nicolai urged, pausing so Jewel could get a visual.

The first person that came to mind was his brother Leo. Sharp around the edges, but loyal and trustworthy as they come. At least to those he cared about. He thought of Father Frances next. *God rest his soul.* And then to Brother Malachi, Sister Isabelle. *Speaking of sisters, I wonder how Page is doing?* Then he winced. Page should have been his second thought, if not first.

"Now that you've got them in mind"—Nicolai leaned into the cage, head pressed between two of the bars—"imagine none of them being as they appear. Rather they are a wolf in sheep's clothing. Imagine this conversation between you and I, not between you and I at all, but between you and Abaddon."

Nicolai clenched his teeth at the thought, and Jewel wondered if Nicolai had fallen prey to such a scheme before.

"It can be the most vile of betrayals ever imagined." Nicolai leaned back into his prison.

"Vile indeed." The longer Jewel reflected on such a power, the more his stomach turned. He decided to change the subject. "What about that ring? The one Abaddon took from you. What's the significance of it?"

"That ring was worn by King Solomon himself. A gift from the heavens, presented by the Angel Gabriel. It gives the ringbearer clarity to find answers to the incomprehensible. I was entrusted to protect that ring and the ringbearer long ago. And after Solomon's death I retrieved it." Nicolai waved a hand in the air. "Soon enough, Abaddon will figure out why he's unable to conjure the Giants of Orion."

Jewel felt the slack in his chain draw tight, then loosen. When he turned, Agnen wasn't as deep in his own thoughts as he'd first appeared. "We've got an eavesdropper."

"I know." Nicolai regarded Agnen. "He that has ears to hear, let him hear."

Startled to his feet, Agnen dropped hold of Jewel's chain and Nicolai began to laugh. "Fecking witch bastard!" the Gorronian commander cursed, reaching down to regain his grip on the chain.

Jewel couldn't contain himself and let out a laugh of his own, which came to a screeching halt when Agnen tugged the chain so hard Jewel sprawled out onto the ground.

Inside his cage, Nicolai rolled with laughter as Jewel picked himself up off the ground with what little dignity remained. If Jewel wasn't mistaken, a wry smile spread across the battlefield of Agnen's face before the Gorronian sat back down.

***

After the tribal war band finished pilfering for supplies, available horses in Chamood were few and far between. It had been two hours since the Tribesmen left for Tamore and panic was starting to set in as Page padded south on foot towards Netche looking for a mount of her own. When the Netche village began to take shape through the trees, Page glided to a stop, hunched over with hands resting on her knees, laboring to catch her breath.

Her sudden stop quieted the forest floor just long enough for Page to hear a second set of feet trampling through the forest behind her. She cast her eyes to the noise only to find a canary goldfinch serenading the woods with its unfettered song. Chest still heaving, she took a deep breath and held it long enough to seek out the bearings of her pursuer.

One of Nico or Chief Dretchel's babysitters, she presumed. "Show yourself," Page demanded, still searching for the source. The silence stretched on and Page put her back to the bark.

The pluck of a bowstring and the twang of an arrow releasing caught her attention. The arrow's tip entered her shoulder from the back and pierced through to the front. She sucked in air through clenched teeth. Before the pain could set in, shock left her staring stupidly at the tip of an arrow glistening with her blood. Another twang sent a second arrow speeding towards her from behind. This one just shy of the mark, it ricocheted off the tree at her back and showered the forest floor with birch bark.

Clasping her wounded shoulder with her left hand, Page took off running, wincing as the arrow jarred back and forth. Another twang, and an arrow flew overheard. She risked a glance back and saw two Tribesmen chasing after her, both of them notching arrows on the run. She ducked and dodged branches, fallen trees, and the rugged forest floor but her already-exasperated legs began to burn fiercely, leaving her with only one other option—she'd have to hide should she have any chance of escape. An overturned redwood would have to do. She dove over it, careful not to land on the arrow that had taken residence in her shoulder.

The two pursuers slowed to a creep like hunters on a game trail. Page wedged herself between the tree and the earth, straining once more to control her breathing and still her pounding heart. The huntsmen exchanged words. Page failed to decipher their meaning but guessed the dialect to be Netchen the way they rolled their r's.

It wasn't hard for them to follow Page's reckless trail to the fallen tree. The two men separated around the ends of the redwood. When they appeared again, both had daggers in hand.

She'd no hope to escape now and no weapons to defend herself. "It's me, you imbeciles. Page Rosewood, betrothed to Nico, son of Chief Dretchel," she plead in Antucha-whahn.

"Precisely who we've been sent to kill," one of them responded just a few feet away from her now. He lowered his dagger ready for the work. When he lunged forward a flash of light hit the Tribesman center mass, launching him backwards over the fallen tree. The second man nervously scanned the forest.

A bone-armored Vratta stalked forward with a star on his left hand. He loosed a second burst of starfire that took the remaining huntsman's head clean off at the shoulders. The headless corpse fell on top of Page.

With one good hand, she cursed and clawed it aside.

"Trechon!" Page exclaimed. The Vrattan enveloped her in a warm embrace.

His shaky hands came to rest on her shoulders, assessing the arrow's damage. "Was nearly too late. You okay?"

The pain seared through her arm and numbed her fingers but she fought the urge to state the obvious. "What the hell just happened?"

"Wish I knew," Trechon replied. He knelt down to regard the dead. "They took care not to be recognized, but I know a Chamood reject when I see one, dead or alive."

"Chamood reject? How can you be sure?"

"Neither of these two have any tribal markings or dress indicators that would distinguish them amongst the tribes. Tribesmen take great pride in whichever clan they belong to, and would no doubt bear some rendering. These two bear no marks. Only a desperate Chamood reject would take such a risk as to kill you. Perhaps they were promised admission into one of the tribes. But to which tribe I cannot say."

Page regarded her shoulder then turned her bloody hand palm up. "You mean to tell me you were following me the whole time and waited till they used me as target practice before twinging your little fingers to kill them?" She shook her head incredulously. "I pray you didn't overexert yourself, Trechon. God forbid you break a sweat on my behalf."

Trechon shrugged. "If you weren't running like a wounded deer, I would have had time to spot them. To their credit, it was a well-planned trap. Another, oh how you say...ejaculator that they're Chamood rejects. All the Tribesmen of fighting age are headed to battle in Tamore."

Page stifled a laugh despite the pain in her shoulder. "Indicator. You mean indicator, you dunce. Now what can you do about this arrow? We have a lot of ground to cover if you're going to follow me to Tamore, and it's well past time you and Chief Ansuke told me the secret behind naming one of those stars."

CHAPTER

2

Leo watched the lone envoy speed off and knew immediately that their meeting hadn't gone well. Juan stomped through the outer wall with clenched fists and murder in his eyes. Leo had known Juan long enough to read his moods—something must have gone terribly wrong for him to have lost his cool.

The captain of the Widow Makers was red-faced by the time he passed through the gate of the inner wall. Even from atop the wall, Leo could see the veins bulging in his neck. "Best ready your wall defenders,

Edger," Juan bellowed.

"Aye." The hunter-turned-Castellan ran a dirty hand through his long forked beard, took a savory swig of red, and limped off.

As Juan climbed the ladder, Leo could hear his murderous mutterings. By the time Juan made it atop the inner wall, he was good and pissed. Leo and the others gave him a wide berth. "War it is, and no sanctuary for the women and children." Juan spat the words like a sour taste in his mouth. "There was nothing I could have said to sway the course. I'm sorry, Marie."

Marie stared over the walls into the sea of Red soldiers, clutching her bow like a defiant mast in a raging storm. Since she joined the Tamore resistance, she'd made a massive transformation. When Leo first saw her, she had flowing hair and a mother's gentleness about her. But like a fine piece of metal work, life had rusted all the soft edges from her, and she'd cut her locks down to finger-length. Abigail took her by the shoulders whispering condolences in her ear. Marie snarled and shook her off. She descended the wall in search of her children.

Wade pushed past Abigail and followed after Marie.

Bruce turned the chew in his mouth over with his tongue. He spit the results over the wall in an oily stream of discontent. "Vile bastards, every one of them. When a man loses empathy for women and children he's no man at all."

"We're all doomed," Abigail declared.

Nestin placed a reassuring hand over his wife's shoulder. "They offered no terms, only war?"

From what Leo had learned of men in his twenty-five years of experience, it's unnatural for a decent man to lie. When a person of conscious chooses to deviate from the truth, even by the slightest of margins, they cannot help but leave tells of their deception. Tiny micro-expressions of the face, touching of the nose or mouth, looking up and to the left, the list goes on. A lifetime of friendship and Leo could tell easily enough that Juan was being uncharacteristically deceptive. Something in the way Juan kept looking at everyone's hairline rather than meet their eyes. A few inches off the mark was subtle enough to go undetected, but Leo wasn't fooled.

Leo sat atop the railing with his back to the battlefield. His right hand busily traced the runes on his shield, but Juan's stumbling demeanor had his undivided attention. *What are you hiding, brother?*

"No terms that were acceptable," Juan replied.

"I didn't ask what your opinion of acceptable was, I asked what their terms were." Panic had apparently given Nestin more balls than caution, and Juan seemed in no mood to be challenged by a soft-handed politician, no matter how decent Nestin had been to them.

"Either we all take the knee while you and your

wife stretch your necks on the chopping block, or we all fall by the sword," Juan answered coldly. "How do those terms suit you, Mayor?"

When the town in which you govern is under siege and not likely to survive, Juan's address was more slight than respect. A jab that didn't miss the quick-witted Nestin who brooded over the results. His skin stretched taut over the flexing muscles in his jaw. "We died the day we took you fools in."

"You ungrateful bastard." Bruce lunged for Nestin's neck. His left paw hit pay dirt, carrying Juan, Natalie, and Abigail to the ground with them in a tangled mess of fisted blows and deadly curses.

Leo lowered his golden shield and plowed through tangled limbs until Bruce and Nestin were separated. "Enough." He stood between them, his glare like daggers cutting into all of them. "Take a look around us, dummies." He swept the battlefield with his shield, nearly knocking Mandy off the wall behind him. "You think arguing amongst ourselves is going to turn the Reds away? I think not." He turned to Nestin. "You made your decision, decisions have consequences."

"Damn politicians," Bruce fumed, shaking free of Juan and Natalie's restraining hands. "Always running their mouths recklessly till it's time to knuckle up."

Nestin rubbed his neck where Bruce's stranglehold started to redden and welt. Below the inner wall, a gathering had assembled to watch the confrontation atop the wall.

"Save it, Bruce. If I had to prioritize our problems, I'd put babbling politicians on the bottom and anyone with a weapon on top, wouldn't you?" Leo shrugged. "No offense, Nestin."

The mayor of Tamore caught himself in the middle of brushing dirt off his hand-spun fustian cotton surcoat. "Perhaps I pushed too hard...pried too much. My apologies, Captain Jaminez." Nestin couldn't bring himself to address Bruce directly. "And to the rest of you as well. I would miss the bond between my head and neck, but I'd gladly sever the ties if I could save lives. But my wife's life is a price I'm not willing to pay. Their terms are uncouth. They ask far too much, and Captain Jaminez was right in refusing them."

Clouds began to cluster in the darkening sky. Nightfall was fast approaching and a little rain would only improve their conditions. At least then they wouldn't have to worry about getting smoked out by fire.

"Abigail, I want you to round up the women and children and get them out of here tonight," Leo said. "It will be dark soon, and by morning the Reds will have maneuvered around Britta Creek to surround us. Take them across the Gorro River, but be quiet about it. Wade will go as well and lead you to Gwonda. Seek out the Antucha-whah tribe and ask for Tekrano. He should provide sanctuary until this battle is over. Tell him it will be the last favor I ask."

"And what makes you think I want to leave?"

Abigail crossed her pale arms. "You think I want all your lives on my conscious the rest of my days when it's my head they want? At what point is enough, Leo? When all of us are dead? Just what are we fighting for here?"

She had a point, but Leo didn't have time to preserve the integrity of her conscious. If he had to sleep in a bed of mourning, blanketed by regrets, so would she. "Take a look around you, Abigail. The brave men and women gathered here within these walls are all that's left of Veronia as it were. This battle is bigger than all of us. If we can hold out long enough, perhaps more Veronians will grow tired of their oppressors and join or fight. A small revolt can breed revolution, I know it can. But regardless of the outcome, when my time to die comes, I'll rest at ease knowing I didn't even bend when they sought to break me."

Below the wall a mother cradled a fussing toddler in her arms, swaying to soothe his unrest. Leo pointed her out from the crowd. "You'll do it for her and him and for the rest of them. We don't have the luxury of multiple choices right now, Abigail."

The mother who cradled the toddler stared at Leo with frightened eyes. His armor wilted against her desperate gaze; the hair on his neck stood on end.

Abigail's defiance began to crumble and she let out a defeated sigh. "And what if Wade doesn't want to go with us? Who will lead us to the Tribesmen and speak on your behalf? I doubt they will heed the plea of a women such as I."

Not far from the mother and toddler, Marie knelt clutching her own two children. Wade stood behind her, a reassuring hand on her shoulder. "Oh, I imagine Wade will find it in him to do his duty."

Abigail went off about her business, Nestin close on her heels. Whether he'd go with her or stay behind, Leo couldn't tell. Didn't much care anymore.

"Now the rest of you, get ready for battle. If they come before dark we must be ready. Natalie, get the outer wall covered with enough arrows to keep them honest and then some. Bruce, take a few of your Swords of Bane to assure Wade, Abigail, and the others make it across the Gorro, but be stealth about it."

Bruce moved about his business like seasoned veterans do.

"A word," Leo said, catching Juan by an armored elbow as he tried to shuffle past.

Juan stepped carefully over a machicolation so as not to fall below and clasped his hands on the rail gazing out upon the battlefield to avoid Leo's stare. Whatever happened during the envoy's visit still weighed heavily on Juan's mind and Leo wanted to find out what it was.

"What were the terms they offered? And don't give me the same bullshit you told the others. It was my head they wanted was it not?"

"Your head, my head, all our heads, it doesn't

feckin' matter much does it Leo? By the end of the week, we'll be buried side by side in a shallow grave if we're lucky, and worse besides if we're not."

Lucky indeed. More than likely, Leo's head would end up on a spike, the centerpiece of some Kiman Hall no doubt. His body probably paraded around the countryside and left for the crows to feast upon. He pictured his head propped next to King Lawrence's. The former king having one last laugh at Leo's expense. "They wanted my head, and the rest of you on bending knees, didn't they?"

Juan turned from the balcony with watery brown eyes. "Their envoy. That bastard Saul Harrington was the one that killed my parents." The name rolled off his tongue with a contempt Leo hadn't known Juan to possess. "Said they trapped them in their chambers with a pair of Heron snakes. The Reds could have sent any other man to give us their feckin' terms but they sent the murderer of my parents to twist the knife in my back instead. I'll have my vengeance or die trying."

Leo could only wonder how the fate of Jaminez and his wife Louralis had transpired. Now that he knew, he wished he'd been left wondering. "Aye, brother. Vengeance or death, whichever comes first, I'll be your shoulderman."

In the distance a battle horn rang out. The sound of its wailing call was enough to steal Leo's breath. A mass of soldiers began to break from the Kiman formation. "Here they come."

***

Their carriage swayed back and forth as the horses clapped along the sand-covered road that led them past Heron's north region and into the desert. Killian wouldn't hear of them traveling in anything less than his two best carriages. Liz, Brielle, and Ambrose rode ahead in the first, while five minor Zodans occupied the second.

The carriages were made of watertight ship-wood with polished brass accents depicting the Heron Scorpion, pulled by the biggest horses Liz had ever seen. They were driven by four of Killian's person guards, two to a carriage. Silk screens covered the windows to prevent the irksome sand from molesting its passengers, but the Heron desert would not be deterred.

Brielle's boot met Ambrose's shin and his log-sawing snore ceased instantly. He startled back to life dabbing drool from the corners of his mouth.

"How long have I been out?" he asked, shifting the curtain aside. Sun filled the carriage and Ambrose blinked in rapid succession to adjust his eyes.

Liz peered out her own window opposite his. Nothing but barren desert. "We're just outside Heron's north region. With any luck we'll make it to Nebula by morning."

"By morning?" Ambrose looked sidelong at Liz, struggling to do the math in his head. "I thought Nebula was at best a two-day ride from the north district?"

"Need I remind you we have friends in trouble?" Liz replied in her least condescending tone. "We'll be traveling through the night so take your naps if you must. Silently though or you'll be riding atop the carriage. With any luck, we'll be in Tamore in three or four days."

Ambrose straightened in his seat. "And we've arrangements for fresh horses?"

"Our time spent in Heron was not a holiday, you know. Kano has taken the liberty of staging fresh horses along the way for us. Every thirty miles or so. At least that was the plan. We'll find out soon enough."

"And when will Master Kano be rejoining us?" Brielle asked.

Ambrose perked up awaiting the response. Fact was, Kano was supposed to have been back by now, and his absence suggested something amiss.

"As fast as Kano can teleport, he has a lot of preparations to make if we're to arrive in Tamore on schedule," Liz said. "And there's still the matter of Nicolai missing. Kano's probably busy trying to locate his whereabouts while we trek north."

Only the churning wagon wheels and clapping of iron-shoed hooves over rock and sand extinguished the silence that pursued. Nicolai's absence was troubling to say the least and the Prothica's brazen violation of the accords suggested it was no fluke. None knew that better than Liz. She arched her back, still thankful for Ansuke's healing touch. She wondered if Nicolai too lie near death with one of Borin's stars in his back.

"It would appear that our first checkpoint is up ahead," one of the Heron drivers bellowed from the front of the carriage. Codoc or Oberian, Liz couldn't say for sure. Codoc was darker-skinned than his service brother Oberian but their voices were just as similar as their physical attributes.

Liz shielded her eyes from the sun and peered out the window once more. In the distance four horses with white sheets draped over their backs stood tied beneath a cluster of leafless trees. A boy no taller than Kano waded through a knee-deep watering hole waving his hands as if the convoy would mistake him for a mirage and ride past.

The carriages rolled to a stop. One of the drivers, Codoc perhaps, wore a brown pleated skirt, brass wrist guards, and chest plate with a black and gold striped headdress. He offered his hand to assist Liz out of the carriage. Brielle was next out, thanking the drivers for their chivalry. It appeared their chivalry had bounds, though, as Ambrose was ignored completely and hopped from the carriage on his own.

Neatly stacked baskets were laid beneath a shade tree. Liz's stomach rumbled at the sight and smell of the buffalo-milk-based Gibna Domiati, which shared a plate with blocks of sesame paste *halawa*, olive-oiled bread, and Heronian red wine to wash it down.

"Well met, kind sir." Liz extended her hand to the boy. He was golden-skinned, dark-haired, and a miniature version of the drivers aside from the bronze armor.

His coffee-colored eyes widened at the sight of Liz's star-patterned hands. "I'm honored to be at your service," the lad responded bowing low, yet careful not to take his eyes off her hands. Whether he was fascinated with Liz's starburns or scared beyond belief, she couldn't tell.

"Nonsense," Liz insisted, turning her hand palm up to reveal a golden crown. "You didn't see us and we were never here." She smiled graciously when he nodded his understanding and Liz dropped the coin into his hand.

Codoc and Oberian dutifully began exchanging the horses and loading the refreshments. The minor Zodans separated themselves just out of pissing distance from one another and began showering the earth.

Ambrose plucked some olive bread from a basket as Codoc passed by. He'd eaten nearly half of it in one bite and only stopped chewing when he felt Liz and Brielle's disapproving glares. "What? Was this food not meant to be eaten?" he asked, swallowing a lump of bread.

The minors who'd just put their pricks away took to the bread baskets as well. Liz's eyes flashed with disdain but she chose her words carefully. "Just how many Zodans are there in this world, Ambrose?"

Ambrose sucked his cheek and shook his head, already aware of where Liz was going with this.

"Including minors...twenty-five or so I'd imagine."

"Probably less than that," Liz clipped in response. "But assuming there are twenty-five of us, and bearing in mind that you are a second-generation starborn no less. How is it that you forget our kind has been scorned into obscurity and yet you pay no mind to the privilege bestowed upon us to bear our celestial markings with pride and honor?" Liz regarded the minors with glowing eyes. "And the next time I see your little peckers will be the last time you need stand to piss."

"Forgive my lapse in, erm...etiquette?" Ambrose replied.

"You're one of the twelve, damnit," Liz spat between clenched teeth. "Never let anyone see you hunger or thirst. Never let anyone see you in doubt or disbelief of anything. And that goes for the rest of you too."

Ambrose straightened and lifted his chin. "My apologies, it won't happen again."

"And what do we say about apologies, Brielle?" Liz asked her former protégé.

"Apologies are a consequence of bad decisions. Bury them before they bury you."

Ambrose nodded his understanding.

"The carriages are ready when you are, Lady Liz," Codoc said.

"Thank you, kind sir. We'll be with you in just a few moments. There's been a slight change of plans. Please break your fast and eat your fill in the meantime.

This might take a few minutes."

"As you wish." Codoc climbed atop the carriage next to Oberian and the two began to break bread.

"Change of plans?" Brielle asked.

"That's what I said," Liz continued. "We can't sit idle awaiting direction from Master Kano." Liz gestured for the minors to come closer.

"This is what we know," she continued. "Tamore has become the battleground for two very different wars. Nicolai is most likely embedded with the rest of the Priest's Council who left Mirta for Tamore. We've also heard reports that the Prothica are embedded within the Kiman Army. The second carriage is dragging ass and slowing us down. It's also past time that Brielle and Ambrose here selected their first protégés."

Liz regarded the five minor Zodans, each dressed in matching grey cloaks, save the vertical stars on front reserved only for the majors. "Since the first twelve children of the stars were marked, it has been a time-honored tradition that each major tutor a protégé of their choosing so the art of naming is never lost."

Blue and white matter danced in the palm of her hand and her eyes came aglow. Without warning, Liz scorched the ground before them, leaving the desert sand charred black. "You five, on your knees!" she ordered.

The minors scrambled over one another but made it to their knees where Liz had scorched the sand. Behind them, the Heron lad and the drivers fought to restrain the startled horses from bolting off.

"Two of you will soon have the privilege of apprenticeship under the direct tutelage of our newest members of the twelve." Liz walked between the rank of minor Zodans as they each knelt side by side. "Brielle, namer of Aldebaran, bearer of telepathy. And Ambrose the namer of Hamal, bearer of invisibility. You have five very capable minor namers before you. If you find one worthy of selection, you shall name them now." Liz regarded the minors once more. "If any of you are cold of the foot, speak up now."

The minors exchanged glances but none of them refused the opportunity.

"Excellent." Liz clapped each of them on the shoulder as she walked down the line. She rounded the end and moved out front to stand between Brielle and Ambrose. Both of whom were in deep reflection, assessing the minors who knelt before them. Once Ambrose and Brielle named a protégé, it was like a marriage that couldn't be annulled. Only death broke the time-honored apprenticeship. Or advancement of the protégé into the twelve, mind you.

"Ambrose, you joined the twelve before Brielle, therefore you have first selection. Choose wisely, but remember we are pressed for time. You should have been pondering the decision as soon as you joined the twelve."

Now it was Ambrose who paced in front of the

minors. Out of the five, Liz found only three of them with any real aptness for the art.

Weston was a fat-ass lack of potential. He spent more time bellyaching over hunger pangs than learning anything the majors tried teaching him. Every group has that ten percent of underachievers and Weston was their bannerman.

Roland was driven to stand out above the rest. So much so that he took every opportunity to smear his peers in doing so. He was pompous and proud, even more so than any nobleman Liz had ever met, but he'd recently learned to manipulate starfire which could be useful in a fight. That was if Liz didn't strangle him before they reached Tamore.

Diddo was a Heronian that Kano had shown a liking to. He seldom spoke but when he did, it was in his native tongue which neither Brielle nor Ambrose was fluent in.

Otis was pretty well-rounded as far as Liz could tell. He knew astrology better than the rest and had a decent grasp of starfire. He was also a devout social introvert and esteemed awkward conversationalist.

Without hesitation Ambrose selected Lamar. He was Kotian-born and, like Roland, had a knack for starfire manipulation. Lamar was once a well-known mercenary leader who left his country to feed the appetite of his growing intellect and was recruited by Hadrian who'd discovered him at the University in Mirta.

Lamar rose, fighting the urge to smile and failing miserably, but found his way to Ambrose's side nonetheless.

Brielle stepped forward to regard the remaining four. She paced back and forth, hesitating towards Diddo, but Liz suspected the language barrier was too great. She paused behind Roland.

"If I choose you, Roland, what is it that others might learn from you?"

"I'm glad you asked. I'd love nothing more than for others to learn from my failures so they don't repeat my own mistakes. One might also learn from my many achievements. I'm a servant of and for the Mozzaroth."

Liz stilled her twitching hands. If Brielle chose him, they'd both be walking to Tamore.

"And what about you, Otis? What might others learn from you?"

Otis looked left and right to make sure it was he that Brielle called upon. He opened his mouth to speak and closed it just as quickly. He stared ahead for what seemed to be ages, till the corners of his mouth twisted into a smile.

"Answer her, you fool," Roland exclaimed.

"I already did."

Roland turned to look at Brielle and found her eyes aglow. "Oh shit," he said, palming his face.

"What is it?" Weston asked. He was late on everything except mealtime.

"Oh nothing, Weston." Brielle smiled. "I choose

Otis."

Roland stood fuming in defiance. "I thought using your ability on starborn was strictly forbidden, save in combat. I was deceived."

Roland had a point. If Liz had told Brielle once, she'd told her a thousand times that her ability would get her into trouble if she abused it. Now she'd caused a hot mess.

"Oh relax, Roland. Now you'll have another mistake you can teach others to avoid," Lamar chided.

"You sonofabitch," Roland cursed, lunging for Lamar.

To Liz's surprise it was Ambrose who stepped forward wrapping his arms around Roland's waist to pull him away.

"Enough!" Liz ordered.

Roland shook Ambrose off. He adjusted his collar and flattened his cloak, careful not to break the deadly stare he fixed upon Lamar.

"Need I remind you that Nicolai, Kano, and I are still without protégés, Roland?" Liz suggested. She didn't expect Roland to be selected in any case, but perhaps it eased the sting of rejection at least for a time.

Roland appeared to consider the prospect. Nicolai was their leader, and Kano in his absence. Becoming either of their protégés would fast-track Roland to a leadership position. Diddo didn't seem to care either way, but Weston appeared just as interested as Roland.

"But I have another task in mind at the present,"

Liz continued. "I need the three of you to travel ahead of us. Go eastward around Crystal Lake into Gwonda and find Ansuke. We have no way of knowing that Kano's made it to him, and without Ansuke, we may have no chance of finding Nicolai and/or defeating the Prothica if it comes to blows. If the Prothica attack again, they're likely to snare Ansuke and Trechon."

"And where are we to find horses for such a journey?" Roland asked.

"You'll have to be resourceful. I didn't say it would be easy. You must also avoid raiders, Kiman soldiers, and perhaps even the Prothica along the way." Liz pulled a leather-bound coin purse from her cloak and tossed it to Roland. "This should be more than enough to acquire food and horses along the way."

Roland shook the coin purse, pleased with its weight. "We'll find Ansuke and meet you in Tamore then. If Kano returns with word, don't bother sending him to look for us. We'll rendezvous soon enough."

***

All that remained of the former Capitol of Veronia had been reduced to a hastily constructed stronghold. It's inner and outer walls comprised of wooden logs, the tips of which were carved into spikes, the trunks buried in a trench for added strength and stability. Natalie's archers stood atop the inner wall ready to fell the Kiman militiamen as they approached. If any were lucky to climb over top, or break through the outer wall, they would run into a slew of tree branches and debris, strung out between the walls to hinder the siege of the inner wall.

"The Red Garden," Edger had called it. "Once they get tangled in there we'll have ourselves a proper bloodbath. 'Less of course the Kimans got a company of beavers in the mix, they'll get stuck like flies in a spider's web."

Leo had to give Edger credit. It was a decent plan and with all the log-cutting to build the walls, the branches had to go somewhere after all.

"That's a lot of men," Mandy thought aloud. She clutched her shield in front of her so a well-aimed or rogue arrow wouldn't catch her flush. A proper archer won't squabble over whether or not a shot was luck or skill long as the end result puts their intended target in the dirt.

He had half a notion to send Mandy with Wade and Marie who gathered the women and children waiting for darkness to cover their escape. Leo didn't waste his breath. Mandy was stubborn and he knew she'd tell him to take a long walk on a short pier.

The Reds advanced, no more than a few hundred strong but Leo could almost feel the walls sway under his feet. They marched in step, driving their heels into the earth. Shiny helms peered over top their shields as they went. A few hundred yards out they met the first of Edger's sinkholes. The land dropped out from under their feet, and half a dozen Reds cried out in horror as pointed shafts broke their fall in the pits below.

Down the wall, Edger clasped a silver chalice, spilling more wine than he drank. The cup looked strikingly similar to one of the Priest Council's Holy Communion chalices. Leo didn't turn to look, but he suspected one or more of the bishops would be looking on with more than a little reproachful contempt.

A little scorn wouldn't stop Edger from admiring his handiwork though. "Take that you bastards! Welcome to Tamore you fucks."

The Kiman militiamen broke formation, cautiously avoiding discrepancies in the earth that might conceal more sinkholes below. As they dodged the traps, others stepped upon jagged metal caltrops. Those who weren't so lucky flopped around the ground clutching their feet which would never be the same. The sharp metal thorns pierced through leather-soled boots like a septa knitting a quilt by the hearth.

Leo's heart began to race. Blood surged through his veins so fast it chilled his spine. The Reds were far from making it to the outer wall, but the anticipation was enough to make his skin crawl. "Archers ready!"

Just inside the inner wall's east gate, Bruce and his Swords of Bane began to roar. If the archers were overwhelmed, they were to deploy into the Red Garden to clean up the mess. The Widow Makers stood ready at the west gate protecting the only other entrance.

The militiamen pressed on, their attention fixed on

displacing the spiked barriers that were strategically placed to prevent battering rams from breaching the walls. Undaunted, the Kiman soldiers reached the first of many spiked barriers and formed a line to push it away. The heavy logs were more weight than any two men could bear. It took half a dozen to grab hold and push the first barrier aside. Soon enough they had a strategy worked out.

As by Edger's design, brilliant bastard that he is, the sinkholes, caltrops, and spiked barriers were strategically laid out to funnel the Kiman soldiers into kill zones well within the deadly range of Natalie's archers.

Leo scanned the line to give Natalie the order. He found her clutching a bow, thumb and forefinger pressed against the notched arrow. At her feet a full quill, and next to it a bucket of boiling tar sizzled. Soot and grime collected in the valleys of her muscled arms, the crook of her neck, just below her lips....

"Loose!" she ordered, drawing back her first arrow. It raced ahead of the others, thudded off a breastplate, and spun to the ground. "Damn." She notched another. Her second shot took a militiaman right in the ass as he turned to flee. His hand clasped the arrow in surprise. The impact jarred him forward, relieved him of any honor that remained, and sent him speeding off.

Arrows rained down, the first rank went down like a giant hand swept them aside, and the militiamen hastened into a full-fledged retreat. Fallen men lie along the ground, lifeless or bleeding out. Those with the strength raised their hands to be seen, pleading for their comrades to not leave them behind. Others dragged themselves along the ground as fast as they could, shields drawn to protect from the metal rain.

"Cease fire!" Leo shouted. They didn't have arrows to spare on retreating men, but Natalie was lost in the malevolent art of war. Leo's voice was lost in translation if she heard it at all over the strumming of her bow, the whistling of the arrows. When she finally stopped notching arrows, her gaze was vacant like her soul hadn't returned from battle yet.

Mandy let the weight of her shield sag down to her side. Eager as she was for a taste of battle when she'd earned her sword, Mother War's ungentle touch left her looking bewildered. "I'm not naïve enough to call it a complete victory. But a battle won at least," she muttered lifelessly. "It doesn't feel as good as I imagined."

She was not alone. Matter of fact Leo didn't hear a single cry of victory from anywhere inside the walls. *A seasoned lot. Or perhaps they fear what's coming next.* "Just be glad we have the luxury of feeling anything," he said, nodding to the corpses below. "A thousand victories won't replace what a single battle can take from you."

Leo scanned the inner ward where the Priest's Council did their best to steady the nerves of the people. Men and women, young and old, each trapped in a simmering pot set to boil. The bishops moved among the needy, their robes a shade darker than before.

Hardened soldiers and toddlers alike peered up at Leo as if he and his golden shield could protect them. Like his words carried enough weight to defy the wind and turn the course of the war. Leo could think of nothing that would help them sleep better at night. He had no more oaths to swear, no more promises to pledge. All the good he'd ever done trying to defend his country left him exiled, flogged, imprisoned, and surrounded by swords thirsting for his blood.

The memories of it filled him with such contempt that he almost spat into the crowd. He fought the urge to voice that they'd put their faith and trust behind a once-loyal sword, but even the ripest fruit has an expiration date, and his love for Veronia was turning sour.

"Wipe the shit from your head, and say something special." It was Natalie's voice that broke him from the bloody mood. "You can wallow in your self-loathing later. Right now they need to hear something worth writing songs about. Something to live and die for." She patted him on the back and whispered into his ear as she passed. "No pressure, darling."

His scowl of armor began to crumble under the mass of expectant stares. Leo searched the crowd before him looking for a scapegoat. Just one glare to justify his brooding hate. A hate that wrapped him so tight he'd forgotten what it was that filled him with such contempt in the first place.

Time stood still but none of them seemed to mind. Their eager faces appeared resigned to wait an eternity for Leo to give them something worth fighting for. And then Leo saw it. A motion below that when Leo regarded it, so did everyone else.

Edger's lips froze on the silver chalice. He eased the cup from his mouth and diverted his eyes from Bishop Isabelle who'd entangled him with her scorn.

Leo stifled a smile and regarded the crowd once more. There wasn't a single foe within the walls. For better or worse, they locked arms to share in the same fate. This sudden realization flooded him with pride. Leo knew if he spoke now, his voice would likely break with emotion so he took another moment to strengthen his resolve.

He raised his shield and sword to the air. "Today they fucked with the wrong Veronians!"

Although short-winded, Leo's words carried the fury of a storm. Gauntleted gloves began to pound against shields, and a few cheers for the Bloody Rose followed soon after. Bishop Isabelle appeared less impressed. She stared sideways at Trion till his roaring sputtered out. The ginger turned his attention to adjusting his sword belt just right.

The first drops of rain began to drizzle. Water patted into Leo's dirt-strewn hair, taking residence with the sawdust that seemed to coat even the river beside them. They cut up every tree within sight, leaving his fingers blistered to the bone. If he never saw a tree again, it would be too soon. Dusk began to drown the sun as it began its slow descent behind Mt. Drago to the west, leaving the sky in streaks of burnt orange.

"They'll be back in the morning," Leo continued. "Their militia attack was nothing more than a lazy jab. The Kiman Empire expects us to bend the knee but offered us no sanctuary for our women and children. They don't want peace, they want our heads and they'll have to cut mine from the spent corpse I leave behind. Until then they'll have to climb over heaping piles of their own dead to reach me. Enough rotting dead to build a wall around them like a tomb they can't crawl out of till they pray for death and we give it to them!"

Another round of cheers rang out louder than before. Leo turned to Natalie. "How's that for a song?"

Natalie regarded Leo like a puzzle missing more than a few pieces. In the age it took for her to gather a response, Leo felt every bit like the monster he'd become. Her green eyes held no warmth for the stranger before her.

"Lust not for blood but for freedom, my love." She put on her best fake smile and brushed past.

***

Page and Trechon made it to the Netche village, where he bartered a vial of sword venom for two horses, a warm meal, and riding cloaks. A deal that didn't take much haggling and left Page wondering what else they could have gotten. Despite the dark of night, they were on pace to reach the Gorro River by late morning. Were it not for the rain, it would have been a peaceful night. As it was, Page wrapped herself in the warmth of her cloak trying to prevent her teeth from chattering. Trechon rode by her side, bone armor rustling as they went.

She fixed her gaze on the clouded sky searching for Regulus, the only vacant major star. It would have been a difficult task on solid ground. Trying to name the Leo star through fog and rain while swaying on top of a horse and shielding her eyes from the torrent made it impossible.

"Damnit." Page brushed a pool of water from her brow and squeezed the reins in frustration. "We need to pull over and at least try before it's lost to the sun."

"If we pull over, we'll likely miss the battle. What makes you so sure Regulus will mark either of us? I've spent the better part of two summers trying to name him, and the last time wasn't so pleasant." Trechon rolled up his sleeves and lit the night with a handful of misty starfire. Beneath a bone-armored gauntlet, his skin was wrinkly white where Regulus had burned him. "Chief Ansuke has healed it twice already. There's no pain but the burn remains."

Page had to admit the burn looked bad but she didn't have a better alternative. Even if they made it to

Tamore before the battle, she'd be no more than target practice against armored men and their swords. But if she possessed the power of a starborn she could turn the tide of battle. "Maybe he's a she." Page winked and turned her horse off the trail. "This place looks as good as any. A little shelter from the rain, and as clear a shot as I'm going to get of Regulus tonight."

Trechon grunted atop his mount while Page tied hers to a tree with enough slack to let it graze. She laid out a blanket, sat down and patted the spot next to her. Trechon stared into the clouds.

"What is it?" she asked.

"It's bad luck naming in the rain. Had to be one of the first things I taught you, wasn't it?"

Chief Ansuke would be less than pleased if he were to find out their little secret. Trechon staunchly refused teaching her anything at first, but over the last two years, Page was relentless in the effort to gain Trechon's trust and it didn't take long for the two of them to become unlikely allies. It also helps when you're the brother to a man who all of Gwonda owe a blood debt, but Page didn't stand on it. She didn't have to. What Trechon lacked in tact he made up for it in wits.

She thought about asking, "what's the worst that could happen?" then her eyes fell back to Trechon's ruined flesh. "Luck's never done much for me anyways."

The clouded sky did nothing to mask the glamour of Leo's brightest star that night. Regulus stood out among the rest like a diamond in the rough. Twinkling its defiance like an unbreakable wild stallion. The last of its major siblings to be named.

Page crossed her legs on the blanket, the hood of her cloak drawn up like Trechon had taught her. The rain angled towards her face but she dared not blink or break her stare. Minutes passed and then an hour before the wind picked up, taking leaves from limbs. The longer Page stared the more violent the gusts became. Branches creaked and began tearing free from their trees.

The horses began snorting with anxiety, whipping their necks against their lead ropes to free themselves. "Bad luck!" Trechon roared above the howling wind.

Creak...creak...crack! The wind howled, and a tree near Page bowed forward. Its branches flailed above her head. "Timber!" Trechon yelled as the tree split and leaned towards Page.

Regulus was so radiant that it began to burn and blur Page's vision. An invisible force pressed down. Her head felt like a mountain on her shoulders. She stared ahead and saw nothing but giant blotches of light that seemed to draw nearer. A gust of wind blew her hood back and tussled her hair. She strained to speak. "Buy me some time, Trechon."

Trechon struggled to stand upright against the howling wind. His cloak bellowed and tattered behind him. The sky darkened save for Regulus and the moon. The creaking tree snapped at last and tumbled down towards them; Trechon's starfire took it center mass as it fell. The explosion that followed showered them with splintered wood. When Trechon turned to Page, she was suspended in midair, right hand and eyes star-bright.

Regulus twirled her through the air like a spinning top. A wounded squeal escaped her breath, a weight pressed down to muffle her cry. Then as sudden as the wind came, it vanished. As did the rain. Page dropped to the earth landing heavily on her back and all air escaped her lungs.

When she opened her eyes, Trechon's pale face was leaning over her. His dark hair matted by the rain. He had a cut over his left eye, and blood trickled from his nose into his mouth. "Are you alright?" he asked.

Her heart felt like it had popped in her chest. Much the same as shrapnel tore through her torso and took residence in the extremities that no longer seemed to function. Her lips moved but her speech hadn't returned although her vision improved so much that she could make out each of the millions of stars that lit up the sky.

"We did it." Her strength had left her. The weight of her eyelids was unbearable. They closed tight like a curtain drawn against the stars.

The breaking of the tree left Trechon on the cusp of burnout. He heard the pounded hooves of their horses scampering off into the night, neighing as they went. Trechon collapsed next to Page.

Twigs and limbs crackled under footsteps in the

night.

"There they are," a voice called in the darkness. "Over here, lads." Chainmail rustled and not long after their red tunics came into view.

"Well no shit, Randle," another one said. "I ain't no feckin' tracker, but even a chambermaid can see a couple starborn blowing shit up in the night."

"She's a pretty little lass," Randle added. He pulled his helm off and tucked it under his arm. "Might be we shouldn't kill her so fast. What says you Henry? We can each have a turn before she wakes up. Quick as you are, you can have two and she might never know you was there."

A light flashed through the trees. "What the feck was that?" Randle held his sword out in front of him with trembling hands.

Again, the light flickered aglow, illuminating a cloaked figure. "Drop your weapons and have a seat. I'll only tell you once."

"Another one," Randle whispered. "It can't be."

"Don't do it Randle. Easy now," Henry said, easing to the ground. "You seen what Borin can do with the flick of a wrist."

Randle darted away and the others followed in a dozen different directions. Starfire pursued them and their bodies tumbled to the ground in teeth-gnashing fits of agony. Their cries were short-lived. In a matter of seconds all but Randle lie smoldering in blue flames.

The cloaked figure knelt next to Trechon whose

chest failed to rise and fall with the breath of life. The stranger's star-patterned hands transformed from blue to green. He clasped Trechon by the head and arm and the Tribesman sucked in air.

The stranger stood, cast his hood aside, and walked towards Henry. His eyes were aglow revealing a sea-weathered, saggy-cheeked face with grey finger-combed hair. "And what did Borin have to say about me?"

CHAPTER

3

Rain drizzled down as waves carried the moonlight, crashing into and fizzling out against the sandy shores of Shield Island. The Kiman soldiers found the wine cellar and were deep in their cups. When hunger struck them, they broke into the kennels and killed all the chickens and nearly a whole herd of goats. More meat than they could eat in two or three sittings. To avoid the rain, the Reds set up cook fires inside the Chapel. A wicked lot they'd become. Hard to believe any of them were birthed in Veronia.

Jewel and Nicolai were left outside to bask in the rain. Agnen had one of his henchmen watch them while he left to break his fast. *How did they become so savage?* Jewel wondered. *Brainwashed beyond reason.* Not two years ago, most of them would have been sword-sworn to Veronia, its king and the church. The oath-breakers had slain their own king, sacked nearly all of Veronia, and pledged new oaths to the Kiman Empire and their blasphemous Book of Light.

Agnen stalked down the dais with a plateful of meat and a tankard overflowing with wine. With his dragon-scaled armor, he looked like a void in the night. His menacing scowl seemed permanently affixed. Jewel took note of the other soldiers who went out of their way to avoid the Reaper and his everlasting dark mood.

"Move along," Agnen ordered, plopping down to eat his meal.

"Aye sir." The soldier dropped Jewel's chain and made for the Chapel before Agnen could get the last word out.

He chewed through half his plate before Agnen felt Jewel's gaze on him. Agnen paused in reflection. "Want a piece, Priest?"

Despite the darkness, Jewel put on his best glare. Wasn't much else he could do in chains. Not that he had any real hope of besting Agnen with fist or sword. "Savage," Jewel spat in disgust. His stomach disagreed and rumbled with hunger.

"Well fuck you too then." Agnen's words lacked

any real malice. With a Red name like Reaper, he didn't usually have to say much. "You don't stay my size by skipping meals."

Nicolai leaned back against his dragonglass prison. Fingers interlocked across his stomach, hood drawn over his head. Jewel suspected he'd been sleeping till he spoke. "I'm still trying to figure out why you're wasting your time down here with the two of us. Any number of your men seem more than capable of goaling the two of us. I'm sure Abaddon's already told you that dragonglass prohibits my accessing the celestial else, and Brother Jewel is quite useless bound in chains."

Agnen set his plate down, sucking the final scraps of meat off a chicken's bones. "In case you forgot, I tried to bury most of these bastards a few winters ago. I know they sure haven't."

Nicolai shifted restlessly within the cage. He adjusted his hood and made his hands a pillow behind his head. "Not many things escape my attention, Commander. With or without my ring. Just wanted to hear your version of it."

"Up, Berinon, get up!" Abaddon stomped out of the Chapel with fire in his eyes. Berinon stirred from the fetal position he'd fallen asleep in. Beside him, Lyle appeared just as drowsy yet he'd received no scorn for it. "I've found the remedy to our failed attempts."

"All hells," Nicolai blurted as Abaddon stormed towards them.

Abaddon regarded the pentagram that had done

nothing but vex him thus far. He cast his fiery eyes at his starborn prisoner. "You knew all along, didn't you Nicolai?"

Nicolai turned rigid, and Jewel remembered why. He recalled what Nicolai had mentioned earlier, when he said Abaddon would figure it out soon enough. Abaddon's glee left knots in Jewel's stomach. Whatever he'd discovered couldn't be good.

Abaddon's evil laughter continued. "Ah yes. The ever-knowing Nicolai." The Prothica leader clasped the dragonglass bars of Nicolai's cage. "Or at least you used to be, before you became my pet bird. It must have been quite entertaining to watch us fail. Not quite as entertaining as it will be watching you lose all your wits in that cage."

"I'd just assumed you and Lyle had developed a knack for failure. But who am I to judge?" Nicolai clipped.

"Ha," Abaddon mocked. "You ought to savor that sarcastic jab. It might well be your last." He leaned his head against the bars of the cage. "Perhaps I can parade you around my new kingdom. You'd make an excellent jester. In time you might even learn to juggle in there."

Nicolai lurched forward reaching for Abaddon's head, but the Prothica leader moved easily away.

"The Mozzaroth must be complete with twelve starborn to successfully conjure." Abaddon rubbed his hands together matter-of-factly.

"And good luck naming the last," Nicolai brooded.

"Regulus hasn't been named in what, two thousand years now?"

"Hahaha." Abaddon approached Nicolai's cage just out of reaching distance. "You can't feel it in there, can you?" he mocked, regarding the prison that bound Nicolai.

Nicolai sunk back in the cage and Jewel wondered earnestly what it was that Nicolai suddenly realized.

"It can't be," Nicolai muttered.

"Oh but it is," Abaddon answered.

Abaddon turned away, stretching his hands to the sky. "Regulus has been named. The Mozzaroth is whole again!"

"But how?" Nicolai asked. "By whom?"

It was one of the first times Jewel had seen Nicolai lack an answer. Something felt wrong about it.

"Now that even I don't know." Abaddon regarded the Ring of Solomon he still wore. "But this ring allows me to sense starborn far beyond the limitations I once knew. Given time, I'll find out. And I'll have to build more cages when I do."

Abaddon twisted the ring past his knuckle and off his finger. When he did, his fiery eyes dimmed like water squelching a flame. He held up the ring and peered through its center at the moon. "Knowledge is perhaps the most valuable resource among the twelve and you wasted it Nicolai. Oh, but I won't."

If only Nicolai's frown could kill, they'd both be free.

"With this ring," Abaddon continued, "I'll conjure the Giants of Orion and the monsters of the sea. I'll have an army of cherubs at my beck and call. No army, mortal or divine, will stand before me. Your god preaches of heaven in the afterlife. Let him have it. I'll create mine here on earth."

"Blasphemy," Jewel rebuked. "You're nothing but a wretched demon." He braced himself for Agnen's sure hands to yank the chain and bring him to heel, but it didn't come. When it didn't Abaddon lost his temper.

"Kill him, Commander. Or have both of you outlived your usefulness?"

The chain rustled in Agnen's hands. Jewel sprawled to the ground.

"When I summon the giants, and summon them I will, they will be all the army I need to erase all that was Veronia."

Jewel lifted himself to both knees and Agnen pushed him down again. The Gorronian stared down at him for a time, then with a grunt he unsheathed his sword.

"Master Abaddon," Berinon squalled, shuffling forward with the Book of Light. "If you have no further use of the vile priest, would you be so kind as to allow me the pleasure? With Jewel and his brother's blood, I might be able to perfect my Eternal Potion."

Eternal Potion? That's what the fool's been up to? Spilling innocent blood as if it were a common alchemy ingredient? Before Agnen could swing his sword Jewel was on his feet barreling towards Berinon.

The Light Priest held up the Book of Light but it did little to shield him from Jewel. It wasn't long before Jewel had both hands wrapped around Berinon's sweaty neck. Jewel felt Berinon's feet kicking under him. The Light Priest's fleshy, sweaty little hands clawing at his own. Jewel dared not let go until the deed was done. Berinon's eyes bulged from their sockets, his face turning shades of purple and blue as he fought for breath.

Agnen lifted Jewel up off the ground by the chain and slung him away from Berinon. When he looked up again, Jewel saw Agnen's sword rise and he closed his eyes as it fell.

***

The rain in Tamore was relentless. It lashed down at impossible angles and showed no signs of letting up. Leo sat atop the inner wall emptying water from his boots.

"Give it up," Juan said, elbows propped against the railing as he leaned over the wall. He closed his eyes and raised his chin to let rain wash over him. "We'll just have to make do with wet everything. Never heard of a man halting in the middle of a swordfight on account of some wet boots. You gonna start flower-scenting your hair too?"

Leo squeezed his foot into his wet leather soles.

"Eat shit, Juan. You know I got a thing for dry feet."

Who could blame him really? Hell, the Frostbite was named after all those poor bastards who lost limbs to the chill. Their fingers and toes a little red at first. Then looked as if they'd been dipped in candle wax. After that their digits would swell up, turn black, and in some instances the skin would split. There was no saving them after that. Had to be cut off then, lest it fester and take your whole limb or life with it. As far as Leo could tell, it wasn't cold enough for the chill to set in, but trench foot was frostbite's angry cousin.

"They about ready down there?" Leo asked.

Juan regarded the anxious women and children lined up next to the west gate. There were almost as many men, not all of them past their prime. Neither Juan nor Leo could blame them for swallowing their pride to live and fight another day. "I reckon most of them have been ready to leave since the Reds arrived."

Wade anxiously shifted his weight from one foot to the other at the front of the line. Beside him, Marie wrapped her son in her arms, his legs straddling her hip. Her daughter clung to her leg.

Leo wondered if a true leader, one better than he, should have been down there patting backs, shaking hands and saying goodbyes. He wasn't particularly suited for that kind of thing. Figured he'd only make things more awkward than it had to be.

Truth was, Leo could have done a lot of things better. Juan for example was a better man than the

Bloody Rose would ever be. Leo had come to terms with that long ago. Juan had a prideless sense of love and duty to everyone he met, and the people loved him for it. Sure Leo could change his ways if he'd only make the effort. Become a better brother, leader, and friend. Instead he chose to please Mother War. Or perhaps she'd chosen him and he couldn't get out of her snare.

"Let's get on with it then," Leo muttered. He found Bruce at the gate and gave him a nod.

The west gate rolled open and the line slowly filtered out in groups of three. They were to cross the Britta, follow it north then cross the Gorro as soon as they lost sight of the Kiman soldiers.

Abigail was next to go. She stood locked in Nestin's loving embrace. A vision of Drew holding onto Mandy before getting killed in Gwonda flashed through Leo's mind. He clenched his teeth and diverted his eyes. *Perhaps I deserve nothing less than to cradle that razor-edged memory.*

When Ole Faithful, Sergeant Wade Holloway, looked up to meet his eye, Leo found he was grinding his teeth to keep it together. Wade raised his sword. Leo lifted his shield in return. A soldier's farewell.

Wade clasped Bruce's hand one last time and then trotted off into the night. Bruce and his Swords of Bane stood at the open gate, poised to deploy should the Kiman soldiers send an attack.

Leo regarded the Kiman camp that hadn't bothered

to stir in the night. Either they didn't notice the group fleeing, or King Xalvador had decided killing women and children wasn't in the best interest of his new empire after all.

Juan rested his hands in the collar of his breastplate and they watched Wade disappear into the night. "Well, I suppose that's the last of them. You think they'll make it to Gwonda?"

Leo tilted his head back but the rain failed to wash away the thought of Wade, Mandy, Abigail, and the others getting cut down in the woods. "I'd say they have a better chance than we do." He regarded Juan with a red smile. "I don't know about you, but I'm okay with that."

***

Slain while trying to choke the life out of another priest. As deranged a clergyman as Berinon had come to be, that was the legacy Jewel had left behind. A lifetime of walking in the light, trying to do the right thing for God and fellow man, ruined in his final moments. Jewel always thought it would be Leo who allowed his anger to consume him to the point that it carried him through the last door and yet there he was, the High Priest of Veronia, taking the spiritual flight to be judged.

He felt light as a feather, but darkness wrapped him as he floated in what was sure to be the afterlife. His eyes swam for light. A light that would guide him to judgment like a beacon through the night. But all that surrounded him was a labyrinth of cold, dark nothingness. *Purgatory! No, it can't be. Heavenly Father, please have mercy on my soul.*

When no answer came, Jewel felt the cold scorn of rejection wisp towards him like a frozen wind. His head spun in search for something, anything that would reassure him. Again, only nothingness. A flood of panic washed over him. He darted high and low, left and right, but found only darkness.

Please Father. I beg of you. Don't leave me here!

A slow creaking sound caught his attention. When he found the source his heart plummeted to his stomach. At the far end of the abyss a door creaked as it closed. On the other side of it, a bright light filtered into his purgatory. *No!* Jewel pled, trying to close the distance as fast as he could. The door creaked further and further.

No! Please, take me with you! Please don't leave me here!

He was almost there. Jewel stretched his hand out to catch the door before it closed shut. Closer and closer he got as the door creaked along the hinges. His outstretched hand was almost there when something began tugging on his heels. He kicked to shake himself free, scared to take his eyes off the door and return to the black abyss. But the force clawed more and more at his feet until he could move no further. The door creaked and creaked. Jewel looked down where swirling shadows of monstrous hands grabbed hold of him and pulled him back.

No. Let go of me. Let me go. Jewel's plea was cut short when he heard the door slam.

"No. No!" Jewel screamed.

A hand wrapped around his mouth to muffle his cry. "Silence you fool, or you'll kill us both."

Jewel's vision slowly returned. With it, a headache the likes of which he'd never felt before. He tried to blink the grogginess away. When the world shifted into place, Jewel felt Agnen's paw covering his mouth. The Gorronian's other hand clasped round Jewel's ankle. *Is he dragging me? Wait a second. I'm alive?*

Jewel ran his fingers through his hair and his hand came away bloody. The metallic smell of it turned his stomach. He found the source of his headache where a fist-sized knot had taken residency on top of his head. Jewel shook Agnen's hand from his mouth and sat up.

He filled his lungs with the blissful salty air. It tasted like he'd taken a drink straight from the sea. Jewel looked back and saw the rut his dragged body made all the way down the hill. To his surprise, on either side of the drag marks, four Kiman soldiers lie slain. The first few looked to have died quick and clean. The last one looked to have almost made it atop the hill as he fled, before being cut down from behind.

Agnen dropped Jewel's foot and began walking towards the dock where a skiff rose and fell on the waves. "Get in the boat. They'll wonder why I haven't returned soon. Doesn't take long to bury a body in the sea."

"You saved me? But why?" His hand rose once more to his head. Agnen must have hit him with the flat of his sword. Otherwise they wouldn't be having this conversation. On further inspection, he could almost feel the width of Agnen's blade on his head.

The dock creaked under Agnen's weight. He tossed his golden-horned helm into the skiff and began to unravel a knot in the rope. "I've got my reasons." Agnen made quick work of the knot and tossed the rope into the skiff before easing into it. He reached down and came up with a paddle. "You Veronians talk too much. Either shut up and get in or go see how much forgiveness Berinon has in 'im."

"Can't say I saw this coming," Jewel said, hopping into the skiff.

Agnen pressed a paddle into Jewel's chest. "Paddle."

Jewel took the paddle and began sweeping the ocean. Agnen did likewise on the opposite side.

"What about Michael? Erm, Nicolai."

"You want to go back for him, be my guest."

"Blast!" Jewel fumed, paddling harder now.

***

Kano stretched his head out from behind a palm tree that rooted in Veronia's mainland. Squinting through the darkness, he could barely make out the skiff that rowed north from Shield Island. He saw two men, one wearing a violet-colored robe, but didn't sense Nicolai. Maybe he'd follow down the coastline and question them about the missing bishop once they docked.

Kano 'ported to Shield Island for a better look, landing on a creaky dock. "And what do we have here?" Just up the hill he regarded a few slain Kiman soldiers. But more profound than that, he began to sense starborn on the island. Two of them if he wasn't mistaken.

Kano eased up the hill, careful not to draw alarm. If he could sense starborn, they no doubt sensed him too. If it were Nicolai on the island, then he shouldn't be accompanied by any other of the twelve. Something was very wrong here.

More Kiman soldiers shuffled around the island, none of which appeared to notice their slain companions by the dock, or the skiff sailing away. Short as he was, Kano crouched to mask his silhouette.

"Well what do we have here?" Kano regarded the candlelit pentagram situated at the foot of the Chapel's dais. Lyle stood within it, holding a radiant summoning orb. Beside him, a Light Priest thumbed through a massive book just outside the pentagram. Then a cage caught his eye. Inside it a prisoner stirred. Kano couldn't tell who it was from that distance in the night, but he didn't sense whomever it was to be starborn.

Abaddon strolled down the dais towards the

pentagram. His eyes like flames sweeping the distance and flashing towards Kano.

"Shit!" Kano cursed under his breath. He dove to the ground and lie prone. Surely he'd been sensed, if not seen. He readied himself to 'port away but a song froze him in place.

Lyle's orotund, singsong voice began to carry across the island. When Abaddon slipped a ring from his hand and handed it to Lyle, Kano's heart sank. There was only one ring he knew of that bore any significance to the starborn.

Kano regarded the cage and the sleeveless prisoner once more. Could it be Nicolai in there? And why couldn't he sense him if it was?

Lyle cupped the precious ring in both hands then carefully sat in the center of the pentagram. The rolling tide behind Kano turned placid and the wind sputtered out.

Kano's chest began to itch with starache. He clasped a hand to his chest but it provided little comfort. Panic set its claws in him and Kano began to wonder if Lyle had cast some sort of spell on him. Gasping for air, Kano named Sadalsuud to 'port him anywhere but there. For the first time ever, the star failed to heed his call.

Lyle continued to sing. The candles lost their flame and smoke billowed from the wick. Lyle's summoning orb brightened as if he held the moon in his hands. Abaddon's twisted smile broadened as he knelt beside

Berinon. The Light Priest rubbed his hands together and wet his lips anxiously. The glowing orb took flight and hovered in the air just above Lyle's outstretched hands. The stars of the sky recoiled into the night and even the moon began to fade as the constellation of Orion mustered more and more light.

Lyle knelt down to retrieve Solomon's Ring. When he situated it atop the hovering orb the sea began to swell and Kano heard the waves crashing violently ashore behind him. He wiped saltwater from his eyes as the wind began to howl and thunder loosed its vengeance on the Iron Sea.

Kano's teeth clicked together when a bolt of lightning touched down much too close for comfort. The copper taste of blood filled his mouth where he'd bitten into his cheek. He felt no pain. Only the roaring thunder shaking the world around him.

The island creaked and groaned, shifting underfoot. Like a madman, Abaddon stood welcoming it with open arms and starlit eyes. Berinon shielded himself with the oversized book. It would do little more than soak up the pouring rain.

Lyle continued to sing. He stepping cautiously out of the pentagram, leaving Solomon's Ring resting atop the summoning orb that swirled within the confines of the pentagram.

Another bolt of lightning crackled down to earth. This time hitting the orb. When Kano's vision returned, a dozen or more giants knelt on the ground, silhouetted by the lowest-hanging moon Kano had ever seen.

One giant, taller than all the rest, stood at the center of the pentagram holding the Ring of Solomon between his massive forefinger and thumb. A golden crown enameled in rubies rested atop his head. Golden wristbands wrapped each of his forearms. Even the braids of his beard were fastened with gold. The only clothing he wore was an embroidered shendyt that covered his waist. The giant closed his eyes, inhaled a lungful of air, savored it for a time then blew it out. His first taste of earthly air in nearly two thousand years would not be wasted.

Starborn power derives from the else, an invisible current of energy that surrounds the earth like the atmosphere. When the giant spoke, Kano felt his own knees quiver as the monster's words rippled through the waves. Kano fought the urge to 'port the hell out of there. For now at least.

"Who dare summon King Delbec, the last of the Nephilim?" The golden giant swept Lyle and Berinon with hungry eyes. Only Lyle had the courage to meet them with his own. Berinon wilted once more behind his Book of Light.

"It was I, old friend. Abaddon, namer of Antares, and my starborn brother Lyle the Summoner, namer of Pollux." He spread his arms wide. "Welcome to the Kiman Empire."

"Anakim rise," Delbec bellowed. The other giants stomped to the sides of their leader. Each of them clutched a dragonglass shield in one hand, heavy wooden clubs in the other. In a frightening display of uniformity, the giants rested the weighted ends of their clubs on their right shoulders.

The giant entourage, or Anakim as Delbec had called them, were every bit as menacing as Kano had imagined. Unlike their Giant King, they had grizzly beards and wore intricately engraved light armor and helms. Given the distance, Kano couldn't tell if their armor was made of brass or copper. What was even more troubling than their size was their battle-scarred armor. Each nick and groove, slash and stab, the only mark their foes left behind.

Delbec sniffed the air with disdain. He regarded Berinon who must have been musty with fear. The King of Giants spat at the Light Priest's feet. "Your fear is wretched, little man." He peered around the island to take in his surroundings. "And where is the third starborn?" Delbec turned his frosty glare towards Abaddon. "Do you think I cannot sense him? That I cannot smell his fear either? Do you aim to deceive me?"

"Most certainly not," Abaddon responded, not bothering to seek out Kano himself. "I'm afraid that would be Kano, namer of Sadalsuud, who spies from the shadows." He made a *tsk tsk* sound. "Much has changed since your confinement, King Delbec. You might be pleased to hear that the Mozzaroth are no longer united, which is why I've sought to summon you and your Anakim."

Delbec regarded the ring he held between finger and thumb then wrapped it in his mighty palm. "The starborn have never been united," he spat, jaw muscles flexing tight beneath his ebony skin. "Not even when you and Nicolai bound us within Orion. You must be mad or desperate to have summoned us now. Which is it?"

Abaddon forced a chuckle. Eyes shifting back and forth to the ring Delbec clutched in his palm. "Only the man without cunning and vision stoops to desperation. But mad I may be. There's little hope to restrain your giant will on the earthlings now that the Mozzaroth is divided. However, the mere fact that you've returned to earth at my summons should be more than enough reassurance of my good will." Abaddon held out his hand, palm up. "My ring please?"

Delbec considered his options. "I could swat you down like a fly without this ring," he finally said. "What makes you think I'm so keen to trade a celestial prison for the end of your chain? Why did you summon us, Abaddon? I'll not ask again!"

"Oh I think you'll find any chain of mine has more than enough wiggle room. But without it, your second coming will be rather short-lived, don't you think?" Abaddon spoke flatly. Perhaps he was cracked in the head, Kano thought. Standing toe to toe against those giants, he had to be.

Abaddon regarded the cage where Nicolai sat

brooding. "Here before you, we have one of the twelve bound beneath my will. You remember Nicolai, don't you?" Delbec snarled and Abaddon continued. "With your help, soon the others who pose a threat will be just as bound. That would leave me in complete control of the Mozzaroth and together we could take back what is rightfully ours. The way it was before the flood, in the Days of Noah." Abaddon stepped forward, one hand clenched into a fist, the other outstretched for the ring. "A heaven on earth, and an empire to control the world."

The King of Giants regarded his Anakim. After a time, they nodded in return.

Delbec held the ring. "To the Days of Noah," he said, dropping it into Abaddon's hand.

CHAPTER

4

It was the dawn of their second day on the road. They parked their carriage just outside Nebula to avoid attention. The tavern where Hadrian was killed had a new roof as far as Liz could tell and despite keeping their distance they drew more than a few cold stares from villagers as they passed. From what Kano and Ambrose had told her it was quite the battle. Liz tried her best to push Borin's vile metal stars from memory but the sight of the tavern felt like the wound between her shoulder blades was reopened.

Ambrose leaned against the carriage, one arm pressed against his stomach. "I feel strange. Like I've got the runs but can't get any of it out." He scrunched his face and cupped his jaw. "Matter of fact, I haven't shit since we left Killian's."

"I can't be the only one who isn't surprised that you're full of shit," Brielle said. "An ailment with witless side effects, not even the star Aries could cleanse you of." She looked just as queasy. The loose strands of her hair clung to her pale, clammy face but she resisted the urge to dunk her head into the depths of the horse trough like Ambrose had.

Starborn don't get sick. At least among the twelve they don't. The celestial energy that courses through them is a repellent to mundane disease such as poison or plague. For Brielle and Ambrose to be in the shape they were in meant only one thing to Liz. Someone had named the last major star. The twelve were whole again.

"Feels like my chest bones are rubbing together trying to start a friction fire," Ambrose muttered. "What the hell's wrong with us?"

Liz rolled a golden crown across her knuckles waiting for the horses to be changed. "I'm afraid the two of you are suffering a bout of starache."

Ambrose drew in a shaky breath. His chest swelled and then he winced it out. "Starache? What's that...?"

The air shifted around them, then Kano appeared.

"Kano!" Liz exclaimed, wrapping him in her arms.

He smelled like salt water but Liz didn't mind. "Where have you been?"

He pulled himself from her grasp and Liz noticed for the first time how pale he was. "I found Nicolai," he said, running his stubby fingers through his disheveled hair. "The Prothica hold him prisoner on Shield Island. But that's not the worst of it. Abaddon and Lyle summoned the Giants of Orion."

"They imprisoned Nicolai? But how?" Liz asked.

"I'm not sure," Kano answered. "I'm afraid I've returned with more questions than answers."

Ambrose staggered over to greet Kano and nearly fell on top of him.

Kano reached out to stabilize him. "What happened to you?"

"Afflicted to the core," Ambrose muttered. "Liz called it starache. Whatever that is, feels terminal."

"Ah yes, starache." Kano reached up to put a reassuring hand on Ambrose's shoulder but gravity had never been kind to Kano so he settled for Ambrose's tricep. "I forgot to warn you about that. Didn't think we'd have a full dozen any time soon though. Using your ability should help take the edge off it. You can try it on the road." He pointed at Brielle. "Remember what I told you though. Stay out of our heads. Using your ability on another starborn is likely to end in a fight. Try it on Killian's guards."

"So what's the plan now?" Liz asked. "Keep moving north to Tamore, or should we go straight for

Abaddon's head on Shield Island?"

"Listen, I want to get Nicolai back as soon as we can, but now that Abaddon's summoned the giants we need to be careful. Who knows what they're capable of. And there's something I haven't told you. Abaddon has the Ring of Solomon."

She'd nearly forgotten all about the ring Nicolai had worn for so long. A sickening realization washed over her. "And I'm guessing the full dozen just activated the ring's power."

"What ring?" Ambrose asked, invisible now. "You never taught me anything about rings."

Kano waved the scrutiny of his former protégé away. "And for good reason. There are many things only privy among the twelve. Anyone listening, Brielle?"

Brielle had her attention divided elsewhere, between the minds of Codoc and Oberian. "Not of the mundane variety. Killian has them well trained it appears. Any time one of their thoughts wander towards us, they think of scorpions crawling on them. Like they're clearing their minds on purpose."

"Mind Wall," Liz decided, shaking her head. "Those clever bastards. We need to have a talk with Killian when this is all over. The man knows more than he should and I want to know how. You don't think he's found the book, do you?"

Ambrose blurred back to visible form. His head cocked to the side, both hands on his hips. "Oh now there's a book you haven't told me about."

Kano sighed. "Listen, there's been a lot going on lately. I'll bring you up to speed on everything I know as soon as we free Nicolai and avoid ending up in one of Abaddon's cages for the rest of eternity."

"Abaddon's cages?" Liz asked.

"I know, I know. Like I said, a lot has happened lately, but they've found a way to bind Nicolai in a cage so he can't access the else."

"And what about the book?" Brielle asked.

"Right, the book," Kano answered. "The Book of Baraqiel is as real as talking unicorns and gold-toting Leprechauns. I should know. Nicolai's sent me to every corner of the earth searching for it. He's mad about his books, you see, and that one hasn't been seen or heard from in thousands of years. If it ever existed at all."

Liz wasn't so quick to write it off as a fairytale. She'd heard Nicolai ramble on about the Book of Baraqiel more often than his Holy Codex. The latter of which he'd been assembling for centuries to unify the Christian scriptures into one book. Nicolai would go on and on about Baraqiel, the infamous Watcher who had left behind answers to many starborn secrets. The Holy Grail of forbidden knowledge.

"Did you know about any of this, Brielle?" Ambrose regarded his companion with the same flamboyant scrutiny.

Brielle was lost in Codoc and Oberian's thoughts as the two Heron guards sat talking to one another at the front of their carriage. So much so that sweat began to bead on her forehead as she tried to break down their mindwalls. "Nope. Never heard of any books or bracelets."

Liz made a flicking motion with her hand and Brielle's head pitched forward like she'd been cuffed on the back of the head.

Brielle shook herself from the Heron guards' thoughts and clasped the back of her head. "Hey, I though you said we couldn't use our abilities on each other."

Now it was Liz, waiving off her former protégé. "Pay attention. This is important."

"Alright, alright." Brielle flattened the sleeves of her cloak. "So why aren't we going to kick Abaddon's ass right now?"

"Because even on the verge of burnout, Abaddon's more powerful than the two of you combined." Kano pointed at Ambrose and Liz matter-of-factly. "And now that he's got Solomon's Ring, the Prothica behind him, and the Giants of Orion at his side, it would be suicide to attack him now. Not to mention, now that the twelve majors are named, he might have enough power to possess multiple abilities."

"You can possess multiple abilities?" Ambrose asked.

"It's not unheard of," Kano replied. "When the Mozzaroth is full, the else produces more energy to keep up with demand. Long before the twelve split up into the Zodans and the Prothica, they were known to possess at least two abilities. I've heard stories that the original twelve might have even possessed them all. Nicolai would never admit to it, but I've long suspected him to possess more than one."

Liz's mind wandered to a vision of Abaddon shape-shifting into a mirrored image of Codoc or Oberian, and naming her wind to kill them. The thought sent a chill up her spine. She straightened and made a mental note to be more alert to such an attack. "We need to get that ring back. If we have to take him out to get it, so be it. Or perhaps..." Liz snapped her fingers. "Perhaps we should take out another member of the Prothica. A vacancy in the Mozzaroth should nullify the power of Solomon's Ring."

"That's not a bad idea. But then there are the giants we'd have to contend with," Kano thought aloud. "We can't do anything without Ansuke though. You guys get back on the road to Tamore, and I'll catch up with you later. I've got to warn Ansuke before he ends up in a cage as well. If you don't hear from me, I'll see you in Tamore."

Kano was gone in an instant. Liz stared at the blur he left behind till it faded. "Let's move," she ordered, climbing into the carriage. "Double-time."

***

Page woke to a green, florescent light on her shoulder.

She found its source coming from the hand of a cloaked stranger hovering over her. Startled, she crawled away from his touch, tripping over Trechon's limp legs beside her. "Who are you and what are you doing?"

The stranger held his palms up in good faith. His eyes faded from florescent green to ocean blue then masked by the night. A star pattern on his right hand marked him as one of the twelve. The dozen or more minors on his left hand indicated he was very powerful. More stars than Page had ever seen or heard of.

"Reasonable enough questions, given the circumstances." The stranger smiled but it did little to reassure Page and he knew it. "My name is Boyce. I'm a friend of your brother. Or at least I thought we were. I once shared a dungeon with him in Bresdan, so an old roommate if nothing else. But that's neither here nor there. How are you feeling? From what I've read, Regulus mauls like a bear when it marks you."

She held up her aching hand, eyes tracing the star pattern recently burned into the back of her palm. The warrior rune at its center. When she rotated her hand, she saw the first of the dead Kiman soldiers between her fingers and startled to her feet. "Oh my God. What happened?" The more of the scene she took in, the more bodies she saw. Ten or more at least. The last of which sat cross-legged, his headless torso leaned over his knees. Cauterized just above the shoulders. Not a speckle of blood to be found. "Trechon." She pushed and pulled to wake him up. He looked just as dead to the world as the others, but his chest rose and fell.

"Trechon, wake up!" she cried. Tears blurred her vision now. "Help him. Please help him."

Boyce brushed dirt from his knees. "He's burnt-out but he'll survive."

"Your hands were green. I saw them." Page accused with her finger. She measured the distance from herself to the sword of a dead Kiman soldier and nearly leapt for it. "How did you come by Chief Ansuke's healing power? Did you do something to him?"

"Relax girl, Ansuke is fine." Boyce was calm as placid water. "At least for now he is. When he gets to Tamore, who can say. He'll have his hands full against the Kiman soldiers, Borin and Elias besides."

"You were healing me," she realized. "But how?"

"Clever girl," Boyce declared, sitting on the ground. He kicked his feet out and rested his elbows on his knees. "Well read or well trained, one of the two. I tried to tutor Leo as best I could, but he's stubborn as they come. The ultimate realist in a complex world. Perhaps now he'll be more apt to reconsider his non-belief. A starborn sister should do what I could not." His mouth hinted at a smile that got lost in his weathered face. "I imagine Leo seeing you now—will be quite the sobering experience."

A stubborn realist. That was Leo alright. But Page still had apprehensions about Boyce's intentions. Once again Boyce dodged her question about his healing ability. He was hiding something. "The Reds. Did they follow you here? I hope you at least got some answers from them before it was off with their heads."

"You truly are your brother's sister." Boyce pointed to the headless corpse setting cross-legged. "Harold I believe his name was. A bit reluctant at first to betray his Master Borin, but abandoned and alone at last, Harold didn't have many other options. His candid disclosure earned him a painless death."

Boyce's calm demeanor was chilling. The position of Harold's corpse appeared to have been a sudden execution at the conclusion of a casual conversation. It left Page wondering if she'd suffer the same fate. Boyce could have easily pushed Harold's corpse onto his side to cover it up. It would take only the nudge of a boot. He'd left the soldier in place to send a message. She'd have to be careful with this one.

"And it's only by happenstance that I stumbled upon the two of you out here. I was actually on my way to see Ansuke. When I sensed Trechon's presence I followed the scent." Boyce regarded Trechon who still lie motionless. "He probably would have sensed me if not for your naming in the rain. That's bad luck you know. No wonder that tree nearly squashed you like a bug. I've never seen a minor namer destroy a tree like that. Quite impressive actually. Now I've got to ask," Boyce said, regarding the dead all around them, "with all the Reds in the area, what were you two doing so far south?"

"We're headed to Tamore to find my brother. The Tribesmen wouldn't let me go with their army so they must have sent Trechon here to follow me. We got attacked by two others just north of here. Trechon thinks they were Chamood rejects."

"Hmph," Boyce muttered. He tilted his head and raised an eyebrow. "And you thought you'd just join the twelve in the middle of a storm on your way?"

It seemed batshit crazy, she knew. Truth be told, she hadn't wrapped her mind around naming the major star just yet. Two years she'd spent trying to name Regulus and now she bore its mark, and didn't know the first thing about using it.

Page found herself laughing at his question. It really did sound absurd. She raised her right hand in wonder. "This was a rather unexpected surprise. I've tried naming minors before but didn't really know what I was doing." She regarded Trechon once more. "Trechon and Chief Ansuke weren't exactly forthcoming with assistance. I suspect they taught me just enough to keep my mouth shut and protect their secret."

"Wait a second." Page cursed her loose lips. What the hell was she thinking? She didn't even know this man and she'd already begun confiding in him. "What were you trying to find Ansuke for, and how do you know who I am?"

"Another excellent question, my dear." Boyce rose to his feet, brushing dirt from his cloak. "But there aren't many blond-headed Veronians running around the Gwonda Forest in buckskins. And our headless foe Harold here confirmed my suspicions. Listen, Page. I'd tell you not to worry about me, that I mean you no harm. That I'm someone you can trust. But the majority of the time, it's the people you trust that let you down the most."

"Your timing is very unfortunate however," he continued. "I don't know how much Ansuke and Trechon have told you, but the starborn have locked horns in battle that will impact not only Veronia, but every nation across the globe. Unbeknownst to your brother, he's crossing swords against an empire with enough brute force and celestial power to conquer the world over."

Boyce's eyes flashed green once more. "Now then. I think I've recharged enough to get our friend Trechon on his feet again. We'll have to hurry if we plan on making it to Tamore before the battle is over."

***

There wasn't much of a sunrise far as Leo could tell. Grey clouds filled the sky, threatening to give them more showers. Leo wiped a thin layer of dew from his hands. The fog covered everything dirt and blood had not yet soiled. The men began to stir within the walls, strapping on armor and lining up for a bowl of pottage and a cup of ale.

Edger was already up hollering at his wall-defenders to boil the morning's tar. They'd taken to calling him Redbeard now. Whether it was on account of his newfound wine appreciation or his siege defense efficiency, Leo couldn't say. Either way, Edger was proving to be one hell of a hand and Leo left him to his business.

"Got you a killer's breakfast here," Bruce said, balancing two bowls and two cups in his hands. He handed Leo his share and took a seat to eat his own.

Juan clanked down to his right, and Natalie and Mandy completed the circle. Leo wasn't much in the mood to eat, but didn't want to die hungry a few hours from now either. He shoveled a mouthful and down the hatch it went. Before he knew it, he was cleaning the bowl with a piece of rye bread.

"That's the spirit. Hearty meals will keep the Reaper away." Bruce fingered a leather pouch, drew out a handful of tobacco, and wedged it between his cheek and gum. "Not the Gorronian one, mind you. Fuck that bastard, we'll let him come. I mean the one with the cloak and scythe."

"Maybe you should start carrying a more distinct weapon, Master Bruce," Mandy suggested. The baldheaded swordmaster had told her to drop the "Master" business when she addressed him, but Leo insisted she give him the proper respect. *A good teacher teaches life's hardest lessons. Pay attention and you'll make fewer critical mistakes of your own,* Leo had told her. An echo of his father long ago. "Something more intriguing than a common sword. Like a mace or a bearded axe," she continued.

"A more distinct weapon, you say? That's a fine idea," Bruce mocked. "Maybe I can get Jonas to melt my sword down into a Guardian Spoon." He cut the air with his eating utensil and they all had a good laugh at it.

Their chuckling didn't last long before the nervous fidgeting returned. Leo found himself tinkering with the straps of his shield like they had an additional use. He stilled his hands and drew in a deep breath. "Guess we'd better get on with it. Looks like the Kimans are off to an early start."

Beyond the wall, a mass of soldiers broke from the ranks, heading west towards Britta Creek. They ambled methodically along, each of their helms facing the stronghold as they went. Inside the keep, the defenders climbed atop the wall to get a look at the Kimans who stretched out to surround them.

Edger's mouth slacked open as he stared mortified at the defenders climbing atop the wall. It swayed as more and more weight piled on. "Off the walls, you dummies. It's a shield not a damn catwalk."

Like a snake stretching from its coil, the Reds reached Britta Creek, careful to stay out of bowshot. And just like that they were surrounded.

"Isn't that lovely." Natalie moved across the wall carefully regarding each of the whitewashed range markers she had painted on the ground surrounding their walls. Soon enough, they'd be trampled into the mud and muck, but it was the best she could do for now. "Archers to the wall! I want a crossbow for every five long bows."

Leo was nearly pushed off the wall as archers scrambled into position. Edger paced through the Red Garden barking orders. This time there was a sharp edge in his voice.

"Guess I better get down to my men." Bruce drew his Guardian Sword, dangling his feet over the wall ready to leap down. "The east gate will hold, or I'll fall with it." Bruce hopped down and jogged towards his Swords of Bane."

"And so shall the west gate." Juan adjusted his helm. He turned to Leo. "You staying up here?"

Leo clasped Juan's hand, wishing he'd wiped more of the sweat from his palm first. "Save me a spot. I'll be down there soon as the swords start clashing."

"I imagine that won't be long," Juan added. "Take care of yourself, Leo. Remember you have an army at your side, so you don't have to do anything foolish. I'm afraid if you fall here, volatile as things are now Veronia will fall with you."

Juan hopped down from the wall, careful not to crush the earth as he landed. As Bruce and Juan ran to their gates, Leo felt oddly alone. The golden shield hummed against his forearm. Leo regarded it as if it could read his thoughts. He hoped not, or else it would sense his fear.

"Something wrong?" Mandy squinted at him in wonder.

"It's nothing." Leo shrugged and cracked his neck. "There's no place I'd rather be."

"Here they come," one of the wall-men announced from the outer wall.

The Kiman Army appeared in no mood to play games as they did the day before. Their formidable ranks spread out to swarm in a blitz formation. And why not? The Reds had plenty of men to impose their will.

Kiman war cries started to ring out as they began their charge. They beat their weapons against their shields. It sounded like a drum line. Slow and menacing, the beat quickened as they drew closer.

"Here they come indeed." Leo tightened the straps of his shield. His heart raced like he knew it would. The familiar rhythm so warm he began to sweat beneath his armor. "Stay close and keep your shield up," he ordered to Mandy. "And stay off the bow."

Mandy muttered some derogatory remark but dropped her bow and arrow all the same. She drew her sword and pressed her shield against her breastplate.

Leo glanced down the wall and found Natalie gripping the rail with both hands, her eyes fixed on her distance markers out in the field before them. As the Reds closed in their drumming waned as they started stepping over their fallen from the day before.

On the east side of the Red line, the first of their battering rams wheeled into view. It was a rolling mass of bundled logs. *Shit.* Leo peered to the west and found two more. *This is it then. A red day it shall be.*

"Archers ready!" Natalie bellowed as the Kimans approached the first of her range markers.

To Leo's surprise the Reds halted at once. "What are they doing?"

"Incoming!" a voice cried from the outer wall.

From the west, a loud noise rang through the air that Leo couldn't quite place. When he turned to find the source it was too late. The boulder crashed into his shield and upended him from the wall. The Red Garden's tangled embrace broke his fall. His head hit first, landing on a tree branch that dented his helm and wounded his pride. Disoriented, he wollered around in the branches that wrapped him like quicksand.

His sword had taken a flight of its own but his shield was firmly attached to his forearm. "What the feck was that?" he asked, not hearing his own words leave his mouth. His eyes watered, his vision blurred, and his legs felt lifeless when he ordered them to lift him up. He resorted to crawling overtop the mound of branches till he found solid ground.

A set of boots ran towards him, then halted. When Leo looked up, Edger stood in front of him with a hand extended. Another stone crashed into the wall behind them. Edger continued to yell at him but Leo couldn't hear a damn thing. He read his lips clear enough though. "Get up!" Redbeard yelled. "Can you walk?"

Wine trickled from Edger's beard and landed on the back of Leo's hand. The Castellan tossed his chalice aside and extended his other hand as well. Leo took both of them and was lifted onto his shaky feet.

"What the fuck was that?" he asked again.

"Catapults!" Edger yelled too loudly into his ear and Leo flinched away. "I ain't never seen such a perfect shot. Knocked you right off the wall." Edger patted Leo's boulder-notched shield in amazement. "Un-fucking-believable."

Leo still couldn't hear his own words. "I have to get back to the wall."

Edger's eyes lit up with wonder. "You sure about that? Not necessarily the first place I'd want to be when the stones are raining down. You of all people should know that by now."

"Out of my way, Redbeard."

"Suit yourself," Edger answered palm up. "You might wanna take that with you though." He pointed out Leo's sword in the Red Garden.

Leo bent over to pick it up and fought the urge to lie down beside it. He found a ladder and used it to scale the inner wall. The barrage of stones halted and Leo scanned the walls to assess the damages. The west wall had taken the worst of it. Five or more gaps at least a man wide stood out like black eyes. The Widow Makers strained to heave the fallen logs back into place.

After obtaining the desired effect of shock and

awe, the Kiman soldiers began their blitz. They ran towards the outer wall with blood-curdling cries. Their hot heads triggered the rest of Redbeard's hidden traps, and waves of them disappeared in the ground beneath. They hit the remaining spiked barriers and pushed them out of the way. By the time arrows began raining down upon them, the battering rams were creaking forward to do their worst.

It went without saying that the rams were the first targets of choice but Leo called for them to be taken out immediately.

"Rain of Fire!" Natalie ordered, running down the line. Her arches retrieved their cloth-tipped arrows and set them aflame. One by one the rams began to catch flame until the Kiman soldiers abandoned them where they smoldered. No man wants to stand next to arrow fodder. The Kiman soldiers continued on without them, running headlong into the outer wall.

The Reds were well equipped it seemed. Not only did they have plenty of men, catapults, and battering rams, many were closing the distance carrying ladders to scale the damn walls.

Their ladders hit the walls and Reds started to ascend. "Burn 'em down!" Redbeard bellowed from his garden.

His wall-men scaled ladders of their own with boiling pots of black tar. They spilled it liberally over the side of the wall. Men cried out below their pots, writhing in pain as their flesh burned away. Smoldering skin tinged Leo's nose and turned his stomach. Arrows and bolts continued to rain down but where one had fallen, two other Kimans took his place.

A cloud of arrows rose into the air, and Leo noticed they were heading the wrong way. Only then did he spot the rank of archers in the rear of the Kiman assault. "Shields up!" he yelled too late for some, as the arrows began to pelt the stronghold. For the first time, cries of pain and agony rang out within the walls. Their songs so emotionally charged that Leo recognized the voices from the curses they shared.

Natalie's archers returned fire as fast as they could. The sky filled with pointed people-killers doing their worst on both sides of the wall.

"Bloody hell." Leo crouched down beneath his shield, back against the battlements. Arrows thudding into everything around him. He knew it wasn't the most motivating sight for his men to see their chosen Shield nearly curled up in the fetal position but he'd be damned if he got knocked off the wall again. "To Sheol with archers and trebuchets," he hissed.

"I can't believe what I just saw," Mandy said almost too casually. She scooted her ass over next to him. *At least she still has her shield up,* Leo noted. "A stone like that should have put you in the dirt. Maybe you truly are Unbreakable."

"Not true." Leo worked his jaw to the side with an effort. "I'm pretty sure I swallowed a tooth down there." His tongue found a gap where one of his premolars should have been. "My flawless smile will never be the same."

The Kimans were all over the outer wall now. A few of the more agile ones even managed to scale over and into the Red Garden. Their triumph was short-lived as they were gunned down by crossbows. At least most of the Kiman archers had stopped blind-firing now. Wouldn't do them much good if they shot down their own men.

Leo risked a glance over his shield and saw Edger wrestling with a man in the garden. "Shit!" he barked, scrambling to his feet. "You stay up here. Grab a crossbow and try not to shoot me with it."

He hopped down the wall careful not to get tangled up again. By the time he made it to them, Edger had found himself on top and went to work opening up the Red's face with short, slicing elbows. More of them began to climb over the outer wall and Leo met them with his kwatina. The hatchet cut easily enough through the skin, and broke bones where it met chainmail and armor.

A battering ram bludgeoned its way through the outer wall and into the garden. Kiman soldiers began spilling through, tripping and falling in the brush. The walls rocked again from the outside where another battering ram did its worst. Between the slits in the log wall, Leo could see the Kiman bastards and set to stabbing them through the wall with his sword. Thrust after thrust he felt more armor than flesh but his sword was wet from the effort.

A Kiman soldier scaled the wall and took a bolt to the hip for his troubles. He toppled over the wall and fell on top of Leo. The Shield of Veronia had checked out when the blood started to spill and the Bloody Rose took his place. He grabbed the man by the bolt in his hip and tossed him aside. Leo rolled on top of him and rained down the pommel of his sword so viciously that the man's orbital socket quickly turned to mush.

The spatter blurred Leo's vision when he blinked through the crimson sea. The Red Garden began to fill as the Swords of Bane and the Widow Makers joined the fight. Juan's bastard sword flickered in the distance, cutting souls from bodies on his way towards Leo. Sergeant Jaxon was at Juan's side and happened to get knocked over by a charging Kiman.

On his back now, Jaxon shielded his face from the blows but his forearms weren't big enough to cover both his face and stomach. The sword took him just above the belt and Jaxon was left on the ground staring lifelessly into the sky. No one could help him now.

Juan cut the Kiman soldier down before the Bloody Rose could get there. Juan's wild stare found Leo's just as a horn blasted three times and the Kimans began their retreat.

***

They were south of Mt. Drago when Agnen called for

Jewel to get out of the boat and pull them ashore. The huge volcano smoked in the distance and a cloud of soot loomed above it. The Gorronian had been quiet through the night and Jewel didn't have to wonder why. Agnen was exiled from his native country and there were bounties on his head in Veronia and the Kiman Empire now.

Jewel slid over the side of the boat into the waist-deep water. He sunk down into it, submerging the aching knot on his swollen head. The cool seawater washed over him, stinging the wound. When he rose above the water, he found Agnen staring impatiently at him. Jewel latched onto the boat and began pulling it ashore. "Have you heard any word from Tamore?" Jewel asked.

"I imagine they're under siege by now. That was the plan anyways. Not my problem now."

"Right," Jewel replied. He wasn't exactly sure why Agnen had made the decision to save his life, but like all things there must be strings attached somewhere. Perhaps Agnen felt he'd outlived his use within the Kiman Empire. Or maybe he'd grown tired of all the swordplay. The Gorronian sure looked tired of something far as Jewel could tell. His feet trudged up out of the water to the sandy shoreline where he pulled the tow of the boat out of the water.

Agnen stepped out onto the shoreline, stretching his back and taking in the view. This close to Mt. Drago, the earth was more rock than soil, but not near as desolate as the Winsoot Mountains to the north.

Jewel watched Agnen regard their boat once more. It was of little help to the Gorronian. Too small to cross the Iron Sea, and the longer they coasted along the shoreline the more attention they would draw. "Where will you go?"

"I've got only one place in mind, Priest." The Gorronian regarded the Winsoot Mountain Range to the north and a smile threatened to spread but died quick as it came on the Reaper's battlefield of a face. Like the muscles weren't supposed to stretch that way. He lifted his fist and pointed with his thumb. "What happened back there changes nothing. I saw a way out and I took it." He stepped in close. "Next time you'll get the edge of my sword. Best be on your own way now. I've got places to go and something to find."

Agnen pulled at the leather strap around his dragon-armored breastplate, repositioning the sword at his back. Satisfied with the result, he brushed past Jewel and stalked off in a northward direction carrying his helm by the horn.

Jewel watched the warrior without a country step it out. As curious a fellow as Agnen was, Jewel thought there might be a glimmer of decency in the Gorronian he hadn't seen before. He wondered if anyone else had ever seen it too. Reminded him a little of Leo.

He stared at Agnen's back as the Gorronian walked up a rocky slope until he was out of view. The sun overhead began to break through the clouds, and all the rain they'd been getting lately made for a very humid afternoon. Jewel set off to the west. With any luck he could find a mount and reach Tamore in a day or two.

Not long after he set off on his own, sweat began to bead on his forehead. He wiped it away with the sleeve of his robe. He wetted his chapped lips, tongue like sandpaper, and longed for a drink. He quickened his pace through the trees towards Britta Creek. Surely he could barter for a mount and a hot meal in Mt. Drago, but that would cost him valuable time to backtrack and he and Tamore had none to spare.

Jewel's mind was in another place as he walked. He could almost taste Britta Creek and had a mind to swim the last leg to Tamore. So lost in thought he was, that Jewel hadn't noticed the man on the trail before him, until the cloaked figure raised a hand to halt him. Jewel reached for the dagger at his waist; his hipbone reminded him it wasn't there. "Blast."

CHAPTER

5

The cloaked figure regarded Jewel and then the trees beyond. "You must be Bishop Jewel," he said. "Where is the other man who I saw you sailing with?"

Jewel weighed the question and his answer. It wasn't uncommon to be recognized as a bishop, but rarely had he ever been called by name. Something about this half-man unsettled him. "My shipmate has set out on his own. Forgive my suspicions but these are troubled times. Might I ask what your name is and how you found me?"

"Fair enough questions, but you and I don't have time to waste on pleasantries. My name is Kano. I was looking for an old companion of mine, Bishop Michael, and saw you sailing from Shield Island last night."

"So you're a Zodan then." Jewel let out a sigh of relief.

"I am indeed. I trust Bishop Michael's true identity has become known to you now."

"It has, among other things. Abaddon summoned the giants last night, and Brother Mi...erm, Nicolai, has been bound in a cage. Where are the rest of the Zodans?"

"On their way to Tamore. There are Prothica embedded within the Kiman Army that surrounds your brother's stronghold. We've been looking for Nicolai for some time now."

Jewel edged forward. "So my brother still lives?"

"As far as I could tell. But it doesn't look good. The Kiman Army has them outnumbered and surrounded. Their walls will only hold for so long. We were on our way there to provide assistance should the Prothica decide to intervene. That was until I found Nicolai bound on Shield Island."

If the Zodans decided to abandon Tamore in lieu of saving Nicolai, then all of Tamore would fall. "There's something I must tell you," Jewel said. "Abaddon doesn't mean to harm Nicolai."

Kano turned and began to walk away. "I have to go. For the love Nicolai bore you, I've not left you stranded. You'll find two destriers tied to an oak a mile or so west of here. That cavalry unit in Tamore cut them loose. The Black Widows or something to that effect." The air around the Zodan started to shift and Jewel risked reaching out to grab Kano by the sleeve.

The Zodan's cold eyes met Jewel's hand with a warning and Jewel let him go. "Listen, Bishop Jewel. I know you want us to help your brother, and the Zodans tend to do just that, but we must save Nicolai first. We cannot allow the Prothica to dig in deeper than they already are."

"They're called the Widow Makers," Jewel corrected. "Did you see my brother there? Or the rest of the Priest's Council?"

Kano regarded the ground, finger and thumb pressed against his half ear. The look he bore didn't inspire much confidence and Jewel started to assume the worst.

"The stronghold stands, as do most of the people within it I'd imagine but both sides have already lost many men. Who still lives I cannot say. I didn't risk getting too close. I could sense the Prothica, Borin, and Elias among the Kiman soldiers. If your brother's men can find a way to hold on for a while, the Tribesmen aren't too far out."

The Tribesmen? Then Jewel remembered the blood debt they owed Leo. "Tekrano's doing I'd imagine." Jewel was almost giddy with the news. Then he paled. "Does Leo even know the Tribesmen are coming?"

"I have no idea. Listen, I must go now. I wish you the best of luck."

"Abaddon wears the Ring of Solomon," Jewel blurted out desperately. "And you must have seen his Giant army. I could make them out sailing away in the dark of night."

"Of course I saw them. That's why I must gather the Zodans."

"And how many Zodans do you have at your disposal?" Jewel spat. "Four, maybe five? You think a handful of starborn can storm that island and defeat Abaddon, Lyle, and an army of giants?"

A cold wind blew between them and Kano's eyes flashed aglow. A threat that should have stilled Jewel's tongue but did not.

"Abaddon doesn't seek to harm Nicolai. He's trapped him in a dragonglass cage that prevents him from drawing power from the else. You said so yourself that you have to prevent the balance of power from tilting more in the Prothica's favor. Abaddon plans on using his army to capture the rest of you Zodans. Killing you will only allow another to name the star in your place. But if he can bind you all to a cage, he and his armies will have no one that can stand against them."

Kano's eyes swept Jewel up and down. "If what you say is true, how did you discover Abaddon's plan? That man you were with. His name is Agnen, isn't it? The commander of the Kiman army, is he not? I saw the bodies you two left behind. Must have been in an awful hurry."

"I was held prisoner along with Nicolai. I would thank the heavens for allowing me to slip away, but I know my freedom was the result of one man. A man who's raised the sword against Veronia for years but now grows tired of the fight."

Kano chuckled at that and turned to walk away once more. "Listen Bishop Jewel, I know you want to save your brother and the rest of Tamore, but we Zodans have a duty to free Nicolai first."

"Helping Tamore withstand the siege and my brother's army will no doubt help you get Nicolai back. As will I." Kano stopped in his tracks, the way men do while making a decision. A weighty one indeed. "If you Zodans are already headed to Tamore, then between Leo's army, the Tribesmen, and your starborn we can defeat the Kiman Army and the two Prothica you mentioned before. Then together we can attack Abaddon and his giants to free Nicolai."

"And just how can you be so sure, Bishop?" Kano's question was more a challenge and Jewel didn't miss the condescending tone of it. "The Tribesmen are more than likely only fighting to save face in lieu of a two-year-old blood debt they owe Leo. And who's to say that what's left of Veronia will be so willing to attack the Prothica and the giants once they are made known to them?"

"Because Abaddon is the real threat and we both

know it. As long as he and the Prothica still reign over the Kiman Empire, there will be unrest in the world over." Kano stood still for what seemed an eternity. "You have the ability to teleport, do you not? Perhaps you should go to Tamore and ask Leo yourself. Send him word of my escape and the Tribesmen who you say are marching to join their ranks."

Kano's gaze met Jewel's once more. His mouth parted to speak then closed as he disappeared.

***

It was the dawn of their third day under siege in Tamore. Their walls didn't take much damage after the militia attack on the first day, but the Reds broke through the outer wall on day two, and Leo hoped it wouldn't be the inner wall he stood upon that they infiltrated today. He scanned his men, most of them eating dried meat and cold stews for breakfast, while others released their pre-fight jitters outside the east gate.

Leo descended the wall, nodding to his men as he walked along. He didn't bother having Juan and Bruce conduct a headcount after yesterday's bloody battle. Counting the living only reminded him of their dead and Leo knew better to dwell on the past when they had a sea of swords still threatening. He knew the count close enough. About six hundred men between the Swords of Bane and the Widow Makers. A hundred more or so archers and then there were Redbeard's wallmen who had taken the brunt of it yesterday and now numbered less than fifty.

"Commander Rosewood." It was Lieutenant Cederic la Mare, Juan's First Horseman. His black tunic was tattered and he stood favoring his left arm where a sword slash had bitten into his elbow the day before. Dark bags of restlessness swelled under his eyes which didn't look to have dried since he'd buried Jaxon during the night. "We, erm, have a visitor."

"A visitor?" Leo couldn't see over the walls, but he was certain the Red Army remained ready to put their stronghold to the sword. "Who is it, and how the hell did they get to the wall without my knowing?"

"That's precisely what Captains Soberal and Donnell are trying to find out now, Commander." Cederic drew his right hand from his hurt arm. When it came away moist, he regarded it with a welfare sniff. Satisfied with the results, he dabbed the blood on his tunic. "He's a short man, almost childlike in stature but I hear the Drago Smiths and the Priest's Council have already vouched for his credibility. I hear he has a message from your brother."

Leo was off, shouldering through the crowd before Cederic called at his back. "He's at the west gate, Commander.

Even with Cederic's warning, the visitor's short stature caught him off guard. He stood waist-tall between Jonas and Juan, while Bishop Isabelle put him to the question. He wore a star-embroidered cloak. A pink scar started at the corner of his mouth and ended where his right earlobe used to be. When Leo shouldered past Trion, the half-man saw him for the first time and crouched into a fighting stance with starlit eyes.

A sorcerer, Leo thought, remembering his former dungeon-mate Boyce. All around him, soldiers palmed the grips of their swords. "Sheath your weapons!" Leo commanded.

"His eyes," someone said.

"A sorcerer!" exclaimed another.

The half-man's gaze dimmed and he slowly recoiled from his crouch. Leo felt the visitor's eyes swimming all over him, searching for something he'd yet to find.

"Silence," Leo barked to the crowd. He regarded the star-patterned marks on the visitor's hands. Similar to the ones he'd seen on Boyce, but not as abundant. It occurred to Leo that the sorcerer just might have been doing the same thing. *Is he searching my hands? He thinks I'm a sorcerer.* Leo felt something wrap 'round his torso constricting him as he stepped forward. Whatever it was took his breath away. He winced and halted. "Your name and message, sorcerer?"

"My name is Kano. You must be Commander Rosewood, the Shield of Veronia." The half-man stepped forward with a knowing grin. "Something paining you, Commander? An ache in the chest, perhaps?"

Leo fought the urge to step further back. Now that Kano mentioned it, that's exactly where the sudden ache resided. He wondered if the sorcerer had put a spell on him. Leo felt suddenly compelled to cut the half-man's other ear off. But if this visitor was anywhere near as powerful as Boyce, he knew his sword would never be quick enough.

"I hear you've a message from my brother. What is it?" he croaked.

"The Tribesmen ride south to combine their swords with yours against the Kimans. Your brother managed to escape capture with the help of a rather unlikely ally yet Bishop Michael remains prisoner. Bishop Jewel rides here from the west."

"Oh thank god," Trion said. Bishop Isabelle and Malachi appeared only half satisfied.

Leo would have smiled himself had it not been for the pain in his chest that grew stronger, radiating up into his head. The weight of the golden shield on his back became unbearable; he fumbled the straps to shed its weight. When he latched onto it, his hands turned numb and he lost feeling in his arms. The tingling began to spread towards his torso, dulling the pain in his chest. Leo slid his arm through the strap of many colors, letting out an exasperated sigh as the pain in his head began to subside.

It wasn't until he noticed the whites of Juan's eyes that he looked down and saw the runes on his shield burning with light. The runes on his hatchet like fiery coals. His right hand drawn to its wooden handle. When he clasped onto it, a warmth coursed through his limbs.

"Now this, Nicolai didn't tell me about," Kano said, regarding Leo.

"Who's Nicolai?" Leo asked.

"I'll let Bishop Jewel explain that when he gets here. Tell me Leo, have you ever wished upon the stars?"

"Hmph. You sound like a man I once knew. What is it with you sorcerers and all your pining for the stars?"

"It's time for round three!" Mandy called down from the wall. Across the battlefield the Kiman soldiers left the comfort of their bedroll and fires to get in formation. Most of them didn't seem in any hurry to get there either.

"To the walls," Redbeard bellowed. Natalie, Juan, and Bruce began to ready their own men into position.

"Tell me, Commander." Leo had to look down to see Kano strolling beside him. "Was this friend you once knew starborn?" Kano made a circular motion with his hand. "A sorcerer if you will. Might I ask his name?"

"A name for a name then." Leo climbed the wall as he spoke. Somehow Kano beat him there. Leo did his best to conceal his surprise. "First, tell me who this unlikely ally is that helped my brother escape."

A wry smile spread across Kano's face. "Oh I think

you're rather familiar with this particular person. Why it's none other than Agnen the Reaper."

"Bullshit," Leo declared. "That bastard lives only to wet his sword. He'd kill my brother just to spite me." Leo set his jaw and squeezed his hatchet. "Is the Gorronian on his way here too?"

"Oh you won't find Agnen at your walls, I'm afraid. When he fled Shield Island with Jewel, he turned his back on the Kiman Empire once and for all. He's probably the most hated man in the Free Cities right now. Now a name for a name," Kano reminded.

Leo searched the half-man for deception but found none. "Humph," he said at last. "His name is Boyce. At least that's what he told me. Spent some time with him in the dungeon, so take it for what that's worth. But he's a sorcerer alright. Had stars on his hands, same as you. Used his magic to spring us from Bresdan when the Reds sacked the city."

Kano leaned forward like he hadn't heard that right. "Boyce...in the dungeon you say?"

"That's what I said." Leo shrugged and rotated his neck left and right till it cracked and popped. "Now if you'll excuse me, I've got something rather pressing to attend."

"Right. I've got an errand or two to run myself. Should only take a few moments."

Kano disappeared. Leo blinked and blinked again. He moved forward peering at the place where Kano once stood. He twisted around and found no sign of the half-man. "Fucking sorcerers."

***

They were west of Crystal Lake when Liz felt her carriage creeping to a stop. After sending Roland, Weston, and Ditto off, Liz had taken sole occupancy of the first carriage, while Brielle and Ambrose rode behind with their new protégés. She needed time alone to gather her thoughts. She wondered how the mundane war was going and whether or not the Prothica had broken the accords yet again and intervened. Liz also wondered who had named the final major star. Where was Nicolai now and why hadn't Kano returned yet? And what was Abaddon's endgame in all of this? So many unanswered questions.

Liz peered out her window and caught a glimpse of the Bay of Bones through the trees. They were getting close now. If they pushed hard they could make it to Tamore by this time tomorrow. If they got rid of the carriages they'd make the trek even faster. Liz made up her mind to ditch them at Sweetwater Creek. A day's ride on horseback would make all of them saddle-sore and they'd need every ounce of energy if they were to face the Prothica and the Kiman soldiers in Tamore.

She stepped out of the carriage and welcomed the westward breeze that caught her hair and cooled her neck. A heavy trodden horse trail was the only road on which to travel northward from Nebula to Sweetwater

Creek. The previous kings of Veronia didn't encourage any travel that led to Mt. Drago and the smiths that inhibited the region were even less enthralled to have a road leading to their precious mineral-laden land.

The checkpoint was marked by a small homestead. Abandoned most likely as a result of the civil war that ruptured Veronia from coast to coast. The log cabin was sturdily built, but the mortal holding the rocky smokestack had been neglected for some time and was threatening to collapse. Nonetheless their horses were spotted easily enough on the backside of the cabin.

Brielle and Ambrose hopped out of their carriage while Otis and Lamar busied themselves in search of refreshments to restock their supplies. When they didn't see any in plain sight, the two protégés ventured toward the cabin, announcing themselves to anyone who might be inside. Lamar knocked on the front door. When no answer came he gave it a push to no effect. Must have been barred from within. Otis abandoned the front door, making his way to the side of the cabin where a window was boarded shut. Shielding the sun from his eyes with both hands, he peered between the planks for a look inside.

Liz heard Ambrose's spine creak and pop when he arched his back. "Ahh," he exclaimed, satisfied with the results. "I'm no master of cartography, but I can smell salt water to the west, and just beyond those giant redwoods to the east is Crystal Lake. Should we ditch the carts and ride horseback from here?"

"Not just yet," Liz replied. Beside Ambrose, Brielle flipped a coin into the air. She suspended it in mid-air then reached out with her sorcery to spin it. Liz flicked her fingers and the golden crown twirled up and away. It came to rest in the palm of her hand. She smiled at her former protégé then slid the coin into her cloak.

"Hey!" Brielle exclaimed. "I was only trying to dull the starache."

"The two of you need to start conserving your energy. You'll have plenty of time for games provided you don't get yourselves killed when we get to Tamore. Help your protégés get the carts loaded, and try to make water without soiling your cloaks."

Ambrose moved his lips for a witty reply and Liz silenced him with a raised eyebrow.

Liz made her way to the horses tied next to an unattended feed trough. She untied the first one and led him by the reins to her cart.

"My lady," Codoc called at the front of the cart, his deft hands busy unbuckling the leather straps that secured the horses to the front of the carriage. "Please allow me." He hustled over to relieve her of the reins. "Master Killian would be quite displeased were he to hear that Oberian and I allowed you to do our work."

She shook him off and led the horse past his outstretched hands. "Do I look like the type of lady who's afraid to get her hands dirty, Codoc?"

"Not at all m'lady. I was just—"

"Master Killian will hear only the highest praise of you and his chosen shields, but that's only if we make it to Tamore in time."

"As you wish, m'lady," Codoc replied, moving twice as fast to change the other horse.

Liz carried the reins in her right hand. With her left, she brushed through the horse's coarse mane. Suddenly a cold nail raked across her spine. "There's no sheets on them." She regarded the other horses tied to the trough. Not a single one of them were draped in one of Kano's white sheets.

"Brielle! Ambrose!" she shrieked like a momma bear who'd lost sight of her cubs.

"What is it, Lady Brielle?" Lamar turned away from the front door just about the time it flung open. Chainmail rustled and Kiman soldiers spilled out with crossbows in hand. A bolt took Lamar in the chest as he turned around. He went down to a knee before his weight carried him face first into the ground.

The twang of crossbows filled the air and a volley of arrows darted towards them as Liz dropped to the ground to avoid a similar fate. She was tackled on the way down by Oberian who tried to shield her from the onslaught of arrows. Two or more of them already lodged firmly in his back. His ivory white teeth stained with crimson clamped shut as he grimaced in pain. His strong brown eyes held hers, until his body turned limp, and his dead weight pinned her to the ground.

Codoc and the other two Kotian guards drew their

swords looking for targets. They were met with another flurry of bolts and arrows. Codoc and his brothers weathered the volley but were not unharmed. Bolts pierced them from all angles. They charged forward despite the pain slashing and stabbing. Codoc grabbed Liz by the arm with bloodied hands. He strained, spitting blood as he pulled her to the carriage for cover.

"We're undone, m'lady. Ambushed like..." he trailed off, wincing in pain. Two arrows, one in his thigh, the other in his shoulder, had begun to drain the fight and life from the Heronian warrior. "I must get you to safety," he moaned as another bolt thrust into his back and jolted him forward.

Codoc's eyes glistened and he clutched his teeth like his valiant brother Oberian had done just before him. It was then that something inside Liz snapped. Her eyes turned aglow and she opened the carriage door and pushed Codoc gently inside.

The flood of sorcery that Liz called upon chilled her to the core. Her wintry gaze found the Red soldiers reloading their crossbows, while Ambrose, Brielle, and even Otis flung starfire into the tree line where more soldiers began to spill forth. Most of them abandoning their bows and charging forward with naked steel.

"There's too many of them!" Ambrose shrieked.

An arrow took Brielle in the shoulder and she spun to the ground. Ambrose grabbed her by the collar and dragged her to the second carriage. "Liz. Help us!" he cried, panic-stricken. Despite his trepidation, he managed to pull Brielle with one arm while fending off their pursuers with violent blasts of starfire.

Liz moved past them with clinched fists. The wind gusted and a funnel swept around them. Encircling them like a wall. The bolts and arrows that met it were sent spinning away. As the Kiman soldiers charged, Liz swept a hand towards them. A gust of wind lifted them off their feet and sent the soldiers flailing through the air. Their cries rang out until their bodies crashed back into the earth. Others met the solid trunks and branches of the mighty redwoods which had no give in them. Another flick of her wrist and a howling wind swept the cabin away plank by plank.

The earth trembled like cavalry charged behind her. When Liz turned, two giants chewed up the ground towards her. Their faces twisted in rage. They carried clubs the size of men and shields of blackened glass. Her mind reached into the depths of the else. Like a rushing river it threatened to sweep her away. Her senses heightened to the point she could smell the foul stench of the giants barreling towards her.

Little Otis intercepted them, flinging starfire at the giants as they ran by. Their attention seemed fixed solely on Liz. Otis's starfire took the first giant off his feet, and the giant tumbled to the ground, writhing in pain like a wild boar.

The second giant raised his shield to ward off the starfire, and swung his mighty club at Otis. It struck the protégé with a thud and sent Otis flying through the air.

The impact so bone-crunchingly fierce that Otis was likely dead before he hit the ground. The giant's momentum was unaltered by Otis or the wind that Liz struggled to rain down upon him. It did little but rustle the giant's hairy chest and arms. Liz scrambled out of the way barely missing the business end of the giant's second swing.

The giant dug his heels into the earth and slid to a stop, just a few feet away from Brielle and Ambrose. With a mighty roar he reared back to strike Ambrose who disappeared in the blink of an eye.

The giant spun around looking for his prey but found only his starfire that jarred the giant from behind. The giant grunted hellishly. He swung his club wildly until it crashed into the carriage. The giant pulled at his club, rocking the carriage back and forth, but his weapon was lodged between wooden planks that seemed to cinch down at each pull of the club.

Ambrose's visible form fluttered back into view. He was sweating through his cloak, eyes stark white from the effort of it all. He rained down starfire from both hands and the giant's tunic caught flame. The monster abandoned his club and shield, to beat out the fire.

"To hell with you," Ambrose yelled behind one last burst of sorcery. The giant raised a clenched fist and cried out one last time in his ancient tongue. He left behind only a heaping pile of smoldering soot.

Ambrose clutched his chest with a sweaty palm

and sank to the ground. Liz ran to him, taking his cold hands in hers. His face pale and turning blue. "Ambrose!" she cried, shaking him back to life. "Ambrose wake up!"

It wasn't until Liz heard Brielle's sobering cry that she realized the first giant, whom she'd thought dead, hadn't left the same pile of ash. When she turned, the giant had Brielle lifted up off the ground. Her feet kicked violently as the giant pressed her back to his chest with his left arm, still clutching the mighty club in his right.

"Silence," the giant roared, pressing Brielle into his massive chest.

"You vile abomination," Liz spat, letting go of Ambrose's cold hands. Trembling to control her rage.

"That's as far as you go, starborn." He stretched out his club end at her. Brielle kicked once more and the giant nearly dropped her. "Be still!" he roared loud enough to deafen her.

"Everyone stay calm." Liz took a deep breath. The first one she remembered taking in a while. She swept the scene of bodies and swallowed a lump of gravel in her throat. Otis's body began to rise as his star called him home.

"What is it you want, giant? There's been enough killing today. Let her go and you can have me in her place."

"Isn't that just the cutest thing I've ever heard." It was Roland who sauntered out from behind the second carriage to stand next to the giant. To solidify his treachery, he wore a black cloak now. His smirk caused bile to rise in Liz's throat.

"You traitor!" Brielle screamed, kicking once again as the giant fought to still her in his arms. When his grip drew tighter, she spat towards Roland. Her disgust hit him square in the cheek.

Roland chuckled, dabbing at his cheek with his sleeve. "More of an opportunist really. You pissed my loyalty away when you chose Otis and Lamar over me." He scoffed once more. "Some good it did you, huh Lamar?"

Lamar didn't respond. Most dead men don't. Instead his body burst into light and he joined the children of the stars with Otis.

"And what of Weston and Ditto?" Liz wondered if they'd turned coat too. Their absence led her to believe otherwise.

"Dead and dead." Roland was enjoying this. "That shouldn't be much of a consequence to you though. None of you found them worthy of anything but busywork. Why would the Prothica want to employ all of your rejects?"

Liz shuddered. All the fight seemed to flee from her at once. She wondered if she could muster enough strength to at least wipe that smug grin off Roland's face once and for all.

Standing there beneath the towering giant, Liz felt small and alone. Her company was lost and defeat starting to rear its ugly head. Liz resolved to die before she'd beg mercy of Roland. "What is it that you want, Rol—"

"Shhh." Roland waved his hand to silence her. He gestured past Liz to where Ambrose lie crumpled on the ground. His breathing no longer visible in the rise and fall of his chest.

"Ambrose!" cried Brielle, fighting once more to escape. The arrow in her shoulder rendered her bloodied right arm useless. "Ambrose, no!"

"It won't be long now. He's burned-out. We might as well watch the show." Roland's laugh turned audible and Liz felt her blood boil once more.

"You sonofabitch," she spat, calling the wind with all her strength.

The giant hesitated then slung Brielle aside. Liz knew the decision before he made it. Either club Brielle or reach for the shield at his feet. He didn't have time for both. He went for his shield and crouched behind it. Liz's windstorm rushed past him on either side.

A starball amassed in her hand the size of a human head. So large that Liz trembled to control it lest it backfire on her.

She loosed it at the crouching giant who tried to block it with his shield. The blast took him in the shoulder and rocked him on his back. The giant's shoulder erupted at once and his arm twisted away. The wound blackened. The starfire spread like webbing around his body. A binding that constricted him to ashes and dust.

"Now!" Roland screamed. His eyes swam through the trees. "Do it now!" When nothing happened he loosed his own attack at Liz but his sorcery was no match for the howling wind that swept him off his feet.

"Stay with Ambrose," Liz barked at Brielle.

Roland patted the ground with his hands, crawling up and onto his feet. He sprinted off, cloak billowing behind as he went. The wind pushed him faster than his feet could churn but Liz was fading. Roland ran at an angle as one might swim against a riptide.

"There's no escaping the death I bring," Liz called out. She halted her wind and glided towards him, flicking starfire at his heels. Blood trickled from her nose. Her head throbbed but she couldn't stop now, not while Roland still lived. She pressed on, each step heavier than the last.

Lost in flight for his life, Roland regained his bearings. His only hope was to reach one of the mounts still tied to the trough where the cabin once stood.

He reached for the reins; the horse snorted and kicked wildly. In a panic, Roland struggled to untie the simple loop knot. "Silence you stupid fucker, or I'll break your legs and skin you alive." He elbowed the horse in the snout for good measure. "Aha." He untied the knot at last and mounted with haste. He dug in his heels and the horse bucked, nearly losing its rider before galloping off. "Easy now, you fecking cunt." Roland tugged at the reins, lifting the horses head to slow its gallop. The horse kicked and thrashed in circles. "Run you fecking... Argh."

Roland lost his grip on the reins when the bolt plunged into his throat. The horse took the opportunity to buck his rider off the ass end and sprint away. Roland clutched his neck, fighting for air. His strained breaths came out hollow and bubbly sounding.

When Roland went down, Liz breathed a sigh of relief. Never before had she been so pleased with Brielle ignoring her commands. But it wasn't enough to stop the crippling pain in her chest that dropped her to bending knee. Liz pawed the earth with both hands, the ground beckoning her to lie down and stay a while.

When Roland looked up, Brielle stood over him with another bolt notched in her crossbow. She favored her own shoulder with a slow mocking regard. A matching wound in Roland's neck. She cradled the crossbow awkwardly in her left hand. Roland wasn't worth the sorcery it would take to kill him and Brielle was weak enough as it was.

If it weren't for the arrow that lodged in Roland's throat, Liz was sure he'd be begging for his life like the coward he was. She crawled forward, close enough to hear Roland's wet wheezing. She wanted to tell Roland that his death would go unnoticed and his life a stain best forgotten. That he was the lowest piece of shit she'd ever seen and that she'd cut his hands off, tie him to a tree, and let the wolves have what's left of him. If in fact she could only make it to him before Brielle finished him off. Her throat spasmed shut and she couldn't find her voice.

Brielle met her gaze. When it did, it shifted past her as Liz crawled forward, wide with shock. Liz's senses had all but left her but she felt the earth shake where her hands and knees met it. Brielle stared slack-jawed, her eyes wide with fright. The crossbow fell at her feet.

Liz felt strong hands clasp her by the shoulders. She was lifted off the ground and shoved into a cage. A latch clicked home and she wrapped her hand around the jagged glass bars. Another giant lifted the cage and as she was carried away, she saw several more of them walking towards Brielle. She swayed in the cage, until it was hefted up and into a wagon. Another cage was next to her own. In it, she saw Nicolai.

His solemn gaze was full of pain and Liz found she couldn't hold it. Her eyelids were too heavy. Utterly exhausted, her head sagged forward, asleep at the touch of the bars.

***

Kano 'ported to Yusolf's homestead where he'd set up the last of the checkpoints. He met Yusolf years ago on a mission to add another rare book to Nicolai's collection. You would think someone with the ability to teleport wouldn't do much walking. The proof of that myth was evident in the heavily trodden soles of Kano's footwear. Thus befriending the best cobbler in all of Veronia seemed like a reasonable thing to do, and Yusolf was more than happy to oblige Kano's frequent business.

With any luck Kano could find the other Zodans and get a new pair of boots at the same time. He pushed the thought aside when he 'ported to the cobbler's cabin. Or at least where it once stood. Now there were just planks strewn about the foundation, and dead bodies peppered in the mix. His heart sank to new depths when he saw the wrecked carriages.

"Yusolf!" he cried out, voice high and anxious. He ran to the nearest corpse. A Kiman soldier who'd had his head taken clean off. The stump of his neck, charred black at the shoulders, let him know that his starborn companions had been in the midst of the fight.

He ran to another corpse and another but it was more of the same. He found the splintered front door of the cabin near the road. Kano ran to the collapsed cabin. "Yusolf," he cried, digging through thatch, wood, and stone. Beneath a wooden support beam he saw a foot. Kano pushed the beam aside and found Yusolf staring lifelessly into the sky. Blood had already dried and crusted around the slit in his throat. Kano shielded his eyes with the back of his hand. "Dear God." He shuffled away and his foot landed on something soft. When he peered down, he was standing on Henry's stomach.

Henry, who was just a boy, no older than ten and

barely taller than Kano. He shared the same fate as his father. Kano dropped to his knees gathering thatch to cover the boy's body. In doing so he uncovered Yusolf's wife. She lay on her back, skirt scrunched up above her waist.

"No!" Kano cried into the palms of his hands. He wept for some time, then staggered out of the rubble into a patch of grass where he found the first pile of ashes. "Prothica," he forced the words out through clenched teeth.

He found three of Killian's guards near the carriages. The Heron warriors had arrows sticking out from every limb. Each had died with swords in hand. By the looks of the butchered Kiman soldiers at their feet, they'd fought well.

"Ambrose," he cried again. "Brielle," he rasped, sifting through more bodies. "Liz." He made it to the first carriage. It looked as if a tree had fallen on it. Kano ripped the remnants of the carriage door aside and peered in.

The fourth Heronian warrior lie on his side within. He reached out to Kano with a bloodied hand. "Codoc," he breathed, taking the warrior's hand in his.

"Forgive me, Master Kano. There were too many of them."

Kano climbed inside, crouching beneath the caved-in roof of the carriage to hold his countryman. "No, no my friend. There's nothing to be sorry for." He trembled to get the words out. A pool of Codoc's blood wet the floor and started soaking into Kano's cloak. "Can you tell me what happened, brother? And what of the Zodans?"

"The Kiman soldiers attacked with great force." Codoc's voice was weak. A mere whisper. The strain of speaking almost too much to bear. "They had giants among them and a starborn besides. We were ambushed." He broke into a fit of wet coughing that spattered onto Kano's face. "It was Roland who betrayed the others."

"And are the others dead?" Kano urged an answer before Codoc could speak more.

"No. Captured from what I could hear. Carried away by the giants."

He wanted to thank the heavens but learning of a dying warrior who'd given his life to protect Kano's friends was no time to do so. "Do you know where they've been taken?"

Codoc sucked in a lungful of air and wheezed it out. "Promise me you won't let my brothers and I rot here. Bury us in our homeland and preserve our akh-spirits."

"I promise you, brother." Kano wept when Codoc's grip slackened. "May your spirits wander in peace, across the beautifully strewn paths of the west. And thank you my friend."

Codoc closed his eyes for the last time.

CHAPTER

6

The Kiman soldiers were making an awful lot of racket when their Red King, mounted atop an armored white steed, rode down the length of their front lines shouting words of encouragement to his men. From atop the inner wall Leo couldn't hear what Xalvador was blabbering on about, but he had a hunch that there'd be songs written of the valiant king's everlasting courage long after today's battle was over. Leo also suspected that whatever Red speech Xalvador delivered had probably been rehearsed again and again over the first two days of battle. The mere fact that the Red King chose this day to let his presence be felt meant two things. The siege would likely end today, and Leo wouldn't live long enough to hear any of the songs.

There was a pause in the Red King's battle speech, where an impregnable silence drew out uncomfortably long. Leo's heart felt like it pumped fire into his veins. He wiped sweat from his palms and wrapped his hand around the familiar grip of his hatchet. Within the stronghold, Juan and Bruce's men pressed their faces between cracks and gaps in the wall to watch the Reds methodical advance.

Leo's gaze swept over the Gorro River, the Netche Bridge, and beyond. The water was placid, as if it stood ready to receive blood and bodies to carry away. Leo imagined what his own body would look like being swept away in the current. Probably better than the alternative though. Should his corpse fall into the hands of the Kimans, he suspected it would be torn apart limb from limb. A piece of it hung over the mantle of every Kiman lord's hall from Chaucer to The Shield. If the Tribesmen were coming they were too late now. The stronghold would fall before the sun swept across the sky.

Was it all for nothing? To stand so few against an army of so many? He need not look back at his shouldermen for answers. When a fight comes at the warrior he stands firm or dies trying. Let a man push you around long enough, and you'll learn only to kneel.

There's no kneelers in this lot. Let all of Veronia remember. Let the whole world remember.

The outer wall, having been pummeled for two days, would be little more than a hurdle to the Kiman soldiers now. Edger's men stood in position to protect it until the last log fell all the same. "Redbeard," Leo called below.

Edger paced through his Red Garden, sword in one hand, chalice full of red in the other. "What is it? Can't a man sip in silence before he dies?"

Leo shook his head. "Get your men inside. There's nothing they can do for the outer wall now. Post some of them with the arches if you must."

Edger continued his walking and drinking, not bothering to look up. "You heard the Shield didn't you? To the inner wall!" His wallmen scurried in through the east gate and fell in with the Swords of Bane. Edger did not. Instead he unslung the wineskin from his shoulder, filled his cup one last time, and tossed the empty skin aside. He took a sip and stared at Leo overtop his chalice. There was no challenge in Redbeard's gaze. More disturbingly, it was the look of a man who knew his fate and welcomed it.

Leo set his jaw and turned away into Juan's gaze which looked much the same as Edger's. *God save them, or take them.* The defiant fire in him grew stronger. "The afterlife awaits us all, whether we meet it this day or the next. But first we shall wet our swords. For what warrior wants to meet Saint Peter any other way?"

The clamoring of swords on shields and battle cries rang out. If the priests took offense to Leo's words, they hid it well. Bishop Isabelle might have even pursed her lips to fight a smile as Trion beat his shield beside her. Even she looked at peace, ready to meet her maker. May have even been looking forward to it.

Across the battlefield, King Xalvador pointed his Guardian Sword towards the stronghold and dug his heels into his mount. His soldiers ran behind for all their worth. Natalie's archers began their fletching, enough arrows to blot out the sun. There was no point in rationing them now.

"Climb down and help Trion and the Drago Smiths protect the priests."

Mandy craned her head. "What will you do?"

Leo stared at her, like the answer was obvious. "I've got a king to kill."

"But you'll be—"

"No buts, Mandy. Just do it." Her eyes began to water. He'd seen her swell with sadness too many times since he'd found her the night Bresdan burned. He promised himself today would be the last. "Keep your shield up until it becomes a burden, then cast it aside like you would any other. Life's too short to carry anything that slows you down. Oh, and I'm proud of you." The last words shocked even him yet his only regret was that he'd been too stubborn to mutter the words to the rest of his shouldermen. "Go on now."

She hesitated, almost spoke. Leo yelled something down to Edward, and left her standing there. "Right." She nodded, then carried on dutifully.

The battering rams creaked forward once again. The number in which they'd multiplied must have meant they'd been up all night fashioning more of them. At least ten of them rolled forward from every direction. It was a red day to be an archer atop the inner wall. There was only so much surface space around the wall for the Kimans to get at. Rank upon rank of the others stacked up behind, waiting their turn. Easy enough targets that Natalie's archers didn't need to do much aiming at all.

King Xalvador rode on amidst the metal rain and was first to the wall. Leo turned his scorn towards Natalie. No way the bastard should have made it to the wall unscathed, but he did. It hadn't missed Natalie's attention either. She notched another arrow and turned it towards the Red King, but his horse circled wildly and her shot narrowly missed the mark. Xalvador's men closed the distance behind him with a fury. They hit the outer wall and liked to have pushed the whole damn thing over at once.

They met Edger alone in his Red Garden. He went to work, chalice in hand. His speech was slurred by drink but his curses were beautifully timed with killing blows.

Watching Redbeard do his work caused Leo to lose sight of the king he meant to kill. His head spun back into the crowd, but Xalvador was nowhere to be found. Not even the snorting steed could be heard in the chaos.

Below, Edger's blade rose to block a downward slash. His arm must have already grown tired from all the work, and his sword was knocked out of his hand. In an unbelievable turn of fate, Edger tackled the attacker to the ground and struck him about the head and neck with his chalice until the soldier's legs quit trying to buck him off.

Another Red charged Edger from behind, sword lowered for killing. No warning from Leo would have stopped the blow. Leo reared his hatchet back, assessing the distance. When he let it loose the runes blazed as it spun forward. The bearded blade bit through chainmail and broke through backbone. The Kiman soldier arched in pain, shoulder blades pressing against the blade in his back, then went down wincing.

Edger spun around, ready to bludgeon another with his cup, but the would-be foe had a hatchet sticking out of him.

"Had your fill of fun yet, Redbeard?" Leo called down.

"Um, not yet. But I reckon I could use another sword."

"Well come get one you crazy bastard. And kindly retrieve my hatchet would ya?"

Another Red advanced on Edger but was shot down with more than one arrow. Edger pulled the hatchet free and dealt another hack to the face for good measure. Redbeard ran to the inner wall and the arches lowered a ladder for him to climb up. Edger leaned heavily onto the railing, beard wet with blood and wine. He offered Leo his kwatina, wet handle first. "Your hatchet, sire."

Leo took it, not bothering to wipe away the crimson. "There's a fine line between an honorable and a foolish death."

Edger coughed and spat, winced as he did. He held up his battle-worn chalice for a refill. "Wine damnit. Get me some wine." He coughed some more and Leo noticed for the first time that Edger favored his stomach.

"You're wounded?" More an observation but it rolled off the tongue like a question. The inner wall shook as the Kiman soldiers began their assault on it. Arrows still raining down upon them.

Edger inspected the empty innards of his cup and wiped a spatter of blood away. "Dying, most likely," he said, not bothering to look up. "I've not done that before so I can't be certain. Wine I said, damnit!" One of his wallmen slid into view and began to pour with shaky hands. Redbeard drained most of it in one pull. The rest ran from the corners of his mouth and soaked into his beard. "Now about that sword."

Leo nodded solemnly and the same wallman who'd poured the wine, eased the sword from his own scabbard and rested it across Edger's lap. The inner wall rocked once more and Leo lurched forward, nearly toppling over the side.

A quick survey revealed that the east and west gates of the inner wall were both under attack. Archers rained down their worst upon the Kiman soldiers but it was a numbers game now. The east wall was the first to break. Coincidently the Reds attacked it with logs from the outer wall. The Swords of Bane welcomed them in. Leo watched Bruce run through a Kiman with both ends of his blades. More swords collided and Kiman corpses began to stack up at the gate.

"Hold!" It was Juan at the west gate. He could see the Reds spilling in through the east gate and his men itched to go help their comrades. It would be a bloody mistake to abandon their gate now though and Juan knew it.

Bruce's blades continued to flash sending limbs flying and men dying. The Reds began to hesitate at the gate and wanted no more of the Swords of Bane. That was until the west gate fell into the crowd of Widow Makers. More than a few weren't able to get out of the way and were pinned beneath its weight and trampled over as the Kiman soldiers began to use it as a walkway.

Not to be outdone by the Swords of Bane, the Widow Makers slashed and stabbed for all they were worth. Juan's bastard sword arced back and swept forward. From Leo's vantage point the Kiman soldiers were pretty much fucked. They'd have to create a third or fourth hole in the wall to have any hopes of causing any real damage. Their numbers were negated with only two points of entry, neither of which was very wide and filling up with more bodies all the time.

King Xalvador must have come to the same conclusion. Leo spotting him still mounted atop his white steed, ordering his officers around the battlefield. Moments later, his men scurried off beneath their shields to carry out his orders. That left the Red King with only a handful of mounted guards to protect him.

"Leo. No!"

He heard the voice cry after him. Natalie's most likely. It was drowned out by the cries of men both killing and dying. Didn't matter to Leo anyways. No words of reason could have stopped the Bloody Rose when he found his scent. He lashed down into the Red Garden. He felt his hatchet meet bone and crunch through it, not entirely sure of what he'd struck or whose side it was on. By the time he made it to the wreckage of the outer wall, more and more Kiman soldiers thought it better just to let him run past.

The Bloody Rose cut his way onto the battlefield. He felt many eyes on him, but the challengers were few. He found the Red King where he'd last seen him. Hidden behind his mounted, blood-sword guardsmen. "Xalvador!" The Bloody Rose's challenge sucked the warmth from the air.

The first of the Kiman king's retinue charged forward brave enough atop the safety of his horse. Its hooves stormed forward kicking clumps of soil into the air. Leo readied himself to block the sword blow. As the rider approached, the Bloody Rose stepped in front of the horse and knelt down behind his shield, sending horse and rider toppling over him in a tangled mess of broken limbs. He stood upright ready for another charge. The remaining kingsguard circled 'round him instead.

"Aha, Leo Rosewood. I would expect no other fool to separate himself from his own army." Xalvador slid from his mount, taking his time to draw his Guardian Sword. It looked ridiculous inside a Kiman scabbard. The twelve-pointed star etched into brass and gold inlay. "You can't win here. You know that right?"

Leo craned his head, mindful not to take his eyes off the circling horseman. Xalvador's voice was thin and distant as he readied for the fight. The Kiman king was once a renowned swordsman, but like all great men, time is the great leveler and Xalvador was ten or more years past his prime. His ornate armor a work of art, truly fit for a king. Intricately embroidered on all sides. It did little to conceal the greying streaks in his long flowing mane, and he made no attempt to hide it.

Leo slid his hatchet into his belt, reached over his shoulder, and drew his sword. Fingers laced across the grip like an old friend welcoming him home. "I don't have much to lose anyway." Leo maybe, but not the Bloody Rose.

Xalvador stepped forward, sword and shield at the ready. "Nothing to lose, or nothing to live for?" He didn't wait for a response. The Red King pressed forward with a flurry of strikes that sent Leo peddling backwards blocking blows with his shield.

The Bloody Rose thrust his shield forward, until it met the weight of the Red King, then he drove him back. Xalvador's feet got tangled and he fell to the ground. Xalvador landed on his shield side and sent a well-timed thrust as he met the earth. Leo felt the blade tear through his waist and grind against his hip bone.

He knew better than to assess the damage in the middle of a fight. The Bloody Rose followed Xalvador to the ground with a thrust of his own. It missed wide, and his blade bit into the earth and twisted his wrist. He landed atop the Red King and the two snarled at each other.

Leo let go of his sword and shook his forearm free of his shield. He leaned in heavy, pressing an elbow into Xalvador's windpipe. The Red King squirmed to his side, hand feeling for the grip of the dagger in his belt. He drew it out but Leo's right hand wrapped 'round his palm before Xalvador could insert it into the Bloody Rose's side. Leo pressed his hand down, pinning Xalvador's dagger to the ground.

He dug his forearm deeper into Xalvador's neck till the Red King's face started turning blue and veins swelled in his temple. Leo pulled the dagger from his hand and thrust it into the Red King's side. The blade slid in easily enough buried to the hilt. Leo twisted his grip and felt Xalvador's internals shift around by the blade.

You would think a man who climbed so far in life as to be the king of an empire might have more to say as he drew his last breaths, but Xalvador's speech had left him as his eyes drew wide. When Leo determined him quite dead enough he eased his arm from Xalvador's neck.

The clamoring of hooves drew Leo's attention from that mortal moment, and sent him scurrying to his feet with his sword and shield at the ready. He made it up just in time to see Xalvador's blood-sworn guard's shagging ass.

Leo spun towards the stronghold but found his path blocked by more Kiman soldiers than he could ever hope to kill in one sitting. They looked around at each other trying to digest what they'd just seen. Leo looked back at them hoping they'd have the same notion as Xalvador's guards.

"King Killer! Off with his head!"

For fuck's sake. No such luck today. Leo rammed the first soldier that charged him with his shield and hoped the bastard stayed down for a while. Then Leo did what any reasonable man would do. He ran like hell. He ran left and right. Nowhere in particular, just anywhere the men trying to kill him left a gap. His feet pounded the earth with reckless abandon and he found his refuge in the Gorro River. If only he could make it there before getting stabbed or shot in the back.

He risked a glance back and saw them gaining.

Had to be twenty or more in the chase for his head. In his mind, the ground seemed to have inclined to the point Leo could reach out and touch it. Horseshit, he knew, but his legs and lungs burned all the same. His pace must have slowed but his will for survival at that moment had never been stronger.

The river was so close he thought he could hear the water, the stream drowned-out by the footsteps padding along behind him. Leo felt a hand reach out to grab him. Felt the fingertips brushing against his shoulder. That's when he jumped. Truth be told, it was more falling than diving, but the river didn't care one way or another.

Leo at least had the peace of mind to get a lung full of air on his way in. Beneath the water's surface he heard his pursuers plunging into the river behind him. Holding his breath he kicked his feet and swam for his life, letting the current take him far as it pleased. Swimming strokes didn't come very easy with a sword and shield in his hands, but he'd held on to them thus far and figured he might need them again when he resurfaced.

He held his breath long as he could then risked bobbing his head above water for more. When he did, he saw Kiman soldiers running along the bank, trying to spot him. More than one finger pointed his direction. He refilled his lungs and went back under.

The farther he swam the more he realized he wasn't swimming at all. It was the current that moved him now. His arms and legs were spent. He puffed the air from his lungs one last time. The water bubbled around him like a fiery dragon. A vision of Edger drinking his wine in the Red Garden came to mind. Now it was Leo's turn to meet his fate. He clutched his sword and shield, feet searching for solid ground by the bank. When he found it, he sprung out of the water as best he could and saw his Kiman pursuers running the opposite direction. Those who hadn't run fast enough were pelted by arrows.

Across the river, the Tribesmen had arrived. Their painted faces slipped out from the trees with hatchets, spears, and bad intentions. Their skull-crafted death whistles pierced the air, rattled the brave, and broke the weary. Chief Dretchel was easiest to spot, front and center among them. The huge Antucha-whah chief led the charge into the river; his younger clansmen swarmed the bank.

***

Borin agonized as he watched King Xalvador killed and Leo Rosewood being chased off into the river. If that wasn't bad enough, the stronghold still hadn't been conquered and now the Tribesmen had arrived to put their noses where they didn't belong.

"Master Borin!" One of Xalvador's kingsguard pulled up fast, barely managing to slow his mount before riding into the platform. "We're undone, sir. The flatheads have attacked our flank."

Borin slouched in King Xalvador's old commander's chair. It was a solid oaken affair, perched upon a platform nearly ten feet high. The closest thing to an aerial view on the Kiman side of the battlefield. Since they had arrived in Tamore, Borin and Elias took their seats atop the platform. Not even King Xalvador had been so brave as to challenge them. Borin and Elias had done nothing to intervene thus far but that was about to change. King Xalvador had done a fine job of buggering up the siege and got himself killed for the effort.

"Undone?" Borin sat up, put a fist on each of his knees, and leaned forward. "That the chivalrous term for getting your asses kicked by a peasant militia?"

"Perhaps we should call our forces back my lord. Captain Visney was right. We should have starved them out."

Borin stifled his rage, running a hand through his hair. "You hear that, Elias?" He turned to his starborn companion. Elias was newly admitted into the twelve, his loyalty untested. But the namer of Lightning seemed brutal enough for Borin's liking so far. "This lackwit says they're undone. What say you?"

Elias's chin propped against his fist, elbow resting on the arm of his chair. He regarded the palm of his left hand. With a flick of his fingers, he detonated the rider's head. The horse startled and took off; the corpse swayed in the saddle a good thirty yards before falling.

"Ha! My thoughts exactly," Borin exclaimed. "Who's in charge here?" He regarded the Kiman officers in attendance, but most had their eyes diverted to the leather of their boots. The battle raged beyond them, but Borin didn't seem in a hurry.

The officers looked around and after a time, Saul Harrington cursed under his breath and stepped forward. "Um, you are, my lord."

"Nonsense." Borin's smile did little to ease the envoy's state of mind. "Where's that earless bastard with the wonderful smile?"

Saul looked to have aged ten years as he stood there. "That would be Captain Visney, sir. He led a company to the river to meet the Tribesmen but Rosewood's men are out of the stronghold. It appears to be a free-for-all now, my lord."

Borin nodded his approval. "A man of action, that Visney is. Ugly as sin, but made of iron." He felt a tug in his chest and squinted towards the Gorro. Saul continued to ramble; Borin silenced him with a raised hand. "Do you sense that, Elias?"

Elias rose to his feet, beady eyes searching among the Tribesmen like a hawk after prey. "Zodans."

"It's hard to find a good set of assassins anymore. We should have taken the task of killing Ansuke and Trechon ourselves." Borin stepped off the platform and strode towards the battlefield. "The siege ends here and now. Elias, take care of the Tribesmen for me. Ansuke is strong but his starfire will be no match for your lightning. I'll only need a few moments of peace to take out what's left of the stronghold and then we can be rid of Tamore once and for all."

***

Jewel heard the battle long before he saw it but his horse was in no hurry to cross Britta Creek. He removed the saddle and halter from his riding companion then sent the horse off to do horse things. His first view of the stronghold was worse than he imagined. For some reason he expected Leo's army to be safely confined behind thick stone walls. The reality of it was far less impressive. The wooden walls were torn down and men on both sides of the rubble converged on one another with sharpened steel like a giant meat grinder.

For a fleeting moment he stood there watching the battle as if he were peering through the portal into another world. He'd never seen men at war of this scale before. What he'd never forget were the screams that permeated through the air. He felt like an ant looking out into the wide world. So small and insignificant that a mild wind might sweep him away into oblivion.

"You still think your brother's army will help me rescue my friends?"

It was Kano's voice from behind him. Jewel didn't seem to care who it was. He couldn't turn away from the horrors that unraveled before him. "My brother has always managed to eke through sharp times but how could anyone survive that?"

"My question remains." There was an edge in Kano's voice that wasn't there before.

When he turned, Kano looked taller than earlier. Jewel doubted the sorcerer had grown an inch but there was a threatening glint in his eyes. A weariness in his stance that Jewel recognized in men with little left to lose.

"I can swear no oaths on my brother's behalf. Nor for the men and women who've sworn their swords to him."

"Humph." Kano crept forward. They stood there watching for a time. A Kiman soldier sprinted their direction. He was holding his wrist where his hand used to be. When he saw them, he changed directions and scurried off into the trees like a startled rabbit. "An honest answer from an honest man. And yet for some reason, I wish you'd have lied to me. Would have made what I'm about to do seem justified."

The first and last time Jewel saw Kano, the sorcerer was looking for his Zodan friends. Judging by his cold mood, Jewel suspected the news wasn't good. "You'll help us then?"

Kano regarded the star-patterned marks on his hands. "When a starborn strays too far from the light, breaking oaths and the accords, he can expect an eternity of anguish twice or thrice the burden of hell upon his death. May our god and the Mozzaroth forsake me not."

In the moment that Jewel looked away from Kano and back to the stronghold, the sorcerer had taken his leave. Jewel staggered forward, weary from the road and everything the last few weeks had thrown at him. He'd made so many sacrifices to protect his brother and his country and now the fate of Veronia teetered on the edge of defeat before him. Jewel's gaze swept the crowd for his brother. Somewhere out there, Leo might be taking his last breath, if he hadn't lost the heat in him already.

Jewel sucked in a lungful of rotting air and sprinted for the stronghold. Bodies lie strewn out at his feet, and many of the living wounded began crying out to him as he ran past.

"Priest!"

"Father, pray with me!"

It made no difference that they were Kiman soldiers who cried out. When a man's in a bad way such as those reaching out to him, any help will do. Jewel had seen it many times before. When death begins to grab hold of a man, fear of the afterlife starts to settle in. The same men look back on the life they'd lived in what little time they have left, measuring their own deeds for whatever afterlife awaits them.

Their cries were unnerving. They rung out over the clash of men and swords. A Red soldier reached out to him and clasped hold of the hem of his cloak with a weak hand. It left a crimson smear as Jewel pulled away, still running fast as he could to the west gate of the stronghold.

"Forgive me Lord," he said again and again to drown out the crowd. Jewel made it to the outer wall where a mass of Kiman soldiers fought to break through what was left of the west gate's inner wall. He was so close now that he could see the black tunics of the Widow Makers. Jewel froze in place when he saw Juan in the midst of it all. His Guardian Sword rising and falling in a crimson arc.

"Jewel! Jewel, over here."

He swiveled around and found Natalie calling down to him from atop the inner wall. She dropped her crossbow and ran across the battlement. Jewel followed her as best he could, but the thicket of brush, tree limbs, and corpses were nearly impossible to navigate through.

Natalie bellowed orders to her archers and all around him Kiman soldiers began to fall. A Kiman soldier called after him, notching a bolt of his own aimed for Jewel. Just before he settled his aim, his head exploded. The headless corpse remained there with his finger pressed against the trigger. Jewel breathed a sigh of relief when the soldier finally fell.

He heard another man fall next to him. Jewel dared not look back to see the results. He made it to the wall and a rope was thrown over. He wrapped both hands around it, kicking with his feet to scale the wall as he was heaved up.

"Do you have a death wish, Father?" Natalie's

welcome was not so cold as the air around them.

Jewel's teeth were chattering now, and he found no warmth in his robe. "It's so cold," he said, rising to his feet.

Natalie nodded down the battlement. "It's him."

He followed her gaze to Kano. The sorcerer's eyes radiated with light as he cast starfire below. The east gate was under just as much duress. The Swords of Bane were outside the walls in a three-rank square formation with Bruce at its center barking orders to his men.

"Where's my brother?"

Natalie notched another bolt and let it fly. "Apparently death by siege was too slow a process. The jackass...erm, your brother, jumped the wall to kill the Red King. If he still lives, it's only because the Tribesmen arrived in time to save his hide."

Jewel had once overheard General Soberal giving Juan and Leo a lesson in tunnel vision. "In battle or any danger for that matter, one's focus is naturally drawn to the threat in front of him. A man must overcome such limitations by training against multiple threats. You mustn't allow your attention to be drawn to a single threat, when death lies all around us. Your mind is a weapon, sharper and deadlier than any sword. Exercise it often and nothing will confine you."

It's funny how a lesson comes full circle, and you may not even realize it until it passes. Jewel was so enthralled with the battle at the stronghold that he hadn't noticed the Tribesmen battling their way past the river. What was worse, he hadn't seen the black-cloaked figure standing alone outside the stronghold until a battering ram was lifted off the ground and cast against the inner wall like a boy skipping a rock on the water.

The wall rocked by the force and more than a few archers were cast off the battlement. The sorcerer regarded a spiked barrier with a mocking smile. His eyes flickered aglow once more and the spiked barrier rose from the ground and flew through the air. Kano sidestepped the sharpened logs but the men behind him were not so lucky.

The Kiman soldiers split like the Red Sea as the sorcerer approached, and the fighting seemed to have screeched to a halt.

"Where are they, Borin?" Kano asked. "What have you done with them?"

Behind Borin, another black-cloaked sorcerer cast lightning into the Tribesmen's ranks sending men on both sides scattering for cover as bolts rained down on friend and foe singing the earth.

Borin paused in thought as if Kano's question caught him off guard. Lightning struck again and Borin looked over his shoulder to regard his companion. "You've met Elias, no? He hasn't quite mastered the ability, but he sure knows how to put on a show, doesn't he?"

"The Zodans, damnit," Kano seethed. "Don't play coy with me, you vile bastard. Where are they?"

More lightning struck the battlefield and drew Jewel's attention. It was strange to see such spectacular lightning in broad daylight. Elias played with a handful of starfire as soldiers fled his presence. After three bolts of lightning, Elias stood against only one Tribesman. A Vrattan as far as Jewel could tell.

"Shhh." Borin waved a hand to silence Kano, as he regarded Elias once more. "You keep blabbering and we'll miss the battle. I'll never know why Ansuke is so attached to that savage tribe of his. Living worse off than a peasant in that godforsaken forest."

Elias and the Tribesman circled 'round each other for a time. Whatever words they might have exchanged were only for the two of them to hear. Leo had lived among the Tribesmen for two years. Carried one of their weapons and probably knew Ansuke personally, and may have been out there watching the Tribesman square off against Elias. Jewel prayed that his brother would not be so stupid as to intervene. He spied across the battlefield where the Tribesman had mustered to watch the two sorcerers battle, and spotted Leo and his golden shield at the head of the pack. It was hard to tell at this distance but it looked as if others were arguing around him.

Kano's eyes came aglow but before he disappeared Borin called out. "No, no, no. You'll stay here with me, and we'll watch their fates unfold before us. You move to interfere and I can assure you that I'll leave no part of this stronghold standing. Not one heart will remain beating upon your return."

***

The pause in action gave Leo a much-needed rest. At least a pause in the men trying to kill him anyways. Now Chief Ansuke faced off against one of the Kiman sorcerers. It shouldn't have been a surprise to see Ansuke wielding starfire just as he'd seen Boyce in the Capitol dungeon, but even amongst the ranks of Tribesmen, Leo heard the Vratta chief cursed and damned as a witch.

"We going to help him?" Leo rasped. He stood on wobbly knees, head still spinning from running and nearly drowning in the river. His savior, none other than Page's drunken lover Nico, son of Chief Dretchel. Nico knelt nearby nursing an arrow wound in his left forearm. Speaking of Chief Dretchel, where was he? His massive frame had been easiest to spot among the Tribesmen running towards Leo's Kiman pursuers just moments ago. And now he was nowhere to be seen.

Leo didn't remember much of it, other than Nico's strong arms pulling him from the river, and the curses spent from the effort of having to do it one-handed. Trechon had been there too, hacking men down with his hatchet. Leo soured at the score before him. The Tribesmen had settled their blood debt already, now that Leo was alive. At this point they had no dog in the fight, and he could hear mutterings coming to the same conclusion behind him.

"We've tolerated enough of the Vrattas' dark magic," Marchuke spat. He carried as fine a balled club as Leo had ever seen. Its wooden handle intricately etched with dyed-red eagle feathers streaming from the end of the grip. The ball a magnificent sea green stone, the likes of which Leo had never seen before. Despite its brilliance, it looked to have seen little or no use and Leo didn't suspect Marchuke would risk his cush life or his Netchen fortune to earn himself a red name there today. "And look now. The Vratta chief is finally exposed as the witch we've all suspected him to be. Let the pale witch have him. Let the rest of us be gone from here."

That drew hissing glares from the Vrattas. "Still your poisoned tongue, Marchuke," Trechon rebuked. "We came here to fight, not babble." He pointed towards the Netche Bridge with his bloody hatchet. "We can't all be hunters and warriors though. Go back home and gather berries if you must."

Leo knew enough about the tribal culture to recognize fighting words when he heard them. But before it turned bloody, another bolt of lightning struck down narrowly missing Ansuke. The chief limbered away returning fire as he went. The golden shield vibrated at Leo's forearm and its glow caught his eye.

"He's a witch too!" Marchuke spat, pointing at Leo with his club.

Leo turned his full scorn on Marchuke. Hand

twitching on the grip of his hatchet to kill the bastard. The Netchen's eyes went wide and he took a few cautious steps back. "I'm no witch, Marchuke. Still your tongue or I'll skewer you where you stand."

More lightning shook the ground and Ansuke had little time to aim his own shots on the run. Whatever power the Vratta chief possessed seemed to pale in comparison to the sorcerer whose lightning had struck down a score or more Tribesmen already.

"Your name, starborn?" Leo demanded, stepping forward. His shield shone like the sun. The runes on his hatchet thirsted for blood.

"Stay back Leo. He'll tire soon." Ansuke spoke as if the words cut him on the way out. He wielded a ball of starfire in his left hand that grew with age.

Elias regarded Leo with a cold scowl and watchful eyes. Not much of a talker Leo surmised after a few unanswered moments. Leo moved forward to stand at Ansuke's flank. Only then did he realize that Ansuke looked like he'd fallen into a fire and roasted a while. The black-cloaked starborn was far from unscathed. His charred skin smoldered through the singed areas of his cloak.

"What the hell are you doing?" Ansuke whispered.

"Buying you some time. Don't miss."

Leo crouched behind his shield and tried to walk the starborn down. Elias circled slowly, twitching the fingers of his right hand.

"Elias," the starborn wheezed through clenched

teeth. He regarded Leo's golden shield like a cat arching its back, hissing at a threat.

"Well then." Leo rotated his neck. "I wish we hadn't met at all. Be that as it may here we are. Death has come for you at last, Elias. With these blades I'll bury your bones."

Two things happened then. Leo gauged the distance, reared back with his hatchet, and let it fly. It whistled and spun through the air like it was set aflame. Elias was ready for it and dodged the death that span towards him just in time.

Elias didn't look back to make light of the hatchet in passing. He made no boasts of his superior senses and speed. Instead he countered with a thunderous bolt of lightning that crackled from the sky. Leo heard it coming and knew it was aimed at him. He raised his shield but nothing could have prepared him for the impact. When it hit his shield it drove him down into the earth. The spine-tingling impact radiated throughout his bones and his legs felt like they were broken in half. Leo ended up sprawled-out on his ass, regretting more than a few of his life choices.

It took an effort to sit up. His legs and arms tingled numb, dead to the world. Elias stalked forward wetting his lips, so satisfied with himself that he'd forgotten something.

Leo's satisfied smile rivaled Elias's, though it pained every muscle in his face. "Chief Ansuke, if you will."

There was a flash and it took some time before Leo regained his vision. It came back to him blotchy then blurry until it found a pile of dark ash where Elias used to be.

Leo rolled to his side and found Chief Ansuke in the arms of his Tribesman. Ansuke was limp, his eyes closed, dead to the world.

"Ansuke!" Leo wailed, crawling over to him but the crowd of Vrattas wouldn't let him pass. One of them leaned into Leo with a shoulder that nearly pushed him back onto his ass.

All the cold shoulders left Leo looking for an ally. He found Trechon leaned over Dretchel. The blood that covered Nico's hands as he held his dead father made Leo go weak in the knees, and tears began to blur his own vision. "No. God no."

"You did this." The murderous voice belonged to Marchuke who stood pointing his balled war club at Leo. Beside the Netchen merchant, more of his tribe started to fix Leo with their vengeful glares.

All the fight had suddenly drained from Leo. Guilt washed over him so fiercely that breathing became an effort. He stepped backwards as the Netches led by Marchuke moved forward. Leo felt something beneath his foot that nearly turned his ankle. When he looked down, it was his hatchet.

"Leave it," Marchuke spat, encouraged by his strength in numbers. "You'll die with that paleskin sword in your hands."

Looking at the two dead or dying tribal chiefs, Leo had no urge to draw his steel ever again. He heard no battle raging in the distance. His mind wandered to the deaths of his own men somewhere in the stronghold and he wanted nothing more than to be cut down then and there.

The weight of all the blood on his hands brought him to his knees. An old dog tired of the pain and ready to be put down. Marchuke moved forward, eager to please.

Gasps echoed throughout the crowd of Vrattas and they started to push back against the gathering behind them, along with Marchuke and his minions. Leo twisted his gaze to the disturbance.

A bright light hefted Ansuke's body into the air. The star patterns on the Vratta chief's hands beamed with light and his eyes opened once more. It felt as if they found Leo's for half an instant and when they did his golden shield vibrated once more. Ansuke was raised out of the arms of his men into the air. A flash of light made Leo wince. When he looked up again, Ansuke was gone.

* * *

"No!" Kano cried over the battlement. Wood smoldered where his hand clutched the railing.

An impregnable silence washed over Tamore. Jewel clenched his eyelids shut. A fit of quivering made his hands shake. Must have been contagious. Beside Jewel, Natalie flexed the fingers on her crossbow. Chainmail rustled as men from both sides stirred uncomfortably between the two remaining sorcerers.

"And then there were two." The words merely stated the facts. But Borin uttered them as if he were keeping a score. Borin squared off against the stronghold like no amount of blood would quench his thirst. "Tell me Kano, how does it feel?" Borin stepped closer to the rubble of the outer wall. Jaw flexed so tight it looked like a siege weapon. "Does Ansuke's death hurt much? Does it feel like the world's spun a little too fast around this time and cast you off the ride? Can you feel your hands reaching out but finding no purchase?" Borin's pause allowed his words to cut deeper.

The tension was smothering. Jewel started looking for a way out, but dared not move lest he draw Borin's eye. Kano's gaze slowly shifted from the Tribesmen and settled on Borin with a snarl. Jewel saw the half-man mutter something under his breath and then Kano was gone. A blast ensued immediately after and Borin reeled.

Kano reappeared on the battlefield, a few paces behind Borin. Another flick of the wrist and Borin was dodging Kano's starfire.

A sword rose up and out of a lifeless hand at Borin's feet. He turned left and right waiting for Kano to reappear. When the half-man did, the sword sped through the air towards him.

Kano's eyes widened but he managed to adjust slightly and avoid being impaled upon the blade. One of the Kiman soldiers was not so lucky. The sword bit him in the stomach and he crumpled onto the ground. That was the cue for the rest of the Reds to shag-ass out of the way and they did. A moment later half a dozen swords rose from cold dead hands. Their arms stretched out like they were about to rise themselves until the blades slipped from their clutches.

Kano didn't wait around to be their target practice and disappeared once more.

"That's it. Run, you yellow-bellied little fool. Just like you did in the tavern. Didn't even stay long enough to see Hadrian choking on his last pathetic breaths." The swords hovered in the air around Borin as he swiveled for his target.

The Kiman soldiers had all but abandoned the siege. Bruce and Juan ordered their men back into the stronghold. That left the Red Garden clear, except for the dead, and Jewel saw Kano in the thicket crouched low as if searching for something.

"I can sense the fear in you, Kano. You Zodans have always been the weaker breed. Don't tell me that wench of yours has more rocks than you. Ah that reminds me." Borin's rueful smile made Jewel's stomach crawl. "That bitch of yours and the rest of your pathetic clan should be caged and cut off from the else by now. Crawl to me and plead for mercy and I'll see to it that you're put in an adjoining enclosure. Close enough to hear her ravaged by her giant goalers for the rest of eternity."

Another pause and Jewel could feel Borin's patience wearing thin. Jewel imagined the last grains of sand draining from an hourglass somewhere.

"Have it your way," Borin spat in disgust. "I'm here to wipe Tamore from the map. Ansuke was just a bonus. It's well past time I wash my hands of this gutter war anyways."

Footsteps clattered towards Jewel, the boards thumping underfoot. Something jolted into his side, arms clasped firmly around him, and gravity had loosened its hold. A man wailed somewhere far away. Perhaps where he once stood. And then there was impact. Not the jolting kind of stubborn Mother Earth who refuses to soften her embrace for anyone plunging towards her, High Priest of Veronia or not. But the kind of impact that results from someone with a brave heart but little comprehension of physics trying to catch them below. Either that or someone hadn't moved quickly enough out of their way as they fell.

Whomever it was they landed on, Jewel felt bones crackle beneath him as the brunt of Jewel and Trion's weight came down hard.

"Ahh," the load-bearer gasped. "Get your scrawny arses off me."

Scrawny arses? Jewel had no mind in taking offense to the improper address of his station. A slip of the tongue in such a case was a forgivable offense given the circumstances. As Trion rolled off, a calloused, muscled hand reached up and pushed Jewel clear of him. In Jewel's passing he took note that the hand bore the mark of a Drago Smith. Shortly thereafter two more Drago Smiths strained to lift Jonas's mighty frame off the ground.

Jewel stood on his own stammering to give thanks. Trion sat on the ground nursing his right forearm where his wrist and hand sagged unnaturally. Jewel reached out his hand and Trion took it with his left, grunting as he stood.

The inner wall rocked from impact. Another blast and Borin stood in the hole it left behind. Swords, arrows, and maces hovering all around him. "Knock, knock," he said. A flick of the hand and his instruments of war moved forward as if being swung by invisible soldiers. They cut into men from impossible angles and even the Swords of Bane started to scamper out of the east and west gates.

Natalie notched a bolt and put Borin in her sights. Jewel wetted his lips hoping the archer's aim was true.

Twang. The bolt hissed through the air and Borin spared it a knowing smile. It slowed in midair, changed trajectory towards the stronghold, and whistled towards a mass of flesh. It prodded into Nestin's back. The short-lived mayor of Tamore's eyes widened with fright and the bolt lifted him off his feet.

Nestin's head sagged forward. The point of the

shaft pushed his innards out his belly. He rose ten, twenty, thirty feet in the air. Another twinge of his hand and Borin sent Nestin's corpse hurtling down. He hit Natalie with a loud thud and sent them tumbling off the battlement. A blond-headed girl Jewel couldn't place jumped over the wall after her.

"Run. Get out of here!" Juan wailed to his men as if they weren't to the task fast enough. He angled through the mass exodus approaching Borin with a two-handed, white-knuckled grip on his bastard sword.

"I've never been much good at running." Bruce raked the blades of his swords together and they made a sharpening sound. "Besides, you look like you could use a good shoulderman to go knocking on death's door. Let's tear the hinges off that motherfucker, eh?"

Jewel felt a tug on his robe from behind and snatched his garment from Trion's grip. "Come Father. I have to get you out of here." Trion still nursed one arm with the other but there wasn't any rattling in his eyes.

"No. Not yet. We aren't finished here." Jewel searched once more for Kano but couldn't find him.

Borin wielded more than a dozen weapons now, each of them doing their worst to the men in their path. As Juan and Bruce got closer, Borin rolled his eyes as if they were interrupting his playtime and turned his weapons towards them.

A sword swiped towards Bruce and he caught it with a backhanded parry that sent the sword skidding off onto the ground. A shield spun towards his legs, and he jumped over it just in time to swipe a mace aimed for his head out of the air. A ball and chain spun towards him and coiled around the length of his blade, ripping it out of his hands.

Juan was fairing even worse. Without a body to cut down, his size and strength was useless. Out of habit he parried a spear away and countered with a backhanded slash that met nothing but air. Two more swords blitzed him in a hurry and he had only enough time to block the one. The other bit into his breastplate.

The sound of prying steel made Jewel wince as if someone raked their claws across a chalkboard. The phantom blade grinded through Juan's light armor and into his chest. Jewel cringed away as if he'd taken the blow himself. A foolish flash of heroism seeped into Jewel's mind where he'd take Trion's sword and dashed headlong through the chaos to run Borin through with it. He thought better of it before he'd gotten himself killed.

The clamor of steel on steel continued as Juan and Bruce continued their advance. By the looks of it, their progress was little more than a few arm spans and getting bloodier all the time. A gnarly cut on the top of Bruce's bald head split his flesh to the skull. Crimson cascaded down his forehead and into his left eye. How he managed to see anything, Jewel had no idea, but the sword he wielded looked to be getting heavier in his arms all the time.

The sorrowful weight of a defeated man drove

Jewel to his knees. Silently he prayed for a miracle. Had it not been for his hands clasped in prayer, Jewel would have plugged his ears to block out Bruce's violent cursing.

And then a single gasp made the world stand still. Weapons clattered to the ground. When Jewel opened his eyes, Kano stood behind Borin. Holding the grip of a sword, he buried it into Borin's back.

Kano ripped it out and thrust it back in for good measure. This time the light in Borin's devilish eyes faded to black. Kano guided the twice-stabbed starborn to his knees with a gentle hand on the shoulder. Mindful not to take his right hand off the kill switch.

Even on his knees, Borin was nearly taller than Kano. If the sword in Borin's back was painful, he hid it well. Only the fragile breaths around the blade gave any indication he'd be hurt at all. "Stabbing me in the back is going to do little for your reputation, Kano." He winced uncomfortably around the words. Jewel paid it no mind though. He'd never seen a man talking, let alone breathing, with two holes and a sword in his back and the allure of it left him hanging on Borin's every word.

A quick jerk and Kano retrieved the short sword from Borin's back. Air muffled through collapsed lungs and out of the puncture wounds. Jewel felt an odd sensation to put a finger in the hole to ease the bastard's breathing.

Kano had other plans and shifted the blade over the

shoulder to rest its edge on Borin's neck. The Zodan's hand shook with the urge to do the deed. "Why, Borin? Defying the accords and the law of our kind could end in no other way but death and eternal gnashing of the teeth for you. Do you really think Abaddon can summon any number of things that can stand against the sword of God's Angel Army?"

Borin choked out a laugh laden with blood. "If your god's power was so absolute, he wouldn't need an army now would he?"

Kano shook his head, fingers flexing on the grip of the sword. He whispered something that washed all emotion from Borin's defiant grin. A few bone-grating cuts later, and Kano held Borin's head in the air.

CHAPTER

7

Leo knelt down over the soot-stained patch of grass that Borin left behind. He ground the ashes in his fist and watched the wind carry them away. Elias had left the same mess as his Prothica companion. Chief Ansuke on the other hand left nothing behind when he was summoned to the stars. At least that's what Kano determined to have happened. Had Leo heard the story and not seen it, he'd never have believed it. Shit like this was supposed to happen in distant lands, long ago. He imagined years from now, no one would believe what happened here in Tamore.

"You should probably say a few words, Leo. The people are restless in wondering what's going to happen next." As close as Juan stood, his voice sounded distant. After the Kiman soldiers and the Tribesmen left, he'd stripped off his armor to field-dress the gouge on the left side of his chest. Juan thumbed an old scar on his forearm. One he'd earned at the Frostbite in what seemed a lifetime ago. Carrying your friends off the battlefield has a way of agitating the past. Old wounds flare up mixing with the new till it hurts all over. Inside and out.

Leo felt numb inside despite the tiny shards of glass still prickling the scars on his back. A constant reminder that the past was real. He liked to imagine it was just the shock of war that left him empty inside. Emotions will only keep you up at night. He'd taken his teeth to his and gnawed at their strings till something broke inside. Then he clawed into the depths of his soul and buried the taxing remains as far down as he could so the wintry world could envelop him no more.

He raked his fingers through the grass to brush the soot off then stood to face Juan. Leo regarded the nicks, cuts, and bruises on his lifelong shoulderman and those emotions he'd buried fought to resurface. Leo remembered telling Juan that he'd be by his side. Should have been there with him and his men to face Borin. Instead he hunted down a crown that didn't and wouldn't ever fit. "I'm...erm." Leo reached into his word bank but they cut his tongue like little daggers.

"Sorry you mean?" Juan crossed his arms and let the awkward silence ensue.

Leo regarded two men holding down a third, while a fourth took the flaming red sword and pressed it over an open wound. A wounded cry shrilled through clenched teeth then stopped suddenly when the Widow Maker passed out. "I don't know what I am anymore. Stab me with all the judgment you like. I can take it. And if that doesn't suit you, take that bastard sword of yours and cut some more. I won't stop you."

For a moment it looked as if Juan was about to go to work. Then he clenched his fists and spat at Leo's feet. "You keep your shield up all the time and one day you'll be left standing alone, Leo."

Damn the bastard if he wasn't right. Leo swallowed his pride. "I'll work on that. As it happens I could use a lot of work on many things."

"Lord knows that's the truth." Jewel pushed his way between the two. He nodded to Juan then continued. "But I have plenty of faith you aren't a lost cause, brother."

Juan bowed his head. "Greetings your Holiness."

Leo stiffened and regarded his brother who last time he saw was a high-ranking bishop. Now he carried the golden staff. "Your Holiness." *And now it's Jewel's turn to twist the knife.* He looked over his shoulder to see if there was a line behind his brother and relaxed when there wasn't.

"Captain Juan Soberal," Jewel said, shaking Juan by the shoulder. "Your father would be proud to see the man you've become. Bless his bones."

"Bless his bones," Leo echoed. Again that damnable emotion fought to break free at the late general's mention. Leo slammed its door and turned the lock with a grimace.

"He and our father would be proud of you too, Leo. As am I. The Shield of Veronia, savior of Tamore. It has a nice ring to it, doesn't it?" Leo rolled his eyes. "I knew you could do it. If anyone could it was the two of you. Veronia has never had two finer shouldermen."

Juan looked as if he were going to mention something. Probably some smartass remark about Leo leaving his side. On further thought Juan took the high road and bit his tongue. For once Leo was glad his jovial brother blessed them with his presence. It'd be unbecoming for them to bicker in front of the High Priest.

"But I digress." Jewel's smile slacked into a solemn frown. "We've so many left to bury. It would do well for the survivors to hear a few words of encouragement from the Shield of Veronia." Jewel's gaze shifted towards the pint-sized Zodan sorcerer who waited expectantly. The cleanup crews of Tamore and the Kiman Empire shuffled past Kano at a safe distance collecting the fallen. "I'm hearing mutterings of King Leo amongst the men, Leo. Without an heir to the throne, you may have just carved your way to the front of the line. Veronia needs a righteous king now more than ever."

"Don't look at me then. I'm an asshole," Leo replied.

Jewel nodded in agreement. "You certainly can be at times. But Veronia could do a lot worse. The Prothica behind the Kiman Empire are still busy as ever and getting stronger all the time. We may have won this battle but Abaddon will be back with giants in his ranks soon enough. Come now, the people are waiting." Jewel gave each of them a slight nudge and hurried past to lead the way.

Leo eyed the stronghold as they walked past. Nothing but firewood for the most part but he'd ordered the men to leave it be when they started to disassemble it to recycle the wood. What he'd do with it now, he had no idea. Perhaps rebuild it as it was, a memorial to the men who died defending it. Or let it lie as it was till Mother Nature reclaimed it. He shook the thought away when his feet hit cobblestone.

Say one thing for King Xalvador—he must have had at least a shred of decency in his bones. Tamore had abandoned the village to occupy the stronghold. The Red King could easily have ordered every piece of timber and stone torn to the ground but he didn't. Whatever his motivation was, Xalvador wasn't around anymore to be praised for it. The best Leo could do was make sure the Red King's remains were unmolested until the Kiman death cart wheeled him away.

As Leo passed along the town square, men and women straightened their backs and shuffled forward to hear what he had to say. Leo recognized many of them from the group Wade and Marie had snuck out of the stronghold the night before. Perhaps Xalvador didn't want the blood of women and children on his hands after all.

The sun made most of its westward pass and the moon would take its watch in less than an hour. The crowd parted as Jewel led the way and Leo heard a voice calling his name. He swept the crowd to find the source but it was Juan who found it first.

"It's Page," Juan said, pushing through the crowd to meet her. She looked travel-worn but happy enough to see them. Juan wrapped Page in his arms and lifted her off her feet.

So that's what love looks like, huh? Since Chief Dretchel had fallen in battle, his son Nico would become Chief of the Antucha-whahs. Their customs differed slightly among each of the three tribes, but one remained the same. No chief of Gwonda was allowed to take a paleskin as his wife. That left Page out in the cold but Leo couldn't be mad at Nico for it. Nico had just saved his life and took credit for settling their blood debt. An honor the Vrattas and the Netches couldn't deny. Among the Antucha-whahs there aren't many honors higher than that.

But the death of Chief Ansuke and the discovery that he was starborn left the Tribesmen in turmoil.

Trechon was to become Chief of the Vrattas upon Ansuke's death and Marchuke was already calling for Trechon's head lest he spawn another starborn. But wanting a head and taking it was two different things. None of the Tribesmen seemed eager to challenge Trechon now that they'd seen what the starborn could do. If Tekrano had the right of it, there wouldn't be much trade between the three tribes in the coming months.

Page had to tap Juan on the shoulder before he let her go. She flattened her cloak and greeted Leo with an uneasy smile. Her gaze swept him up and down as she stepped through the crowd towards him. Leo's heart skipped a beat when she froze in place and her eyes began to glisten.

Leo closed the distance and wrapped her in his arms. "Sister," he said as she nestled her head into the crook of his neck. He couldn't remember the last time they'd embraced. Much less tell her how much he loved her. He closed his eyes and squeezed her tight, fighting for the right words to say. He settled on silence. It was safer that way.

"I'm so glad you're okay," she muttered into his shoulder. Too quickly her arms loosened around him and Leo her go.

"What's wrong?" he asked when she clasped a hand to her chest and stepped away. Her eyes fixed to the shield slung over his back like it was the source of her discomfort. Leo remembered Kano had a similar

DANIEL L WELCH

reaction when first they met in the stronghold. It was then that he saw the star pattern on her right hand, and a cold hand swept his spine. "No, it can't be," he said, backing away. The curious crowd connected the same dots and stepped back like Page carried the plague.

"Oh, but it is." Boyce appeared at her side and put a hand on her shoulder. Leo's former prison-mate wore a finely embroidered sea-blue cloak. His face looked weathered as ever but not a single strand of his iron-streaked, slicked-back hair was out of place. His brilliant blue eyes basked in the vitality of immortal youth. "It's good to see you again, Leo."

Leo regarded Page and Boyce trying to make sense of it all. His little sister turned sorcerer? It made something burn inside him and he wasn't sure why. And then there was Boyce. The weak-acting con artist of a prisoner who Leo had befriended out of mere pity. The imprisoned sorcerer who had the ability to spring them free and kill everyone in their way, yet for some unfathomable reason Boyce made a home of the darkest, foulest, and most dangerous shit-hole Leo had ever inhabited.

Boyce's charade made Leo's blood boil. Being played was not something Leo typically forgave people for. He remembered Boyce's parting words the night the mage left him as the Kiman soldiers burned the Capitol. *Outside this dungeon, men and starborn grapple for empires, land, power, and gold. Each of us has a role to play, a job to do. You know what yours is. Get to it!*

"You knew the whole time, didn't you?" Leo accused.

Boyce waved the accusation away. "It's no secret that ambition will drive men to take or make what they want in this world. One need only to open a history book to know that. Their plots and names change, but their motives remain the same. Abaddon chose his mortal champion in Agnen the Reaper, and I chose mine in you. It remains to be seen what the outcome will be."

"You played me," Leo spat. His fists clenched at his sides and ached to clasp his sword. Truth was, he liked the starborn, but something ached in his chest and it stung like betrayal. "Each of us has a role to play, a job to do. Isn't that what you told me, Boyce? I'd like to know what your role is since you seem to have it all figured out. You left me in Bresdan. Whose side are you on?"

"Leo." Jewel tugged him by the arm but Leo shook him away.

"Stop it." Page stepped between Boyce and her brother. "He didn't play anyone, Leo. He saved my life in Gwonda, you know? Borin sent a kill squad into the forest and Boyce slayed them before they killed Trechon and I." Leo turned his head at that. "And he didn't turn me into a starborn either. That was my own doing."

Leo remembered back to the dungeon when Boyce tried explaining to him the Mozzaroth. He had paid the old man no never mind and written him off as cracked in the head. It wasn't the first time his unyielding stubbornness had led him astray and now he wished he had listened. "I don't have time for this," Leo spat, thankful that Jewel was still trying to pull him away.

"We'll address this later," Jewel said, spurring him forward. "We've both got more questions than answers. That's usually the way it goes. I need you to keep it together. I need you to be the leader Veronia bled for, not the sword they're afraid of."

Leo pulled his arm away once again and opened his mouth to say something but closed it quickly enough when he realized that he'd been dragged up and onto a wooden platform occupied by a single chair. Leo didn't like the implications.

"What the hell is this?" he muttered to Jewel.

"While you were sifting through ashes, the Priest's Council made an executive decision. Veronia needs a king, and you're it."

"You did what?" Leo grabbed a fistful of Jewel's robe and drew the High Priest into him. "Mutterings from the men. Isn't that what you told me you heard?" He let loose of his priestly brother's holy cloth and gathered himself. "You're my brother and all, but you've tested all my patience. The Shield of Veronia was a stretch and to be King now? Have you lost your wits, brother? I'm a soldier not a king." Leo stormed off the podium.

The crowd watched Leo go, and stared up at the

High Priest with curious frowns. Jewel put on his best reassuring smile and waved a finger in the air. "One moment please," he said before chasing after Leo. Juan, Bruce, Mandy, and Natalie had already corralled him below.

"What the feck is this?" Leo asked any who dared to answer.

Bruce dabbed blood from a gash that ran from the top of his head, down his left brow, and into his cheek. It's a wonder his eye hadn't been cut clean out of its socket. What remained of it was bloodshot and watery and looked to give him no peace. "Would you rather us crown a politician in your place?" Bruce pulled the cloth from his brow and it came away bloody. He regarded it with his good eye and gave it a sniff. "Or maybe we can bury a sword up Saul Holloway's ass when we find him and crown the first sonofabitch that jars it loose. Otherwise Natalie and I can speak for Indigo, and we pledge our swords to you. I reckon Veronia needs a king and you've bloodied yourself enough on her behalf to wear the crown."

Leo regarded Natalie. Nestin's blood still stained her neck. It had dried a bit since his corpse was used to knock her off the wall. Leo had taken the same fall once and knew just how unforgiving the landing was. "And what say you, Natalie? Did you scheme this fuckery up with the rest of them?"

"Judging by our last king the expectations aren't very high, Leo. I have all the faith and confidence that you won't bugger it up too much." She addressed her future king with a mocking smile. "Besides, even Abigail gave you the nod, and she speaks for Tamore in Nestin's place. Bless his bones."

"Bless his bones," they muttered.

"And I can speak for Mirta," Juan said. "We received news from Nebula that they too stand behind you and they're sending men and supplies our way. A rider advised that strange happenings were occurring on Shield Island and giants walked the earth. We just delivered the Kiman army their first loss and Veronians have been taking note, Leo. You may not want to wear the crown but you damned well better or someone with even less competence than you will. It's a shit sandwich with all the fixings and we all gotta take a bite."

Leo thought to argue more but it was starting to sound ridiculous. Most people would cut off limbs to wear a crown and here he was acting like he didn't want it and wasn't sure why. He'd probably defer most of the decisions to the Priest's Council anyways like the days of old. "Wasn't it Kano who said there are other starborn behind the Kiman Empire? And now they've summoned giants? How the hell are we supposed to contend with that?"

"Well that's what we are here for," Kano said. Boyce and Page stood behind the half-man. "You Veronians have a thing about blood debts do you not? Well I made a deal with your High Priest over there." He pointed at Jewel, and the priest shrugged. "You all witnessed my end of the bargain. Now it's your turn to help free my companions who've been taken captive by the Prothica and their giants."

"What are Prothica?" Bruce asked.

"The starborn behind the Kiman Empire," Jewel answered.

"You know of them?" Juan asked.

"They're the same lot that took me captive. If not for Agnen, I'd be dead right now. And without Kano's help I don't think we'd be having this conversation. Whoever takes the crown owes Kano and his Zodans a blood debt to free his friends. One of which you all know. Bishop Michael who in truth answers to the name of Nicolai, the starborn leader of Kano's clan."

Well, I'm glad there aren't any strings attached. A silence passed as the weight of Jewel's words settled in. Leo regarded Jewel and the thought of his brother's captivity was enough to send him on a killing spree that he couldn't start quick enough. He made a note to ask him about that the first chance he got. And about Agnen somehow saving his life. Then there was Page who'd nearly been killed if not for Borin.

"Fine. I'll do it." And like that he took on the deficit.

"You will?" Jewel asked.

Leo's piercing gaze swept the gathering, settling at last upon Jewel. "Am I not my brother's keeper?" He peered down at Kano. "My brother's debt is now my own. Understand?"

Kano nodded.

"Oh and Leo," Jewel said. "Do forgive us, but with all that's been going on lately, we haven't had time to forge a proper crown. The Drago Smiths have assured me that they have more than a few fit for a king in their molten mountains but it will be a few days before they can retrieve one that might suit you. Oh, and Jonas has already sent for more of his smiths to build you a proper throne room."

"It's better I don't wear a target on my head anyways."

"Suit yourself," Jewel said. "Let's get on with it then, shall we?"

The crowd fell silent once again as Jewel and Leo took the stage. Juan and the others shuffled to the front of the crowd. The podium filled up fast with Jewel's council taking their position behind the High Priest.

Jewel raised his golden staff to quiet the crowd. "Brothers and sisters of Veronia, may I have your attention please." Jewel clasped a hand over his wrist behind his back, fingers twisting the staff as he walked and talked. "As we continue to bury our fallen, I need not remind you of the perils our kingdom faces against the Kimans who still occupy much of our land. As we stand here at dusk, God willing, tomorrow dawns yet another day. And with it the opportunity to rid ourselves of our oppressors.

"Our crews will work through the night to bury our dead. In the morning we will bless their bones so their souls may carry on into heaven."

A muttering of "bless their bones" swept the crowd and Jewel waited for it to pass.

"But tonight, as I stand before you as the High Priest of Veronia, I have a few confessions of my own to make."

Every head in Tamore turned at that. "What are you doing?" Leo heard Bishop Isabelle mutter under her breath. Jewel raised a palm out to still her.

"Before I was selected as the High Priest and whilst Leo was in exile, I wrote a letter to King Lawrence requesting him to spare my brother's life."

Leo craned his head at that. He'd known that General Soberal had taken to the king's ear to spare Leo's life but he'd heard nothing of Jewel doing the same. When a bishop earns their chain and joins the Priest's Council, it's well known they mustn't interfere with the king's judgment of his pupils. And if the headless king had granted Jewel's request, he meant to use that leverage against Jewel or the Priest's Council in the future.

"But that was only the beginning of it," Jewel continued while the crowd still worked it out in their heads. "The weapons and armor many of you wear today were bought and paid for out of the church's treasury. I made a deal behind the council's back to equip Leo's army and the Drago Smiths carried out the forging."

Bishop Isabelle gasped so loud that Leo thought

she rolled an ankle and went down. She stared holes into the back of Jewel's head while Bishop Malachi subtly restrained her by the arm.

Once a man starts confessing, all those weighty little secrets start pouring out like water breaching a dam. It was no different for Jewel. Leo tensed, ready to draw steel but the crowd didn't move. Trion must have had similar ideas; he staggered forward cradling his broken arm, his good hand reaching for something sharp no doubt hidden within his sling.

"And that is not all. When the Kiman soldiers attacked Shield Island, I gave myself up. I thought they sought my head to leverage against Leo but I was wrong. They wanted something that Bishop Michael had, though Nicolai is his true name. He might have kept his faith but beneath his robe and his chain of office, he's a starborn. Not just any starborn mind you, but one of their leaders."

The crowd gawked at that and mutterings of discontent for having been played the fools started spreading and a disgruntled mob had formed. Boyce, Kano, and Page started to attract more than a few dirty looks. Boyce stepped in front of Page to address the crowd. Kano went a step further and winked a glowing eye that sent the crowd into an uproar.

"And now I give you the Shield of Veronia," Jewel bellowed into the crowd.

"You sonofabitch," Leo muttered.

"Now, now Leo. That's no way to speak to the

High Priest now is it? Please make it short though. We have to officially appoint you as King after all."

Leo still had a bit of fire in him and stormed the dais. His shield burned with his fury and once the crowd drank it in, one by one they fell silent. Below him, Juan, Bruce, Natalie, and Mandy formed a shield-wall and faced the crowd. Other soldiers started to trickle in at their side and Leo waited for them to fill the ranks. Surprisingly enough Boyce moved to the front of the shield-wall with Page and Kano at either side.

Leo drew his sword and picked at a loose piece of wood with the tip of his blade. "Anyone has a problem with any of our High Priest's actions, speak now."

The silence lingered as Leo carved deeper into the platform.

He shrugged his shield from his arm and set it carefully at his feet. He placed his sword and hatchet next to it, then fingered the leather straps of his breastplate till it clattered at his feet. Last came his shirt till he stood bare-chested in front of the crowd.

He heard sharp intakes of breath from the crowd. More than a lifetime of scrapes with death carved unevenly into his skin. When he turned his back to them, their gazes fell to the ground. The breeze tickled the rigid scars the flogging left behind. He clenched his teeth to bury the ache with everything else that plagued him.

Jewel's eyes welled with tears. "My dear brother." Bishop Isabelle wrapped an arm around the High Priest.

One horrified glance was all it took for her to look away.

"They say actions speak louder than words. I say loyalty lies in our scars." The night started to draw on. His grizzly scars looked angry as they glared against the torchlight. Leo shrugged his shoulders but it provided no comfort to his back. The nagging pain seemed amplified if anything else. Only a strong drink would dull the pain.

"They tell me more men are on the move to join our cause. That they've pledged their swords to me as your king. If pledging fealty were cloth I'd wipe my ass with it. I don't want your oaths or your bending knees. If I'm to be your king, I want your loyalty."

"You have mine, my king!" someone shouted out.

"And mine, my king," said another until the verbal pledges started to wash over the crowd. One man went as far as dropping trou to reveal his loyalty by means of an arrow wound he'd taken in the ass.

"Have a care, you fool," another man said, stifling laughter while shielding a youngster's eyes from the view.

"King Leo!" Juan bellowed, raising his bastard sword to the sky.

"King Leo!" the crowd echoed.

**

Bruce had a stick in hand, nudging the cook pot around

a fiery bed of coals when Leo and Juan made it down to the riverbank. Natalie, Page, and Mandy snickered at something then fell silent when Leo took his seat at the fire.

"Whatever you're eating, I'll have two." Juan made a motion to snatch the bowl from Natalie but she slapped his hand away.

She pointed with her spoon. "Saved you a few scraps over there. Be mindful not to eat it all, Juan. We're in the presence of a king, you know." Natalie tipped her bowl in salute, addressing Leo with a mocking smile.

Juan rummaged for a bowl, wiped it clean with his hand, and filled it with stew. "King or not, last one to the pot usually goes to bed hungry."

Leo plopped next to the fire. He wasn't hungry till he started walking past all the cookfires. A strong drink was what he really wanted though.

"Just fooling around. Here you go, Your Highness." Juan pressed the bowl into Leo's chest and turned to fill his own. Leo fumbled to catch the bowl and most of its contents spilled over and ran down his arm.

"My brother. A king now?" Page sat down beside him then jabbed Leo in the arm. Her face turned and she recoiled like she'd been scolded by the fire.

"What happened?" Bruce peered over the flames, hand on the hilt of his sword.

"I don't know. Something's burning in my chest,"

she muttered, scooting away. Juan dropped his bowl, mostly empty anyways, and shuffled quickly over to her.

Leo carried his shield to the other side of the fire and sat next to Bruce. "It must be my shield." The runes looked to draw light from the fire as the crackling flames died down to mere coals. When Leo set it down, the runes flickered out and the fire came roaring back to life, kicking embers into the night.

"Close," a voice came from the night, "but not entirely accurate."

"Boyce?" Page asked, searching the tree line where three figures approached.

"Yes my dear." Boyce strolled towards the campfire. "Mind if we join you?"

"I'm sure they won't mind at all. Come, let us all sit and talk a while." Jewel brushed past Kano to nudge Juan out of the way with the end of his staff, then offered the short sorcerer the seat.

"Thanks, but I'll stand," Kano replied. He peered around impatiently like he had somewhere else to be. Leo suspected Kano hadn't had a moment's peace since he'd discovered his Zodan companions were captured. But even for an immortal, Kano looked like he could use a few hours' rest. Dark circles, filled with worry, swelled under each of his eyes.

Boyce offered Page his hand and led her a short distance from the fire. "Much of the discomfort you are sensing stems from starache. A temporary side effect that flares up like heartburn, but twice as fierce. Given time and practice you'll be able to harness the energy which flows from the celestial else and use it for power. Now try that exercise I showed you. It should help take the edge off."

Page held her hands up and squinted them into action.

"Hold on a second," Boyce cried, looking at the others. "Not here." He grabbed her hands and led her down to the riverbank. "Now try it."

Leo couldn't see much with their backs turned towards him. But after a moment, a mystical ball of light formed in Page's hand.

"Easy now," Boyce said with a hand on her shoulder. "That's quite big enough." But the light grew brighter. Leo and the others shifted uncomfortably around for a better look.

"Best not get too close," Kano cautioned. "She doesn't have—"

Starfire loosed from Page's hand. Up it went sizzling into the night, lost amidst the stars.

"—any control," Kano finished. Page gasped and sank back. Boyce caught her in his arms.

Leo ran to his sister and helped lay her down next to the fire. Page kicked her legs out in front of her and slouched forward. "Oh man, that's better," she said with a drunken smile.

"She'll be fine," Boyce reaffirmed. "Growing pains is all." He froze suddenly, looking down where Leo's shield rested. Boyce backed away from like it were a snake in the grass coiled to strike at his boots.

"What's with my shield?" Leo bent over to pick it up. "Why are you starborn so skittish around it?"

Boyce and Kano exchanged glances. Kano deferred the question to Boyce. He crossed his arms and cocked his head, waiting on the Water Bearer to answer.

"The short version," Boyce said, "is that starborn have an ability to sense others of their kind nearby. The more minor stars we name"—Boyce held up his left hand—"the stronger our senses are, and the more energy we can draw from the else. That shield of yours is but one of five hundred which were fashioned long ago and those runes about it have an energy which I suspect also draws power from the same else."

"So the shield-bearer can use magic too?" Juan asked. He regarded Leo's shield. "What do those runes mean?"

Boyce paused in thought then shrugged. "The runes are encrypted and beyond my understanding. Kano, correct me if I'm wrong but the shields don't necessarily provide the bearer any special abilities but they do posses certain immunities to starborn ability. A shield in every sense of the word."

"A queer thing, that shield," Kano said. He regarded the crowd cautiously. Trustworthy men and women weren't as easy to spot as bishops who wore medallions around their necks. Far as Leo could tell, if Kano really wanted to free his companions this lot was his best chance. Kano must have come to the same conclusion. "I suspect only Nicolai and Abaddon could tell us more about the shield and what it can and cannot do. I will say this though. It's a dangerous thing," he cautioned. "It can end a life at a simple touch. I've heard it possesses some of the same divine properties as the Arc of the Covenant."

"I've got a question." Jewel regarded Kano and Boyce. "These giants that Abaddon conjured. Nicolai and Abaddon had a few heated exchanges about the Ring of Solomon, and summoning the giants beforehand. In the book of Job, it makes mention of Nimrod being bound in the constellation of Orion, but I overheard Abaddon speaking of a giant named King Delbec. Which one is it?"

"Delbec, I believe. But for all I know they could be one and the same," Boyce responded.

"You believe or you know?" Kano asked tersely. "Since we're on the topic of books and all."

Something in Kano's tone threatened an accusation of sorts and Leo wondered what it might be. When Boyce started measuring Kano with a calculative glance, Leo thought it imperative for his health to put some distance between him and them. One can never be too cautious with their longevity in life.

But Jewel had another question lined up and fired away. "Whether it's Nimrod or Delbec, how did he and the others get bound in the first place?"

Again, Kano deferred the question to Boyce. "It

was Nicolai and Abaddon who did the bounding. The two are said to be among the first of the starborn. But after the fight with the giants, they went their separate ways. Nicolai led the Zodans and Abaddon started the Prothica."

Kano opened his mouth to say something, then closed it with a scowl. Leo remembered Boyce telling him that he held no allegiance to either side. Perhaps that's why Kano and Boyce were wary of one another's intentions.

"Nicolai and Abaddon were among the first of the twelve you say?" Jewel added. "Go on now." He motioned with his staff. "Tell us about the first of the twelve and why they came to be. If we are to take up the sword against the Prothica, the giants, and their blasphemous beliefs, then we should at least know the origin and history of our enemy."

Leo was overwhelmed by questions but figured he could get caught up with Jewel later on. Juan and the others must have been equally confused but to their credit they held their questions till the lesson was over. Only the crackling fire broke the silence.

"Very well then," Boyce said. "Thousands of years ago, in the Days of Noah, there were giants on the earth. They were bred in part by the fallen angels, otherwise known as the Watchers, who descended upon the earth and taught men and women forbidden knowledge.

"Among the Watchers were Azazel and Baraqiel.

It's said that the two were brothers and that Azazel taught humans how to make weapons of war and that Baraqiel taught them astrology. They took earthly women as wives and concubines. Those sons and daughters of the Watchers were giants revered as demigods, titans of the land, but most commonly referred to them as the Nephilim. King Delbec was the leader among them. After a time, even the Nephilim began taking earthly wives and concubines of their own. Their descendants known as the Anakim were also giants but of a lesser size and might, mind you.

"When Azazel began to ravage the earth with war, it was his brother Baraqiel who tried to stop him. Baraqiel turned to his most esteemed pupils, and taught Abaddon, Nicolai, and ten others how to name the stars so together they could stand against the Nephilim and the Anakim who ravished the land. The twelve made up the Mozzaroth who later became known as Children of the Stars. They fought a Holy War against the giants in those days, eradicating all of them but King Delbec who was mightier than them all. So powerful was Delbec that he killed off ten of twelve Mozzaroth before Nicolai and Abaddon could subdue him.

"When the Watchers began fighting one another led by Baraqiel on one side and Azazel on the other, it nearly killed everyone. So devastating was the war that God sent his Angel Army down upon them to subdue the Watchers and bury them beneath the earth. But the Nephilim and the Anakim were left for the members of the Mozzaroth to contend with.

"Just before Baraqiel was bound and buried, he gave Nicolai a book known today as the Book of Baraqiel. And in it were the secrets to unlock the power to subdue the Nephilim. The book led Nicolai and Abaddon to a magical ring, hidden in the land where the Garden once flourished. That ring possessed dominion over the giants' will and with it Nicolai and Abaddon were able to bind them and cast them into a celestial prison.

"But the human bloodlines had been tainted. So much so that God sent the flood to clean the slate. Abaddon and Nicolai were allowed passage upon Noah's Arc, but Noah's son Shem carried on the giant bloodline and the Anakim race lived on.

"One night an angel appeared before Nicolai and Abaddon and instructed them to give the Book of Baraqiel and the ring to a Jewish king named David. King David, mortal as he was, was already a mighty man of valor. Armed with the book and the ring, he and his men took up the fight against the giants of the earth once again and eradicated Shem's descendants from the land. King David passed the Book of Baraqiel and the ring to his own son Solomon before his death. With the ring and the book, King Solomon became the greatest king the world had ever known. It was through Solomon that the golden shields were forged, so that his men could use them to protect the Arc of the Covenant against giants and starborn alike.

"In time, the Jews were conquered more than once but those shield-bearers protected the Arc of the Covenant, while Nicolai and Abaddon fought to protect the Ring of Solomon and the Book of Baraqiel. But with only two starborn against so many enemies, they were unable to protect both the ring and the book so they separated the two and hid them. Nicolai hid the ring and Abaddon the book. In due time the Book of Baraqiel was found and lost. Nicolai dug up the ring, slipped it on his own hand, concealed his identity, and lived among the clergy. After a time, Nicolai and Abaddon taught others to name the stars and the twelve became twelve again. But because Nicolai bore the ring and Abaddon had lost the book, he resented Nicolai for it and eventually created the Prothica."

"And now Abaddon wears the ring and the giants are bound by its bearer," Jewel surmised, cupping a hand to his jaw. "Ha." He must have remembered something that now seemed funny. "Nicolai has always been crazy about books. Collecting them everywhere we went. He had tombs of them back in Mirta. Told me he was trying to assemble a book that would unify the church. Perhaps it was the Book of Baraqiel he was after the whole time."

"Yes and no," Kano resigned. "He's sent me on many quests to look for the Book of Baraqiel, every time he thought he'd discovered a solid lead, but I found no trace or inkling of its existence. As of late, Nicolai's come to the conclusion that it may be just as lost as the

Arc of the Covenant. But Nicolai was indeed working on a collection of books to unify the church too."

Boyce met Leo's eye and held it in firelight. It was rather unsettling until the hint of a smile touched the starborn's lips and Leo turned away.

"I've listened to enough stories this night to last me a lifetime." Leo scooted closer to the fire and drew a blanket over him and the weapons at his side. He rolled an axe-cut branch forward and propped his head on it. "Juan, you set a watch for the night I presume?"

"We did." Bruce placed another log on the fire and stood to regard the full moon. "My Swords of Bane have first watch."

Leo rolled onto his shoulder and nestled into his pillow. "Sit down, the both of you. There are plenty of titles I've yet to assign. I've grown rather fond of one of my own. The *Shield* of Veronia. It has a nice ring to it so I think I'll keep it along with the crown." He stifled a yawn and smacked his lips. "The rest of you pick titles that suit you and let me know what they are by morning. Unless you just can't shake the urge to stay up all night, your firewatch days are over."

***

It was well into the night when the first of three ships docked at Shield Island. Kiman soldiers spilled onto the dock, barking orders at their servants to make haste unloading food and supplies. Two long wooden poles which could have easily been mistaken for ship masts were heaved overboard and clamored to a rest on the dock. Women of different races from the farthest corners of the world were ordered out of the boat and bound at the wrists to the poles. Each of them draped in sleeveless, white silken gowns. Their necks, wrists, and hair enameled with precious stones and metals of every kind.

As the low-hanging full moon cast its watchful eye on the island, it was plain to see that none of the women were chosen by their good looks alone. It was their size that Abaddon was after. If they were to be bred with the giants, only the tallest and broadest of hip would be capable of surviving long enough to bear a child.

"Concubines," Liz exclaimed in her cage. She and the others were perched atop a wagon next to a fire. A handful of giants' goalers sat lazily around the fire charring meat to their liking. Their attention diverted to the silken gowns with the boats pulled ashore though, and most of their meat was left burning unattended.

Nicolai writhed. "They'll all burn for this." He scraped the stubble on his jaw with the backside of his hand. It sounded like wood being filed down. "Their judgment can't come fast enough for my taste." Nicolai snarled at the moon but it did little good. "I'm a fool. I should never have let Abaddon get his hands on that ring."

"You let?" Ambrose asked meekly. "What do you mean? I thought they attacked you and took the ring by force?" Ambrose had not fully recovered his strength from nearly burning out just yet. As far as Liz could tell, his wits appeared to lull behind even further. Ambrose lie on his back, feet raised up against the bars of his cage. Though his long legs went numb often, it was the only comfortable position he could find.

The thought of slapping Ambrose upside the head for his insolence came to the forefront of Liz's mind. Were it not for Brielle's cage situated between the two of them, she would have tried. "Mind your tongue Ambrose, and show a little respect."

Inside his cage, Nicolai hung his head. "No. It's my blame to bear. When Abaddon and his men stormed the island, I tried to buy the priests time to sail away with the Golden Shield. In doing so, I put the ring at risk."

"What will we do now?" Brielle asked. The arrow wound in her shoulder had stopped bleeding but zapped her strength. Abaddon ordered a healer to mend the wound as best he could between the bars of the cage. It would do no good for her to die and another starborn to take her place. Brielle had spat in the healer's face and slapped away the ointment he tried to give her.

Liz watched Nicolai regard the starry sky once more and followed his gaze. Three of the twelve had died that day and Liz could only imagine how it had happened. She prayed Kano wasn't mortally wounded in the fight. Liz swept the stars, resting on Kaus Australis, the Capricorn star of healing. Ansuke's star. Kaus Australis flickered dully as if wounded and Liz knew the Vratta chief had fallen. Her only comfort lie in the hope that Ansuke was lifted up and called home to join the Children of the Stars. Liz imagined somewhere up there, Ansuke and Hadrian were looking down and watching over them now.

Nicolai must have been thinking the same thing for the moon lit up his grin and a chuckle escaped his smile. Liz turned her attention to Borin's star. Rasalhague recoiled into the night as if the moon shunned it away from its light. The same could be said for Elias's star Zubeneschamali.

As if the moon itself pointed with subtle rays of light, Kano's star glistened along with two others.

"Kano's found allies," Nicolai mused. "Boyce the Water Bearer and..." He shuffled closer to the bars to rest his head between them. "Page," he said at length. "Namer of the Warrior star Regulus."

"And who is this Page?" Brielle asked.

Nicolai's knowing smile widened until the stars twinkled in his eyes. "None other than the sister to our shield-bearer, Leo Rosewood. I daresay if ever there was a company viable enough to rival Abaddon and his giants, Kano's found it."

***

In the month that passed since the siege, Leo's new throne room had started to take shape. True to his word, Jonas had called upon his best smiths to complete the work and Leo had never seen so many woodworkers, stonemasons, and blacksmiths in one place. They labored day and night, and despite the constant clamoring of hammers, the chipping of stone and cutting of wood, Leo found peace sitting upon his throne, in the midst of the controlled chaos.

Perhaps only Bruce enjoyed it more. They'd taken to calling him Dead Eye since the siege and it wasn't because he'd improved his archery. The festering remnants of his rotting eye had left the socket black and hollow. Dark webs of decay sprawled out of the wound from forehead to chin, nose to ear. He took to wearing a patch and hammered out his frustrations at the forge. Mandy worried that the wound was driving Bruce mad. Natalie assured her that Bruce had grown up tinkering around forges and woodshops his whole life. Leo told the others to give him space, and let him be.

Where a man finds solace is his own business. Currently Leo found his sitting atop the stone dais throne of his new hall. To a standing audience below the dais, it looked to be a simple grand chair with a budded cross embroidered into its back and pegs on the sides to hold the royal shield, sword, and hatchet. But from Leo's vantage the wooden arms and legs of the chair were a marvelous work of art that served as a constant reminder of Veronia's bloody past.

Where his left arm and legs sat, the carvings etched out a history of Veronia. Much of the symbolism was way before Leo's time. Others appeared to be more recent—it was those he traced with his fingers lost in thought. Like the Kotian Shore where his father had led the Veronian Army that would save the Kotians from Norse invaders during the Viking wars. The Winsoot Mountains where Leo earned his red name. A Bloody Rose was carved into the side of the miniature mountain range and looked to ache like a blistering wound. Next was the Gwonda Forest where he'd led volunteers against the headless king's orders to repel the Gorronian Army. Then a whipping pole crossed by a flail, where he'd taken more than enough lashes to never recover. Even now that etching made him stir uncomfortably in his chair.

And then there was Bresdan. The former Capitol smoldered in flames at the hands of its Kiman oppressors. The Golden Shield rose from the ashes and beside it the stronghold where Tamore repelled the Kiman siege.

Leo recognized only a few of the symbols on the right arm of the chair. The twelve-pointed star which the starborn fancied. The smiths' hammer and sword over the budded cross. Six miniature priests' medallions that made up the High Priest and his council. And the last etching, where Leo's right hand sat cupping the end of the armrest, was a Guardian Chapel, where two soldiers stood guard at the golden double doors.

He twisted Bruce's old chalice in his hand and stared into the swirling red wine. It smelled pleasant enough like a dried-out cigar box. But the longer he regarded it, the darker it got, as if the chalice were dipped in the blood of the fallen. "To better men than me," Leo whispered then drowned the memories.

"More wine, my king?"

Leo shook himself from thought then wondered how long Mandy had been watching him. He swept the crimson carpet to the dining table which sat vacant aside from miscellaneous tools the smiths piled atop it. He found her sitting next to the hearth, leaned back in a chair with her feet propped up. Her watchful eyes peering over the top of a book. She could have at least put her feet down to appear like she meant the offer. Instead she went back to reading before he could reply.

Leo could have had his pick of squires, cup-bearers, or any number of retainers to fill his cup or send his messages, but trusted very few people to do the work. Not that he had much choice in the matter anyways. He'd told Juan and the others to pick titles of their own and the stubborn asses chose to make up the new kingsguard each with the authority of the king. Though he would never proclaim it aloud, it put Leo at ease having Juan, Natalie, Bruce, Wade, and Mandy at his side despite their insolence.

"You've been hanging around Natalie too long," he remarked. She looked up and shrugged then returned to her novel.

Down the length of the hall, just outside the double doors leading into the throne room, Leo heard a commotion of voices. Mandy tossed her book aside and scurried to Leo's side, adjusting her sword-belt as she went.

"Out of my way, Juan. If you won't let me past this door, then I'll make my own," the voice threatened.

"He sounds pretty pissed this time," Mandy surmised.

Kano strode through the doorway and down the hall. Face red as the carpet at his feet which bore the violet Veronian V. Natalie and Juan shuffled along at the starborn's heels, their fingers splayed out like they'd done all they could. Boyce and Page brought up the rear.

Leo clasped the arms of his throne and braced for another tongue-lashing.

"Well don't you look comfortable," Kano said, stopping short of the dais. Any farther would have been considered a threat not that Leo could do much even if he'd wanted too. Kano placed a defiant foot on the lowest step to emphasize his displeasure. "A month it's been. What the hell are we still doing in Tamore, Leo?" The lack of proper address didn't go unnoticed. "You owe me—"

"A blood debt," Leo finished coldly. "And by my bones it will be settled. But we need more time."

"More time? More time for what?" Kano exclaimed. "The longer we stay idle the stronger the threat grows. And at this pace, there will be a whole other generation of giants to contend with."

"And what would you have us do, Kano? Storm the

vault? Fight for every mile against Bresdan, Indigo, Antick, and Chaucer along the way?"

Crowning Leo King of Veronia didn't create the rebellion they'd hoped for. Instead of Veronians fighting to take back their own towns and villages, most of the loyalists fled in the night and turned up in Tamore, but still their numbers were too small to launch an attack. Also, giant sightings kept flooding in. With each account they grew in size and might leaving very few of his men itching for a confrontation. Since the death of King Xalvador, Abaddon revealed himself to all of the free cities and declared himself their rightful king. He'd sent messengers out to every city and town requiring they bend the knee or be swept up in the wrath of his man-eating Giant army.

Although Kano was adamant that there were only a dozen or so giants, word spread that Abaddon had cracked open the gates of Hell and now commanded an army of giants and demons to do his bidding. However much truth there may have been in the stories, it was enough to give even Leo pause. Too many had died already and he was in no hurry to lead the few men he had left on such a red road to the last door.

Leo and Tamore hadn't escaped Abaddon's memory since the siege. Two weeks ago a Kiman envoy arrived to hand-deliver Leo's summons. The scroll commanded that Leo set off for Chaucer at once to swear fealty to the new emperor. It would be only a matter of time before Abaddon led the full strength of his new army back to Tamore for a reckoning. Leo knew the last strands of sand in the hourglass were passing through.

Kano climbed another step to slowly regard Leo from head to toe. "I remember a time, not so long ago, that the Bloody Rose was hailed as the reddest name in all of Veronia. Men muttered it with caution as if you'd burst through tavern doors and snatch their souls." His gaze regarded the golden shield. "So mighty was your name and righteous was your cause that the whole country hailed you as their Shield and crowned you their King." Kano shook his head as if coming to an unsatisfied conclusion. "And now you sit idle like that crown atop your head has weighed you down and zapped all the fight from you."

A chill swept the hall and Leo's kingsguard shifted uncomfortably at the words that pricked their king like weapons. Leo's blood was boiling now and he stood up so hastily that his chalice fell off the armrest and clanked down the dais steps.

"Leave us!" Leo's fury echoed through the hall chasing the smiths out the door. Snarling, he descended the steps until he and Kano were an arm's length from coming to blows.

"Enough." Boyce pushed past the kingsguard and separated the two. "To the council table. All of you. And the first one to stir from their chair deals with me." He put a hand on each of their backs and pushed them down the length of the carpet. At the table he nudged

Kano and Leo to opposite ends.

"The problem we face is evident..." Boyce paused to test the durability of the arms on his own chair. He wiggled them with his hands, deemed them worthy of their craftsmanship, and eased his forearms to rest on them. He turned to Kano. "I'd like to hear your suggestion on how we might free your companions without getting us all killed."

Kano looked like a child in his chair but he had a full-grown scowl for anyone who thought to remark of it. No one did. "Ships," he said at last. "If the recent additions of men are too few to fight across land, then we sail down the Gorro to their front doors."

"It would take months to build enough ships to send our army down the river," Juan said. "And you can't really conceal shipbuilding. Word would spread quicker than the ships are made watertight and Abaddon's army would be here before they touched the water."

"Even if we had the ships built, do you really think two thousand men would be enough?" Natalie added. "It's one thing to hold against a siege with starborn in our ranks, but we'll have no walls between us and their massive army if we set sail towards them. Sitting ducks comes to mind."

"Perhaps we should rebuild the stronghold," Mandy interjected. "Bigger and stronger this time. Let them come to us again."

"This time we won't have the Tribesmen to assist

us," Juan said. "If the Kimans have any wits at all they'll just surround us and starve us out. We don't have the food stocks to survive long against a war of attrition."

Leo still fumed from Kano's wayward tongue. "I'm done cowering behind walls," Leo spat. "I'd rather die in the open field than cooked up like a prisoner within my own walls. Another stronghold is out of the question."

"Then ships it is," Kano said, pleased with his own conclusion. "There is no other way. You've had a month to come up with something better and we don't have another month to contemplate the inevitable. Either we set sail, or they come to us. And we all know what will happen when they come a second time."

A silence carried on as looks were exchanged around the table and fell at last on Leo.

"We need an angle." Leo put his forearm on the table and leaned into it, shaking a finger in the air. "We're thinking too grand of scale. Our few cannot stand against them again. Perhaps we should use our lack of numbers to our advantage."

Boyce rubbed his chin, considering where Leo was going with this, but didn't seem to follow. None of them did.

Leo stared down the length of the table and met Kano's curious eye. "How many men do you think it would take to storm the vault?

Kano's forehead creased in reflection. "More than

what you've got. Maybe ten or closer to twenty thousand. And that's taking into account their number of men alone. Maybe more against such an impenetrable fortress, with giants, Abaddon, and Lyle."

Leo's smile broadened. "Yes. Twenty thousand men might do. Now, how many starborn would it take?"

Kano regarded Page, then Boyce. Then the smartass peered under the table. "I haven't seen what Boyce can do, but Page is still wet behind the ears as far as starborn are concerned. Not only that but the three of us possess only one of the elements. And I don't know how well Boyce's mastery of water might improve our odds on dry land. Even with all those minor stars." Kano sank back into his chair as if the hopelessness of their plight became clear at last.

"Ah, but would the help of your companions improve our chances?" Leo held up his left palm and began to count with his fingers. "Liz and her wind. Nicolai and his wisdom. Brielle with her telepathy. Ambrose's invisibility." Kano stared hungrily at Leo's hands as he counted and named his lost companions. Even Boyce started to bristle as Leo's list continued. "Page with her..." Leo faltered a moment not quite sure what his sister's berserker power consisted of. Surely the sister he knew was not better with sword and shield than he was now.

Leo regarded Page; she stared back at him with a wolfish, rueful little grin. He rolled his eyes and continued. "Boyce the water-bearer. And you, Kano. The teleporter." Leo held up seven fingers now but never before had seven been such a luckier number. "Not to mention all the starfire and other crazy shit you guys can do."

It was Boyce and all the gravity in his voice that turned Kano's thoughtful look upside down. "But we don't have seven. We have only us three. And like you said before, it would take an army of twenty thousand to free the others."

Leo reached into a pocket and fished out his summons to bend the knee. He slapped the scroll onto the table and regarded it with a grin. "Who needs an army when you have an invitation?"

***

It was approaching midnight when Leo sent Juan to go wake and retrieve the High Priest. The rest of the kingsguard sat waiting on one side of the table, while the starborn sat opposite of them. Their chattering ceased when the door opened wide and Jewel and Trion hurried in. Juan barred the door behind them.

Jewel's temper had boiled over somewhere between his bed and the throne room. His cheeks were flushed and his brow creased into a scowl. Leo braced for his brother's fury. "That crown of yours hasn't even settled onto your head, and yet already you're scheming behind my council's back?" Jewel paused to give them all a disapproving look.

Leo sank back in his chair and let out an exasperated sigh. "Sit down, brother. That's not how it happened."

Jewel yanked out Juan's vacant chair and sat down on Leo's right. He turned to Natalie who sat beside him and waved her to shuffle down. The kingsguard shifted down a chair and Jewel waved Trion, the newly appointed Captain of the Guardians, to sit down beside him.

"You all know Trion, I presume," Jewel said interlacing his fingers onto the table. The Priest's Council has reinstalled the Guardians and I've appointed Trion here to be their captain. He reports only to the Priest's Council." Jewel scanned the table but no challenges came.

"That will be fine," Leo agreed. "As long as his Guardians keep their business strictly within the confines of guarding the Church." Leo regarded Trion. "And If I have questions then I'll have answers."

Jewel looked past Trion to Juan. "Likewise," he said. Juan nodded in turn.

"Good." Jewel settled into his chair. "Now, tell me what's going on. I don't much appreciate being drawn from my bed to slither around in the night behind barred doors."

"We have a plan, brother." Page had her own hands resting upon the table. The star on her right hand still unsettled Leo to look upon and it appeared to make

Jewel just as uncomfortable.

"Yes. So I've heard." Jewel frowned at his sister and then back to his brother. "Juan tells me that you plan to use a summons, a piece of paper to break into the vault. A fortress of starborn, giants, and soldiers." Jewel leaned forward and drove a finger into the table. "And not with an army but the occupants of this table. Is that the right of it, Leo? Do tell me just how that idea spawned into action when it should have been abandoned at birth?"

"We're going to spring Kano's companions from the vault," Leo replied. "That will give us the advantage of seven starborn against their two."

"And what about the giants, Leo? Or the thousands of soldiers who guard the fortress?"

"We'll deal with them," Kano said. "All we need is a way in. Or a way out for the other Zodans. If we can catch them off guard then they won't have time to mobilize their whole army."

"So let me get this right. You expect to take that summons of yours to Abaddon, bend your knee and somehow free the other Zodans? How will you get in, and how do you expect to get them out without being detected?" Jewel's eyes glinted with caution. "Listen to me, Leo, and heed my words. Abaddon is a wicked one. And his counterpart Lyle is just as wretched. Not to mention the man-eating giants they have to do their bidding. If you answer that summons and show your face anywhere near Chaucer, Abaddon will kill you on the spot. Even on bending knee you're as good as dead. He has no use for you therefore no reason to keep you alive. Then he'll erase the mere mention of your name from history. Tell me brother. Once the heat in you seeps out and your blood runs cold, how then will your plan work?"

The harsh reality of Jewel's words swept through the room like a violent wind breaking their mast. It deflated their sails and left them stranded at sea.

"I've given this a lot of thought," Boyce said, stirring the silence, "and I've come up with two plausible options." He reached into his cloak and shifted a leather satchel to the front. From it he drew what looked like a rock and set it on the table.

"Dragonglass." Jewel reached over, taking the dark shard of rock to examine it closely. "This is the rock used to bind Nicolai. He's trapped in a cage made of this stuff."

"And I have no doubt that the others are kept in a similar cage," Boyce added. "A prison made of this would cut the starborn off from the else. They are powerless."

"Let me see that." Kano beckoned the stone to him and Jewel obliged. Kano drew the stone to his stomach and his face clenched with stain. "Gah," he gasped, setting the stone down. "It works. Here, hold this," he said, giving the rocky shard of glass to Page. Her eyes went wide and cautious but Boyce swore it would do her no harm.

Kano left his seat to cross the room. "You brilliant bastard," he declared of Boyce. "Now pass the stone along." Page handed the stone across the table to Natalie. "Oh that's good." Kano waved a finger, returning to his seat. "This might work, after all."

"What, what it is?" Leo asked.

"Oh nothing," Kano said coyly.

"They have a right to know, Kano," Boyce said. "If not for the High Priest's candid recollection of his captivity, I wouldn't have discovered it either. But now it makes perfect sense."

"Go on then," urged Leo.

"Dragonglass impedes the flow of energy from the else," Boyce explained. "Kano wasn't able to access his ability or sense Page even though she's right next to him. It basically renders the starborn powerless but that's not always a bad thing."

Leo's wheels were spinning now. "Ahh. So that's our way in!"

"The dragonglass will conceal our way in. I'm told our friend Trion here is familiar with the vault, no?" Trion stirred in his chair, flexing his once-broken arm. He shared a look with Jewel and they nodded in unison. "Good then. We'll have to disguise him a little bit then he can lead Kano, Page, and I through the back door. Our young here king will still have to answer the summons and draw their attention. A distraction of sorts."

"So basically your plan consists of Leo's death

dragging out just long enough to let you sneak in and break the Zodans out?" Jewel fixed a glare on Boyce and Kano. "Maybe they can flog him again before they cut off his head. Would that give you enough time then?" Jewel had a white-knuckle grip on his staff. "I pray your second option has more care for our Veronian king's head."

"It does indeed," Boyce continued. "Had I no concern for Leo's head, I wouldn't have come here in the first place. And surely I wouldn't have revealed what I'm about to now." The council stirred to the edge of their seats.

"I'm afraid the second option is quite as risky as the first. It would still entail us using dragonglass and Trion leading us into the vault while Leo is answering the summons in Chaucer. But this time Leo would have a great deal more bargaining power. So much so that he might even have enough leverage to spare not only his life, but the rest of ours too should things take a turn for the worse."

Were it not his head they were talking about, Leo would have chuckled. He couldn't imagine anything he owned that might be of interest to Abaddon. Not even his shield. But didn't plan on doing any negotiating anyways. Leo's plan consisted of buying time just long enough to run Abaddon through with a blade. Even if it took a bend in the knee. Whatever happened after that, Leo didn't care much. He'd go out spattered in the blood of his enemies, the way it was always meant to be.

Again Boyce reached into his leather satchel, this time drawing out a leather-bound book fastened with leather straps and golden buckles. The cover was blank except for a small crest of squiggly lines of some foreign hand.

Kano gasped. "It can't be." He reached for the book but his arms were too short, Boyce too fast.

Boyce snatched the book and secured it in his satchel. "Oh, it be."

"You bloody fool!" Kano writhed from his chair and paced down the length of the carpet. He made a turn at the throne and came back. His fists shaking in fury. "I knew you had it. How else could you have known the histories without Nicolai's lessons?" He paused in thought and his eyes flashed aglow. "Whose side are you on, Boyce? The time has come you picked one now!"

Chairs clattered to the floor as the others fumbled out of their seats. Leo found himself inching in front Boyce who was the only one left seated at the table. Fool that he was, Leo left his weapons on the throne and Kano stood between them now.

"I wouldn't if I were you," Kano threatened as Page moved forward.

"Enough!" Boyce slammed a fist onto the table and rose to his feet. The others stepped aside and Boyce shuffled forward until he and Kano stood on opposite ends of the carpet. "You're damn right I have it, and a good thing I do or it would have fallen into Abaddon's hands just like the ring. As long as I live, I'll pledge allegiance to neither side. Zodans, Prothica, Veronia, Kiman, or otherwise, so get over it."

"Be still! The both of you." Jewel stepped between the two starborn, addressing each of them with an unfavorable pointing of his staff. "I don't know about you, Kano, but I'd rather have it in the hands of Boyce than the hands of Abaddon, wouldn't you?"

"I want to see it," Kano demanded.

Boyce laughed long and hard at that. His laughter echoed through the hall and Leo wondered if the starborn had suddenly gone mad.

"I bet you do after all the time you and Nicolai have spent looking for it," Boyce replied. He shook off his cloak and reached into the leather satchel to retrieve the book. He held it out at arm's length. "Have a look," he mused.

Kano closed in and snatched the book from Boyce's hand. He beamed with a light that could only be found at the end of a lifelong journey. He unclasped the buckles, wet his lips, and began thumbing through its pages. After the first few pages, his face twisted into a scowl. By the time he'd skipped through to the end of the book he was shaking his head. "What is this? A journal to jot down all your brilliant ideas?" he fumed, turning the book over in his hands. "It's nothing more than a creped old tomb of blank pages? Is this a jest? Do you mean to make a fool of me?" Kano reared back and hurled the book through the air.

Boyce gasped aloud. He lunged after the book and caught it just before it hit the ground. "Careful with it, you fool."

"Careful with what?" Kano replied. "There's nothing there but empty pages. If you think that is the Book of Baraqiel then your judgment's clouded and a danger to us all."

"I'll remember you said that."

"Make it the first entry in that useless book of yours."

"Excuse me." Boyce shouldered past Kano up the dais onto the throne. "Leo, do you mind?" he asked regarding the weapons.

Before Leo could tell Boyce how inappropriate it was to touch another man's weapons Boyce had already grabbed the hatchet by the handle and Leo was left biting his tongue.

"This is a finely crafted instrument of war. One even Azazel would no doubt approve of." Boyce marveled at the fine craftsmanship and the runes which held his eye. He stepped carefully down the dais with the hatchet in both hands. "I heard Chief Ansuke himself forged the weapon as a gift from all three of the tribes. And that the runes are lit by fire when you wield it against your enemies."

Leo fought the urge to grab the hatchet from Boyce's hands. It didn't seem right for anyone else to put their paws on his blade.

"Master Juan. If you don't mind?" Boyce held the

hatchet out.

Juan hesitated. "Erm. We Veronians are kind of particular about others handling our weapons. Might give me bad weapon-luck."

"Oh, I'm sure Leo will think nothing of it. If anyone were to be so worthy of the task, it would be you, no? I'm told that no scrape or battle's been fought where Leo's blade ran wet, that you weren't there by his side. Battle-brothers forged together in the furnace of war. Shouldermen to and through the last door."

Juan grabbed hold of the hatchet. "Fine then. Now what?"

Boyce circled 'round him. "Oh c'mon, Juan. Are you telling me after all this time, you've not been at least a little curious to see if Leo's hatchet would blaze for you too?"

Juan hung his head and extended his arm to give Boyce the hatchet back. "I know it won't. I've already tried it once before."

"Have you now?" Leo asked. Juan shrugged and turned his hands palm up.

"Me too." Leo searched the room for the speaker and found Wade with his fingers splayed out in front of him.

"You too?" Leo asked.

"Sorry, Leo. General Soberal, bless his bones, had me deliver your weapons to Juan in Mirta. It was just before Bresdan was sacked. The road was long and there was little else to do. I got curious is all."

"So what are you getting at?" Kano asked. "Are you suggesting that Leo is the last Bright Eye left?" Kano looked thoughtfully at Leo and didn't like the results.

"Unless you know of any other runesman, he may very well be the last. But obviously not the only one who can draw ability from weapon runes." Boyce spun on his heels and flung the axe across the room. A gasp escaped the crowd and Leo watched helplessly as it spun through the air towards his sister.

Page made a casual swiping motion, snatching the hatchet just before it buried into her chest.

A seemingly impossible feat as far as Leo could tell. He knew he couldn't have moved so fast. Would be a fool to even practice such a thing. That's what shields were for anyways.

Page walked the blade to her brother and regarded him with a wry smile. In her hand the hatchet's runes burned with a fire's light. "Your hatchet, brother."

Leo stood there stupidly, surprised as the others at what they'd just seen. "Give me that before you plague us all with bad weapon-luck," he said finally, snatching it from his sister's hand.

"But how could Ansuke have known?" Kano asked. Mouths hung open and their looks turned hard. "Bless his bones," Kano continued to the relief of the others. "How could he have known that Leo was a Bright Eye? And where is it derived from? He's surely not starborn. I haven't heard of a mortal Bright Eye since...well, King Solomon's five hundred shield-bearers. And they weren't runesmen, but Bright Eyes."

"Chief Ansuke, bless his bones for the duration of our conversation, must have seen something in Leo that we did not," Boyce continued. "Perhaps he was the first to discover Leo was a Bright Eye. We all know that the chief and his Vratta tribe fancied dabbling in dark magics, but none of them could activate the runes they made. Until Leo came along."

It was unnerving to be the topic of a subject Leo had no understanding of. Perhaps Boyce was onto something though. There was an energy in the hatchet, and especially in his shield. Neither of which he could explain. But surely they weren't the reason he'd earned his red name. He had neither of them when he'd earned his Guardian Dagger and Sword. "We fought the Gorronians in the mountains and in the forest before I was given the Tribal Kwatina. I fought against the Gorronians with only a Guardian Sword and Veronian Shield, each of which bear no runes."

"Oh but the sword does," Boyce mused, taking hold of Leo's Guardian sword from the throne. He fingered the blade where the Drago Smith's mark was etched into the steel. "A less-subtle rune, and manmade at that, which is why it doesn't bear the light of a starborn. I believe the Drago Smiths of old were made up of both runesmen and Bright Eyes."

"Tell us what you're getting at," Kano interrupted.

"You might not like what you hear." Boyce eased

into his chair at the table and the others followed suit. Once again Leo found himself on the edge of his seat.

Boyce turned the words over in his head then turned to Kano with a frown. "You already know how it came to be that I named my star. I'll speak no more of it."

Kano nodded solemnly. The rest of the table looked confused.

Leo didn't remember much of Boyce's starborn folklore during their time in the dungeon. He only paid it half a mind at the time. If memory served, Boyce had a wife named Lilly and the two birthed a son named Gregor who was sick in the head. No healer could make the kid right again so Boyce turned to the heavens for answers and ended up naming a star. Armed with this new energy he thought to be healing power, he set to heal his son. Before it was over he'd killed both his wife and his son.

One thing Leo couldn't remember is why in the hell Boyce was in the dungeon in the first place. He remembered having asked him on more than one occasion but didn't get a straight answer. Leo wondered now more than ever.

Boyce stammered to find a good starting point for the story and let out a reluctant sigh. "I became starborn somewhat by accident. Afterwards, not knowing what power I truly possessed, I hurt the only two people I held dear in this world. Kano and the others sensed me shortly thereafter and taught me a little about the

Mozzaroth. But Abaddon had also sensed me and made his own attempts to garner my allegiance. In the end I went my own way.

"For many years I wandered the earth looking for answers. After a time, I suspected the only place to get any of the answers to the questions I sought were in the book that was lost to the world. This book." Boyce regarded the Book of Baraqiel on the table before him. "But to my dismay, even it held no answers. Nothing but blank pages. If not for the place in which I found it, I would have discarded the book long ago. Luckily I held onto it, but continued to wonder why for many years.

"I began to suspect the book was locked. If only I could find the key I'd be able to unlock its secrets. At the time, I was well aware of Nicolai who had embedded himself within the Church. I pondered long and hard why that was. And piece by piece I put it together. The Guardian Church. Why else would such a denomination dub themselves guardians after all? And soon thereafter I realized just what the Church was guarding. The Holy Relics. The Golden Shields of Solomon. The Ring of Solomon. The Book of Baraqiel. Even the Arc of the Covenant."

Leo turned to his brother to see if it were true, but Jewel looked just as surprised as the rest of them.

"My suspicions were confirmed the more I watched their dealings. Nicolai and Abaddon are the only living starborn to have laid their eyes upon the book. They must have known all along that the book was encrypted and that they needed a Bright Eye to find and unlock it again. Then year after year I watched as Nicolai attended the Guardian Sword tournaments with a keen eye on the competitors. But why? Why would he have any interest at all in the winner of such a tournament?

"It didn't make any sense until I started hearing stories of Leo's heroism on the battlefield. About how he cut through the Gorronian Army with his Guardian Sword not once, but twice. My suspicions were confirmed when I heard that he wielded a fiery, runed hatchet, crafted at the hands of Chief Ansuke. Then I realized the sword tournament was not only a test of will but something more. Each of the Guardian Swords bear the Drago Smith's mark. But it isn't just a maker's mark. It's a rune. They were fishing for Bright Eyes to see if any of the winners could activate their rune.

"As Leo's red reputation grew, I began to suspect he was protected, or even strengthened by the runes on his weapons. The runes would have no effect on any but a Bright Eye. When he returned from exile, I planted myself in the dungeon with the book to find out. After a time I befriended him and one night while he slept I brushed the book against the heel of his boot and the book came alive in my hands."

"You did what?" Leo scoffed.

"I meant you no harm, Leo. But after the book was unlocked I had to get it out of there so I helped you escape. As soon as I left your presence the rune began to reactivate. I followed you and the Widow Makers through the night, reading what I could, but it was too dangerous. Opened, the book cast a light of its own and attracted too much attention. There were Kiman soldiers everywhere and I had to get the book to safety before it was discovered."

"It can't be?" Kano was out of his seat again. "Nicolai would not have kept such things from me."

"Like I said," Boyce added, "the book as Nicolai remembers it may not have been rune-locked. Perhaps whoever the runesman was who locked it, did so, so that the book wouldn't fall into the wrong hands. Perhaps that is how the book was lost to begin with."

"Prove it!" Kano ordered. "Give him the book."

"Very well." Boyce carefully slid the book across the table in front of Leo. "All you need do is touch it."

"Hold on a minute. What exactly is a Bright Eye?" Juan asked.

"You'll see," Boyce motioned Leo towards the book.

Leo had never wanted to get further from any book in his life. However, it wouldn't do for the Bloody Rose to be chased from his own throne room by a creped old book of empty pages. Still he feigned annoyance by face-palming with one hand to shield his eyes. As his other hand touched the book it began to shift in his hand. So much so that Leo retracted his hand so fast that he nearly backhanded Jewel in the face.

"Holy shit. I think it bit me," Leo rasped, catching his breath and cupping his hand.

"Hmm. There was quite a bend to your wrist there," Natalie mused. "And was that a squeal I heard?"

"Like the book was about to rape him," Bruce added. "Beat all I ever saw."

"You two can go feck yourselves," Leo countered. "The damn thing moved, I swear it."

"Again," Kano ordered, drawing nearer with his own chair. He slid it next to Leo and climbed up to stand in it. "Go on now. And try to keep it together this time."

Sitting there being prodded along like cattle to do something he didn't want to do, Leo wished he had the comforting weight of his shield on his arm. He'd never live it down though if he crossed the room to retrieve it. As he reached out again, his hand began to tremble so he thrust it forward onto the book to save face. Again the book began shifting beneath his hand but he didn't see or feel any teeth. And there at the center of the cover a rune began to appear. The others diverted their eyes from the blinding light, and Bruce swore an oath cursing everything magical for threatening to blind his only remaining eye.

Leo on the other hand found he couldn't look away. The rune began to wilt like a flower scorched by the sun until only a pile of ash remained in its place. Leo wiped the soot-laden remains from the cover and gasped at the letters that were revealed: *Baraqiel.*

***

The Book of Baraqiel began transforming from a book of nothing to a book of everything. It grew in size before Leo's very eyes and its etchings were of a sort that he'd never seen before. He could marvel at the cover no longer and before he knew it his hands were unfastening the buckles.

"No!" cried Boyce snatching the book from him. He drew it into his chest and wrapped his arms tightly around it.

Leo stirred from the trancelike state and a weariness washed over him. His eyes itched and ached. When they closed his head sagged back into the chair with a thud.

"Leo!" A pair of strong hands grabbed him and threatened to shake what little life remained. Another set of hands lifted him by the legs as they set him down on the floor.

A sharp pain stung his cheek and Leo winced. When he opened his eyes Juan leaned over with a backhand loaded and ready to slap him again. A hell of a healer was Juan.

"He'll be fine," Boyce determined, still clutching the book.

"Let me have a look at that." Kano eyed the book hungrily.

Boyce tucked it away into his satchel. "No. Whatever's written in this book was not meant for us to see. Otherwise it wouldn't have been rune-locked and hidden away. Whoever put it to the rune must have gone through a lot of trouble to do so. I don't know much about runes, but what little I do know is that they fade with time." Boyce eyed Leo on the floor. "And this one had plenty of strength left in it."

"Well what are we going to do with it then?" Kano asked.

"We're going to follow through with the plan." Boyce's face turned grim with thought. "If Leo can buy us enough time, we'll free the other Zodans and wipe out Abaddon and his army. If they go straight to cutting off Leo's head then he can buy some time and use the book as leverage. Abaddon won't be able to resist getting his hands on it."

"Do what?" Kano asked. "You mean to give Leo the book and take it right to Abaddon?"

Boyce regarded Leo on the floor. "Abaddon will know nothing of the book unless our Veronian king here deems it necessary to reveal it. Like I mentioned before, the book is a backup plan. We'll just have to work fast and hope Leo's arrival can buy us enough time."

Kano nodded in thought. "I take it back," he said. "You're no fool at all."

CHAPTER

8

"We're ready when you are, my king." Juan clanked to a stop at the base of the throne. His new tunic, darker than night, offset by the kingsguard sigil dyed into the chest. A crown atop a golden shield.

Leo sat motionless, one hand gripping the arm of his throne, the other cupping his forehead lost in thought. Juan cleared his throat and tried again.

"It's been nearly two full days since Wade set off. The people are anxious and starting to become unruly, Leo. If we are going to do this we must go now."

The people of Tamore didn't take kindly to hearing

their newly appointed king was about to swear fealty to the Kiman Empire. For their plan to work, they had to play the part down to bending knee and news spread fast around town. Many of the townsfolk had begun to openly voice their discord, cursing Leo as the Coward King. So hate- and malice-filled had their hostile looks become that Leo chose not to face them anymore. Rather he'd locked himself in his throne room since he'd sent Wade to announce his compliance to Abaddon's summons.

When he looked up, Juan's eyes widened and stretched tight with concern. "Damn Leo, you look like the walking dead. You haven't slept a wink have you?" Silence. Juan shook his head and let out a heavy sigh. "C'mon Leo, we'll get you something to eat before we hit the road. The rest of the kingsguard is waiting at the stable, and the starborn have staged a few miles out of town. We better get going soon. The Guardians are having fits trying to keep the peace."

Leo couldn't blame them for their hate and discontent. Most of them had shed red to keep their hopes of rebuilding Veronia alive and in one fell swoop, Leo had shattered those dreams, on bending knee no less. The thought turned his stomach and had kept him up at night. No amount of food or wine would console him. If only he could tell them his plan.

It wasn't only his kingdom that had been keeping him up the past two nights. The more time he had to sit and ponder their plan, the more outlandish it seemed.

The fear of failure started chiseling away at his courage even though they hadn't set out yet, but that wasn't the only thing he feared. He was about to lead his closest companions into the belly of a lion's den, and not all of them would return. It was common warmatics really. Killers versus killers equals death on both sides. Victory and defeat care little about who has the highest or lowest casualty rates.

"Let's get on with it then." Leo slung his sword and shield across his back then slid the hatchet into his belt. The length of the room had never felt so great as they walked to the door. Juan pushed it open and sunlight flooded in.

As Leo feared, a mass of people had gathered outside. When they saw him their voices fell silent. Motionless they stood watching their king leave to bend his knee. Trion's Guardians were clad in armor. They hurried over, separating Juan and Leo from the crowd, and escorted them out of the town square.

Juan put one arm on Leo's shoulder and ushered him through the wall of Guardians. That's when the murmuring began, followed by several unpleasant gestures and more than a few verbal jabs at the Coward King. One of the Guardians was pushed back and he shouldered into Juan. "Get back!" Juan roared to the crowd. He placed a hand on the grip of his sword and the unruly spectators backed away.

Something thrown from behind bounced off his shield and Leo quickened his pace. "For fuck's sake.

We should have left at night."

By the time they made it out of the square, they were breathing heavily from the effort. Leo risked a glance back and was pleased to find they hadn't chased them out of the city. He slowed to a walk and straightened his crown. "Well, now that we've got that out of the way."

They made it to the stables and found the High Priest blessing Trion and the rest of the kingsguard. Jewel waved Leo and Juan forward and they fell in at the end of the line.

"Be strong and of good courage, my dear Natalie." Jewel mimed a cross with his hands then dabbed his fingers into a small bowl of oil that Bishop Malachi held at his side. He placed his palm on her forehead then moved down the line to anoint Bruce, Mandy, and Juan. Leo felt his turn coming and wondered if there were any other kings before him—anointed next to a horse stall? The smell of shit wafted through the air. The longer they stood the more Leo feared the scent would cling to his tunic and follow him all the way to Chaucer.

"And you, King Leo." Jewel grabbed the bowl from Malachi and poured the rest of it over Leo's head. Leo's eyes went wide but he resisted the urge to wipe the oil from his brow. "Be strong and of good courage, my beloved brother. You've always been rough around the edges, but your heart is true."

Leo blinked through the oil and noticed Jewel's

eyes glistening. The High Priest turned his head to hide the tears. *Lay all your burdens upon my shoulders, brother. I'll carry them with me and bury them in the shallow graves of our enemies.*

"Trion here will show you the way." Jewel nudged the Guardian captain forward. He will not forsake you. Now then. I must be going. My faith is strong but the flesh is weak and I'm writhe in worry for your safety. I'll fill the heavens with songs and prayer for safe passage and return."

Even though Leo had the bravest companions one could hope for at his side, there was a sense of brotherly deprivation that washed over him when Jewel turned to walk away. Leo buried the sharp feeling next to all the rest but the graveyard was filling up. He mounted his horse and led them out of the city.

A crowd had lined up on either side of the road to watch them pass. In solemn silence they watched their king leave to bend his knee. The widow, Abigail Vorhees, stood at the forefront and Leo met her curious gaze. He spared her no smile. Instead he nodded once and held her stare.

She was no dunce. Even in the distance Leo could see her eyes well up with something that looked an awful lot like hope. She straightened to her full height, nodded dutifully, and turned her back to them.

As soon as she got away from the crowd, her eyes began to water once again. "The Coward King." She placed a shaky hand over her mouth to hide her smile and shook with muffled laughter.

***

It was nearing midday and the sun was doing its worst to melt them in their saddles. Leo shifted uncomfortably atop his mount and cursed his armor for trapping the heat. Bruce rode in front carrying the Veronian standard in one hand, reins in the other. His eye watchful as ever. "There"—he pointed with the standard—"under the willow."

Leo squinted left and found the starborn sitting with their backs against a willow tree. Its weeping branches sprawled out and over the riverbank. Page was the first one up to greet them.

She wore a threadbare, road-stained cloak, similar to the ones Boyce and Kano had donned. "We were starting to worry Tamore had turned on you guys." Shielding the sun, she peered under her hand at Leo. "You look tired already, brother. And what's that shit matted all over your hair?"

"That would be the High Priest's good-luck charm I guess." Leo dismounted and wrapped his sister in a side-hug. He disentangled himself and strode towards the river to wash the oil from his hair. The water was cool in his hands; he had to resist the urge to quench his thirst. He'd been weaker before and suffered the shits for days as consequence.

He felt a presence behind him. Smaller than most.

"Did you get it?" Leo asked.

Kano knelt down beside him with his back to the others and placed a leather pouch on the riverbank. He traced the scar on his cheek. "I did but I don't like this at all."

Leo swept up the pouch and gave the contents a gentle squeeze. Satisfied, he slipped the pouch into his pocket. "Yeah well there aren't many people who like much of anything I do." He craned to his right and found Kano staring off into the river. "Would you not do the same thing?"

Kano stood and extended a hand to help Leo up. "I was pessimistic at first. Rarely does anyone live up to their praise. You on the other hand are everything your brother said you would be." He turned and walked back to the others.

"What now?" Page asked.

"You sure you have enough dragonglass to sneak into the vault undetected?" Leo asked.

"More than enough." Boyce held up his hand and Leo saw the silver bangle set with dragonglass on his wrist. Page held up the back of her hand, fingers splayed wide, and smiled over a similar-looking bangle.

"Okay then," Leo said. "We'll ride together till Indigo. Then Trion will lead you three to the vault, and the kingsguard will accompany me to Chaucer."

"Got it." Page scanned left and right then found Kano already riding slowly ahead. "Someone appears to be in a hurry."

"I would be too." Leo mounted his horse. "Off we go."

***

On the eve of their second day on the road, the outskirts of Indigo loomed ahead in the twilight. Bruce led the pack carrying the standard, Mandy keeping pace at his side. Page and Natalie flanked Juan and Leo. Boyce and Kano brought up the rear, the shorter of which seemed to be the only one amused by Juan's terrible rendition of "Greensleeves". They were met on the road by two very inquisitive Kiman soldiers who were more than happy to accommodate the group and even offered them a security detail the rest of the way to Chaucer. Leo respectfully declined their offer to be put up for the night and requested to be left alone for the evening so they could rest for the last leg of their journey in the morning. All the same, the Reds stretched out their nets and put a loose-banded security detail around Leo's camp for the night.

They left the roadway and set off into the woods to make their fire and lay out their bedrolls. It didn't take long before they were staring stoically silent at each other over burning embers. Leo watched Bruce tie the cookpot over the coals, tossing venison, rice, and red peppers in to complete the stir-fry.

"Forgive me Bruce but I'm not the least bit hungry." Juan sat elbows over his knees regarding the tree line.

Bruce pushed his eyepatch onto his forehead and knuckled his rotten eye. "Won't hurt my feelers any. Might as well get it all cooked tonight if we're splitting up tomorrow though."

"And just how are we going to split up tomorrow?" Natalie regarded the Kiman fires in the distance surrounding their camp like the burning beacons of a goaler line.

Leo rummaged through the contents of his pack and pulled out a bottle, long as his forearm and wide as his fist. He pierced the cork with a dagger and filled Redbeard's old chalice. Their eyes squinted at him over the fire as they watched him drain it in one pull then fill his cup once more, carefully slipping the contents of the vial into the bottle.

He passed the bottle to Juan and encouraged him to do the same. "Let us speak no more of tomorrow." Leo met Kano's stare and then Boyce's and the two starborn seemed to approve very little.

"Tomorrow our fates will be decided," Leo said. He pointed at his kingsguard. "We will go one way"— then he regarded his sister and the other two starborn— "and you three another. I don't know about the rest of you, but I've had enough of this red dance and I eagerly await an outcome one way or another." He took a hearty pull from his chalice and the Netche brew heated him up from mouth to stomach. "So tell me, Bruce. After this is over, what is it you plan to do? When we kill off all the Kimans and I kick your sorry asses out of my kingsguard, where might you go and what will you do to find peace?"

Bruce took his pull straight from the bottle, lips smacking with approval. "When this is all over, you say?" Leo nodded. "I reckon I'd like to spend some time at Mount Drago. Maybe even build my own forge one day."

Leo held up his cup. "Well then, my friend. Let your forge smolder hotter than the rest and your metals find no blemishes." He turned to Mandy. "And what about you, Mandy?"

"I, um…I haven't given it much thought really."

"Nonsense," Leo countered. "Unless you want to end up Bruce's apprentice you better start thinking of something. We can't soldier on forever." Leo paused in consideration. "Look around you, Mandy. We are your family now. You're stuck with us for better or worse. So what will it be?"

"Well, I know this sounds silly." Mandy lowered her gaze to hide from the jests that didn't come. "I want to be a troubadour." More than a few heads turned at that. "My father taught me how to play the lute when I was a child. He used to play at night; my mother and I would sing along."

Bruce leaned forward. "You mean to tell me, we rode for two days listening to Juan defile our ears with his wounded song and you could have been our salvation?"

Mandy chucked as did the rest. "I actually thought Juan was pretty good. His pitch is a little flat, but that's not uncommon for a man his size."

Juan put a hand to his heart as if he were mortally wounded. "Hey now. My song is just ahead of its time is all."

"C'mon now, Juan. Your song sounds like you've been riding hard with your mouth open, squawking like a bird got trapped in your throat," Leo chided. He raised his cup in salute. "To Mandy, the traveling troubadour."

He turned to his left where Natalie sat by his side. "And what about you, Natalie? Think you could find any peace as our queen?"

The brew had made several passes now. Quickened by Boyce who kept blocking Page from the bottle. Apparently he and Kano had no thirst for alcohol either.

Natalie took another pull and boldly reached out to grab a handful of Leo's manhood. "That was the worst proposal I've ever heard." Leo leaned away shocked as the others knocking her hand away with his knee. She smiled devilishly. "But I suppose you and I could find peace between our sheets."

Leo thanked the night for concealing his blush. Had it not been for his sister sitting across the fire, he might have taken Natalie then and there. "Well then…" he stammered.

She advanced again, this time straddling overtop him. Her breath strong from the drink. Leo felt his prick rising up against her inner thigh. "I, erm…" She grabbed his hands, pinned them on her hips, then grinded across his stiffened manhood.

She chuckled once more at his expense before sliding off him. He was left pitching a tent and the firelight betrayed him. "For god's sake," Page said, shielding her eyes from the sight. "Don't mind should the two of you feel the need."

"Nor me," Bruce added with a rueful smile.

"That makes three of us," Juan chimed in.

"Make it four," Mandy added spreading her fingers.

Leo lurched forward to gather himself and hide his short sword. "Fuck you, and you, you and you," he said pointing to Juan, Bruce, Mandy, and Page. He didn't have the courage to face Natalie who, pleased with her work, nestled closer to his side.

"Now let's hear from Juan." Natalie took to her queendom without skipping a beat, mocking an heir of authority. "What would our king's most loyal shoulderman like to do when this is over?"

Juan didn't miss his part in the charade but his speech slurred ever so slightly. "My service to Veronia knows no bounds, my queen." He stifled a yawn and shook off a sudden weariness. "I shall remain at King Leo's side until we shoulder through the last door."

They laughed all around the fire but Leo's heart hardened when he found his sister deep in thought. She was starborn now. Immortal, and powerful beyond belief. That changed many things. He considered asking her next but Page had the look of someone struggling to find an answer.

Instead he turned to Trion. The ginger had stayed true to his Guardian oath and hadn't drunk a drop. "And you, Trion? What would my brother's hand-selected Guardian captain want when this is over?"

Trion was saved from answering when Bruce could sit up no longer. He swayed backward, asleep before he hit the ground.

"Never could hold his liquor," Natalie slurred. Bruce may have fallen the loudest, but Mandy had slipped quietly unconscious first. Natalie leaned into Leo clasping his hand in hers. Her head pressed into his shoulder. He ran his free hand through her hair.

"Sleep, my queen," he whispered into her ear. He kissed her gently on the forehead and guided her back onto the bedroll. Leo took her left hand and slipped a ring onto her finger. Her eyes wild with accusation, twinkling with rage and fear.

"Pa...poison," she declared, heavy eyes pressing closed.

There was a rustling nearby as Trion crossed the fire. Page was close behind. Boyce and Kano sat still, patiently waiting for Leo's plan to play out for better or worse.

"No, my love. Long Wink." The Valerian root and melatonin concoction had set its hooks and carried her into the dream world. Leo didn't trust any local alchemists with the lives of his friends so he'd sent

Kano to the Norse Lands across the Iron Sea in search of a seer who knew his business. Leo lifted Natalie's hand then kissed her ring. "When you wake up my love, this will all be over."

"You vile bastard." Leo felt a tug at his sleeve. It was Juan who lie on his side fighting a losing battle against the sleeping draught. "You did this to us?" There was a glint of betrayal in Juan's eyes that cut into Leo's core. Page leaned over Juan from the other side, her hand on his head to settle him down.

Leo hung his head. "I'm sorry brother. Your battle ends here with the others."

"You did this?" Page accused. "You poisoned them?"

Leo didn't have the courage to face her accusation. Luckily Boyce and Kano saved him from confessing his betrayal. When they pulled her away, her eyes lit up the night and part of him wished she'd strike him down then and there.

Juan writhed against the Long Wink's venom. Panic took hold of him. "Leo, please. You can't do this alone." Juan's surefire grip had Leo by the arm once more, squeezing so tight Leo felt the urge to wrench his arm free. He embraced the pain like a drug numbing his guilty conscious. "We are shouldermen are we not?" Juan continued. "Yet you poison me and cast us aside?"

Just words and yet Leo faltered under the weight of them. Tears welled in his eyes, ran down his cheek and onto his shoulderman. A puddle of torment and misery.

Leo wiped the stain from Juan's brow. Their hands met and Leo felt Juan's strength fading. In that moment Leo wanted more than anything to express his appreciation for a lifetime of companionship but his breath caught in his throat and the words were drowning in his guilt.

"Thanks for always being there," he said at last. Juan squeezed his hand once more and sleep wrapped him.

***

Leo slung his weapons and readied himself to leave. Page stooped over the unconscious forms of Juan, Natalie, Bruce, and Mandy who had been lined up side by side. The sun started to rise for its watch and Leo left dewy footprints as he paced around the camp. "I have to go. Now."

"I don't like this. Not one bit." Page didn't take her eyes off their sleeping companions.

"Don't worry about them, they'll be fine." Leo patted his pockets to make sure he still had the summons. His hands were sweaty and his heart raced. "Kano will stay with them until they wake up. Shouldn't be more than eight hours or so. By then I'll be halfway to Chaucer and you guys should be nearing the vault. Wait till Kano 'ports and then attack after nightfall."

"You might want to take this with you." Boyce drew the Book of Baraqiel from his satchel and held it out.

"No. Keep it. It won't do me any good if they strip it from me before I get to Abaddon. If I need it, I'll tell them it's hidden away in Chamood. I can describe it well enough to hold Abaddon's attention."

"Home of the tribal rejects. A good enough spot to hide anything," Kano added. "If you won't take the book then take this." He tossed something and Leo snatched it from the air.

Leo regarded the black leather sheath and wrapped his palm around the jawbone handle. The beast's sharp jagged teeth nearly broke the skin and when he drew the blade to test its edge, he found it to be a crudely crafted dragonglass blade.

"Keep it in your boot," Kano directed. He sat down to begin his watch. "It will likely only cut or stab once before it breaks so use it wisely."

Leo nodded in turn and slid the dagger into the shaft of his right boot. "Okay then. I'm ready as I'll ever be."

Page turned her back to hide her tears. Leo stepped behind her and she spun around into his arms, burying her head into his chest. He wrapped her tight in his arms. "Take care of yourself, sister. I'll see you soon."

She pulled away at length then turned her back once again.

Leo mounted his and circled it around to regard Kano and Boyce once more. "Attack at midnight." They nodded in unison. Leo dug his heels in and his horse sprinted off towards the road.

CHAPTER

9

"Halt, who goes there?" The sentry stammered up from his campfire spilling a cup of hot coffee into his lap. "Shit!" he cursed, wiping the boiling mess from his crotch. The rest of his companions startled to their feet. Five in all.

Leo slid from his mount to greet them. "When I left Tamore I was King of Veronia. Titles have a way of diminishing like a blade rusted by the sea, the further you get from your homeland." They stared at him for a time, drinking him in. "I know, I know. You thought I'd be taller right?" He smiled. "Don't worry, I'm harmless."

"Where's the rest of your entourage?" asked a thin fellow with an ugly face and a stupid mustache. His keen eye seemed to make up for it.

Leo glanced over his shoulder at the empty road behind him. "If King Abaddon wanted my entourage to come along he should have mentioned it in his summons." He held out the scroll and Coffee Pants snatched it up to give it a read. "I suppose you boys are capable enough to get me where I need to go. I trust you know the way."

Coffee Pants confirmed the legitimacy of the scroll with a nod, but Mustache wasn't done with his questions. "We forwarded that summons along more than two weeks ago. What's been the holdup?"

Leo grew tired of the questions already and set his jaw. "I've never been much good at bending my knees. Had to stretch them out first. You guys look limber enough to the task though. Well-practiced I'd imagine, and pretty mouths to boot." He paused long enough to let Coffee Pants take offense. "Now are you going to take me to your king or shall I tell him it was the lot of you who held me up?"

Mustache bared his clenched teeth but wasn't foolish enough to go further. "Your weapons," he ordered.

"I think I'll hold onto them for now. I'm here to pledge my sword to King Abaddon, not his road guards." Leo turned and mounted. "Now then, shall we be off?"

***

By the time they crossed the Indigo Bridge, Cobalt the stupid mustache-wearing road sentry had worked fast. He sent Coffee Pants off to Indigo with a message for the fief lord that they were escorting one king to see the other. He'd also strengthened his numbers fourfold.

Although the Kimans outnumbered Leo twenty to one, they thought better of turning their backs to the Bloody Rose. Leo rode ahead, biting his tongue as they snickered and sneered at his back. All the same he made a point of remembering their faces and names. When this was all over, he planned to make eunuchs of them all with the dullest, rustiest blade he could find.

They came to a fork in the road just past the bridge and Leo took the north road towards Chaucer.

"Wrong way, dummy!" Cobalt called from behind.

Leo pulled up turning his horse around. "The north road leads to Chaucer, does it not?"

"That it does. But we're going to the vault."

His blood ran cold and he swallowed a lump in his throat. "The summons," he said producing the scroll once again, "summoned me to swear fealty to the king in Chaucer, did it not?"

Cobalt relished in Leo's surprise with a yellow-toothed grin. "It did. But we're going to the vault." The rest of the riders saddled up to Cobalt's side and looked on with mock amusement. "Your friend, what was his name...?"

"Wade. Wade Holloway," said another.

"Ah yes." Cobalt snapped a finger in the air. "Wade, that's it. Your friend Wade was just as surprised. His head decorates the vault's drawbridge now. King Abaddon didn't take too kindly to his summons being ignored for more than two weeks."

Leo swayed in the saddle like an invisible hand punched him in the stomach. A tremor of fury rattled his bones; he squeezed the reins with a white-knuckled grip. Twenty to one were perhaps the best odds he'd see from here on out and he reckoned he might as well wet his sword now or forever hold his peace.

"Something wrong, Leo?" Despite having the numbers, Cobalt's mocking wolf grin waned ever so slightly under the scrutiny of the Bloody Rose's furious gaze.

Leo held his tongue but went to work killing each of them in his head. He imagined staking each of their bodies upon one another with the lengths of their own swords. One by one their smiles faded and Leo waited till Cobalt's eyes turned wide. They tend to do that just before fight or flight. "The vault it is. I'll lead the way."

***

Page and Boyce waited about two hours after Leo had

left before setting out down King's Road. Page road ahead, eyes peeled to the tracks left by her brother's escort. The further they went, the more trodden the dirt road in front of them became which made Page a nervous wreck for her brother's safety. On more than one occasion she stopped to push suspect mounds of dirt around with the toe of her boot. She spurred forward only when Boyce inspected the impressions for himself to reassure her there was no blood on the ground.

"Slow down," Boyce said for what had to be the twentieth time. "You keep pushing the pace and we'll draw the road guards. There will be no shortage of them at the bridge up ahead and no one moves this fast unless they're running to or from something."

A few winding turns later and Boyce proved right yet again. The Indigo Bridge had received a facelift since the last time Page had seen it. The old, wooden-railed, creaky-beamed affair must have been torn apart plank by plank and sent down the river to make way for the new stone-built modern marvel. Three load-bearing arches ran lengthwise and plunged into the depths of the river bottom. A watchtower stood at each end with Kiman banners draped over the sides. For all of its grandeur, Page could only make out a handful of armor-clad, Kiman road guards in each of the towers. One of them sauntered down the steps of the west tower to challenge them.

Page brushed a few unruly strands of hair behind

her ear, and let the hood of her cloak drown out the rest. "Keep quiet. Let me do the talking," Boyce said, urging his horse forward. He pushed his own hood back with gloved hands.

The sentry rested one hand on the pommel of his sword then shielded his eyes from the sun with the other. "Who are ye? What's your business? And where you'ins headed, old timer?"

"Boyce, at your service," he answered, bowing low as one could in the saddle. "This here's me granddaughter Serah. Heard some commotion in town. Me cousin Yusolf says that Rosewood's just passed through on his way to bend his bastard knees and beg for the king's mercy in Chaucer. It ain't every day you get to see a sight like that and we've a mind to watch. If it pleases you that is."

The sentry seemed bored with Boyce soon as he opened his mouth. The guard's wandering gaze turned to Page. He wetted his lips and dressed her down with his lust. "If you mean to see Rosewood kneel you won't see it in Chaucer." He looked as if he were about to say more but his blood was flowing away from his brain. "You know, guarding a bridge ain't too hard, but it can be sharp work when you don't know who or what you're dealing with. Draw back your hood, Page is it? Let's have a look at you."

Two more sentries leaned over the tower wall to have a look for themselves. Page paused and considered cutting off their eyelids. After a time she drew back her hood and fixed them with an innocent smile.

The road guard closed the distance and put a hand out to stroke her horse's mane. "That's better. Tell you what." He continued sliding his hand down the horses neck till it brushed up and lingered against Page's knee. "If the Bloody Rose's fate is anything like his envoy's, he won't have a chance to do much kneeling before they lop off his head and put it skull to skull with all the rest." He turned to Boyce. "A lady fair as Page here shouldn't have to bear witness to such a terrible thing. It'd be my honor to watch over your granddaughter until you return."

Boyce ignored the vile bastard's bad intentions as best he could. "What's that you said about heading in the wrong direction?"

Realization started to wash over Page, leaving her hair standing on end. The crimson she saw on the trail must have been blood after all. And now she knew it was Wade's. She drew the dagger she'd concealed in her cloak and drove the pommel into the sentry's temple. She'd have questions for him in a minute but for now he sank to the ground like a sack of potatoes. Boyce reached out to grab hold of her and swiped at the air. She galloped ahead meeting the other sentries as they filed down the masonry.

"Stop!" she heard Boyce call at her back. Instead of stopping, she buried her blade in the next sentry's chest.

A sword swiped at her, but she danced easily around its bearer, grabbed hold of the man's tunic from behind, and used his forward momentum to upend him over the side of the bridge. He wailed, splashed, and sank like a rock covered in chainmail.

A surge of blue flame flashed in her peripheral followed by bodies hitting the floor at her feet. She drew her short sword, courtesy of Jonas himself. The sword, more runes than blade, swiped through the air pulling her forward at the arm. By the time the red work was finished, Page stood at the far end of the bridge. She turned like a feral cat at the clamping of hooves and found Boyce still sitting atop his horse.

"That was imprudent." He brushed the remains of his gloves from his hands. The sentry who'd first challenged them was bound at the ankles by a length of rope and dragged forward by Boyce's mount.

For Page, the world kept spinning and her head throbbed with the effort of making it stop. "They killed Wade," she said meekly. Her sword clattered to the stone. She rubbed her eyes with heels of her hands.

"Bless his bones but we'll all be dead if you keep running 'round like your berserker brother." He flung the last piece of charred leather to the ground. He sized her up with a disapproving shake of the head. "You could have killed the lot of these idiots with a few bursts of starfire."

Boyce slid carefully from his mount, wrapped his hand around the sentry's jaw, and shook him awake. When the road guard came to, he stared wide-eyed and lost to the world. He gained his bearings quick enough and the pleading for his life began shortly thereafter.

"Please, please don't kill me."

"Shut up." Boyce slapped him with the back of his hand. His fingers left a red whelp. "Where's Leo?"

"They took him to the vault. Please...."

Another slap and blood started to leak from the sentry's nose. "Is Abaddon at the vault?"

"Yes. Yes sir. He's there with the giants. Listen, I'm sorry—"

The next one was more fist than a slap and the sentry was starting to fade from the blow. Boyce shook him awake once more. "There any prisoners at the vault? Four other starborn by any chance?"

"I...I think so. The giants carried them in cages. Had blankets over top them so we couldn't see who it was. Please, don't kill me."

Boyce put his hand on the sentry's forehead. An unsettling sense of déjà-vu gave him pause. The man clawed to get away. Boyce pressed his head down and starfire cut the man's final cry.

***

Leo had heard plenty of stories about the vault, yet he'd never been there. Now that it loomed in the distance, growing more massive all the time, it started to dawn on him that he might have underestimated its defenses. Even the landscape seemed to rise up the closer they got and his horse huffed and puffed for a rest.

They passed through a clearing and into the forest that surrounded its outer walls. He'd never been in a forest so dense. After an hour's worth of ducking branches and a near fall from the saddle, Leo was spit out into another clearing adjoined by rows upon rows of what had to be strategically planted trees which would no doubt divide attacking forces. They were following the trail, zigzagging their way through when Leo saw his first giant.

Lost in the grandeur of the massive stone walls and the Keep that rose up touching the sky, Leo had first mistaken the monster for a tree. Truth be told, Leo's horse had sensed him first and liked to have thrown him from the saddle when he did. The giant's rumbling growl caught Leo's attention first. Then the size of his man-eating teeth as he snarled. Leo shuttered beneath his armor and turned away. Then the earth shook behind him where the giant laughed at Leo's back. Cobalt and the rest of the escort chuckled along too even though the giant showed little regard for any of them.

Leo swore an oath and nudged his anxious horse along. Cobalt called a halt when they'd made it to the murky watered moat Leo had heard so much about. The stories paled in comparison to what sprawled out before him. The moat surrounded the massive stone walls at least fifty feet wide, and God only knew how deep. Chains creaked and pulleys pulled at the portcullis where a massive iron gate bearing the twelve-pointed star started to rise up into the heavens. A score of armor-clad, red-tunic-wearing Kiman soldiers spilled out to greet them. Cobalt led them over the stone bridge to and through the barbican.

Once inside, they passed over another bridge that rested atop another moat even wider than the first. The black water so placid that nothing looked capable of living in its depths. They approached another portcullis, men pulling at the chains within. Rotting skulls sat covered and aligned, spiked to the inner barbican where they caught the last of the sun's rays for the day. Leo didn't have the stomach to sift through them looking for Wade. Another party greeted them, and more soldiers spilled out of the inner wall, led by a nobleman whom Leo recognized instantly.

"Well met, King Leo. We were starting to think you weren't coming." Saul made a show of peering behind Leo. "Could Juan not make it? Tell me he didn't fall in Tamore. I was looking forward to seeing him again."

As much as Leo wanted to strangle the bastard, he fixed Harrington with his best fake smile. Just like Tamore, Leo suspected it was no coincidence they sent the slayer of Juan's parents to greet him at the gate. The Kimans wanted Leo unnerved. Wanted him to lash out so they could cut him down with cold justice. Not that they needed another excuse. He'd defied the Kiman Empire from the start and slayed their puppet king in battle. Why they hadn't taken his head off already, Leo couldn't say. Perhaps Abaddon took pleasure in toying with his prey. Each breath is full of more possibilities than the last and Leo meant to make Abaddon pay for it.

"I'm surprised your tongue hasn't gotten all your teeth knocked out," Leo replied. "Juan sends his best regards. If you longed so much to see him you should have looked for him on the battlefield. Juan's never too hard to miss. All the same, I carry with me his best regards." Leo held out his fist, then turned it over to reveal an empty palm. "Hmmm, must have lost it somewhere along the way here."

Saul reddened, his teeth clinched tight at the slight. His next words came out more like a hiss. Fitting for the snake he was. "Careful, Leo. King Abaddon is looking forward to judging you in person. That's the only reason you haven't been dismembered limb by limb yet."

The blackwater's alcohol scent tinged Leo's nose. He had a vision of drowning Saul in it nice and slow-like. He reeled his wandering mind in. "Have I been summoned all this way to bicker with King Abaddon's help?"

"Ha! Wrap yourself in what's left of your pride, Leo. A threadbare cloak at that." Saul snapped his fingers. "Take his weapons."

Chainmail shuffled behind him and the guards closed in with naked steel. Leo burned holes in Saul as they stripped off his shield, sword and hatchet. "His armor too," Saul ordered with a mocking smile.

They could have just loosened the straps but the bastards took their pleasure in pulling and tugging till the buckles broke and cutting where they wouldn't. Blood trickled from his left forearm where the gauntlet wouldn't give and a blade finished the task.

When they were done, Leo wiped at the blood and flicked it at Saul's feet. "Better now? Or are you going to check my cock for weapons with your mouth? I'll wait."

Comments like that don't generally go over well for the speaker when the recipient has the upper hand. "Shackle him," Saul barked.

The mere mention of bondage didn't suit Leo at all. Neither did the portly fecker who advanced with the manacles; reminded him too much of George the Goaler. He'd already broken one nose and left another a streaming mess before he realized he'd snapped and now had his hands wrapped around Saul's throat. His fingers clamped like a vice around all those vital arteries that send blood to the brain. Leo searched for suitable words that might haunt Saul in the afterlife but curses would have to do.

Leo felt an impact on the back of his head. A blunted mace or perhaps a runaway cart. It rocked him forward but he maintained his grip. Saul was turning shades of blue now and his hands were losing the strength to claw at Leo's face. A second blow came and Leo's world turned dark.

CHAPTER

10

Kano paced anxiously around the sleeping kingsguard. The draught should have worn off by now and he should have already caught up with Boyce, Page, and Trion.

A sparrow squealed as it swooped in the distance. A cold sweat beaded between Kano's shoulders and he pulled at the neck of his cloak for air. He shuffled over to Juan and nudged his boot. No response. He moved to Bruce, toed under his boot, lifted it into the air, and let it drop to the ground. Not even a stir.

"Shit," he fumed, continuing to pace. Kano brought a hand up and snapped his fingers. "Water!" he exclaimed. He hurried to their packs and rummaged through them looking for a water skin.

"That sonofabitch."

Kano froze with an upended pack in hand. He scanned the kingsguard then teleported to Natalie's feet. She propped herself up on trembling arms. "Oh thank God. I was starting to think you guys weren't going to wake up at all."

"Where is he?" Natalie seethed. "I'm going to cut his balls off for this."

Kano knelt down. "I'll be sure and tell him you'd like a word when I see him. Now that you've safely awoken I need to get going. I promised Leo I'd stick around until at least one of you could watch over the others." Kano peered to the road. "It's getting dark. Leo should have made it to Chaucer by now. Boyce and the others will think something must have happened to me or you guys if I dally any longer."

Natalie dragged herself over to Juan, cursing as she went. She propped an elbow onto his chest then awkwardly shook him by the face with what appeared to be a paralyzed hand. "Poison me? What nerve? I'm going to lace his meals with laxatives so strong that he'll be bound to the shitter the rest of his days. Wake up, Juan!"

Juan's eyes opened lazily and closed just as fast. Natalie clamped her finger and thumb down on his nose till he thrashed onto his side in a fit of coughing.

"Good morning, friend. Didn't mean to wake you." Natalie dragged herself over to Bruce and went straight to the nose clamp.

Juan's eyes went wide as he took in the scene. He scowled when he found Kano. "You." He pointed an accusing paw at the starborn. "You helped him poison us?" Juan dragged himself to both knees straining from the effort, reddening with rage. "You bastard."

"It wasn't my call." Kano splayed his fingers out innocently and put a hand to his chest. "Leo would have it no other way." Again Kano regarded the road where the fireflies started their shift. "Listen, I have to go. I stayed back to give you something." Kano fished a scroll from his cloak and set it down at his feet.

Juan's mouth gaped open. "No." He shook his head, eyes watering. When a man leaves a scroll behind, it's a will most likely.

"Leo says he hopes you all find peace." Kano stepped away from the scroll. His chest rose, drawing in a breath to steady his speech. "Said there's no peace for hands red as his and no rest for a bloody conscious. He hopes one day you'll understand."

Kano turned to go, eyes aglow, the air shifting around him. Before he left he heard Juan call out one last time.

***

"Wake up." A fisted blow to Leo's ribcage emphasized the command and left him taking in his surroundings breathless. Two guards heaved Leo forward; he narrowly managed to break his own fall with manacled hands. "Try anything and we'll yank you into the pit." The sentry regarded the flaming pit that surrounded them and held up the end of Leo's chain for good measure. The links tightened as the sentry stepped off the star-shaped platform that stood before the throne's elevated dais.

Leo pushed himself to his feet. Saul stood beside him mopping a bead of sweat from his brow and shifting his weight anxiously.

Four giants, or Anakim as Boyce and Kano had called them, twice the height of a man, guarded the two rounded staircases that wound their way up to the vacant throne. Behind it a second floor where twilight filtered through huge glass windows. Behind the throne a door took its time creaking open and Leo's hair stood on end.

A pudgy Light Priest shuffled into view totting a massive tomb in one hand, a torch in the other. He paused against the wall and regarded Leo with a few dissatisfied *tsks* of his tongue. "Let there be light." The Light Priest dipped the end of the torch into a trough and flames spread across the chamber. Fire ran down the staircase rails and along the walls of the first floor.

As Leo regarded the flaming aqueducts the scent of burning oil tinged his nose. The chemical smell faded as the flames took control. He'd smelled that pungent scent before. His reflection was cut short when another door opened. This one sounded like stone grating against stone as it slid to the side.

Darkness spread across the walls and Saul loosened his collar and straightened his back. Candleholders began to rattle and the four giants took a knee. Darkness filled the room again and Leo noticed for the first time it took on the shadow of a man. Not a man but a giant. The giant of giants.

There was a sound like wind chimes as the giant rounded the staircase coming into view. This giant of giants shrank the room, towering over thirty feet tall if he were a foot. His golden shendyt rustled to rest when he came to a stop at the foot of the two staircases. He ran a muscled hand through his golden-clasped beard. "Humph," he throated after a long pause, staring at Leo.

Leo felt a cold hand twisting a fistful of his intestines but dared not break his gaze.

"Anakim rise," the giant bellowed. The other giants reclaimed their posts at the foot of the stairs. "So you are the champion of men?"

The giant's speech was oppressive. It radiated through Leo's bones and made him weak in the knees. Leo looked to his left hoping the giant was talking to anyone else but him and found Saul kneeling with his head bent low. The urge to boot the bastard into the firepit took hold of him. As it did he felt the chain draw tight nearly pitching him off the side. Leo tugged back, snarling a threat to the goaler who lurked in the shadows.

He fixed his faltering defiance on the golden giant. "I'm nobody's champion."

One of the Anakim pointed his club at Leo. "Address King Delbec on your knees or I'll cripple you with my bare hands."

Leo paid the threat no never mind and held Delbec's glare. He'd come all this way to bend the knee, he might as well get used to it now. Besides, he rather liked his legs the way they were and he hadn't even met Abaddon yet. Leo spat into the fiery pit then knelt beside Saul.

The four Anakim growled in unison. The one who pointed his club nearly leapt over the pit to make good on his threat but Delbec caught hold of him by the arm.

"Be still!" A voice from the second floor. When Leo looked up, a red-cloaked figure sat on the throne. Beside him a black-cloaked Kotian. Leo didn't have to revert back to Kano's descriptions to identify Abaddon and Lyle at this point. Given the tension in the room, he couldn't imagine anyone else brazen enough to sit upon the hellish throne.

Again the four Anakim took to their knees. Delbec grimly followed suit looking pained from the effort.

"Well I see you've met King Delbec." Abaddon leaned forward in his chair. "Rise, King of Giants." Delbec rose to his feet, face still twisted into a snarl. "And now the rest of you, save King Leo there."

"Well fuck you too," Leo muttered under his breath.

"Silence fool. You'll get us both killed." Saul stopped short of cuffing him on the head.

"What was that?" Abaddon questioned with a knowing smile.

"Um. Thank you sire." Saul shifted anxiously. "I bring to you the self-proclaimed king of Veronia, Leo Rosewood."

"I've seen my fair share of ambitious youth turn to brittle old men but my eyes and ears haven't failed me yet, Saul." Abaddon squinted below. "Perhaps you can enlighten me as to why King Leo here looks like he's been dragged all the way from Tamore?"

"Erm." Saul regarded Leo's battered face and turned away from his murderous glare. "He didn't take too kindly to being disarmed, sire. He tried to kill one of the guards."

Lies. I tried to kill you, fool. Perhaps if I choked your dumb ass again it might jog your memory.

"Is this true?" Abaddon scoffed. "Have you come to pledge your allegiance or defy my rule?"

Leo felt Delbec's condescending grin on him. It was hard to see anything with one eye swollen shut but the golden bastard kind of stood out in the crowd.

"I came to bend the knee for all of Veronia. To pledge our allegiance to you and the Kiman Empire. I came ready to kneel not to be stripped like a peasant and herded around like cattle to the slaughter."

Abaddon rose from his throne and sauntered down the dais. His hand gliding atop the flaming rail as he went. "Do tell me, King Leo. What's the allegiance of a defeated king and his peasant people worth to me? Why shouldn't I put you and that whole stain of a village to the sword?"

"That might work for a while. Until it doesn't," Leo retorted.

"Ha!" Abaddon mused. He reached the bottom of the dais and the giants stepped aside to let him pass. As Abaddon drew near, firelight reflected off the Ring of Solomon on his hand. He stopped short of the firepit, only the flames separating the two of them now. Abaddon made a waiving motion. "That will be all, Saul."

Saul breathed a sigh of relief and hurried off to hug the walls with the rest of the Kiman guards.

"On your feet," Abaddon ordered.

Leo rose gingerly to his feet feeling the effects of too many scrapes with death as he did. As he met Abaddon's cold grey eyes for judgment, Leo felt oddly at peace.

"Tamore will be taxed for their resistance and none of them will be allowed to stray from the village. They will live out the remainder of their lives under a perimeter of Kiman kill-guards. Any breeding will be met by the sword, until Tamore is no more."

"Let no one say you aren't a gracious king," Leo spat through clenched teeth.

Abaddon wetted his lips. "Are you not curious what your fate will be, King Leo? Or is there too much pride in you to ask?"

Abaddon poked and prodded in all the right places. "As long as there's breath in me I will curse your name. Any living thing who stands between us will feel the sting of my sword or the strength of my hands until I'm painted red in your blood, less mine runs cold first."

Saul let out a gasp in the shadows that echoed through the hall. Behind Abaddon, the Anakim clenched their fists and snarled like a pack of hungry wolves.

Abaddon's eyes turned to fire and a cold chill swept the room. His hand rose like a beacon of light poised to deliver a killing blow.

To say things hadn't gone quite as planned was an understatement. Leo had one job. To cause a distraction until the others could be freed. In other words, drag out his own death as long as possible. He was vaguely aware that getting killed five minutes into the damn vault wasn't part of the plan, and would do little to improve their odds.

"Trial by sword," Leo blurted. He was pretty sure it was a real thing. He'd suffered through too many of the drunken campfire tales for it not to be. He was out of ideas regardless. It was either that or beg them to spare his life. Given the audience, they didn't look very merciful.

"Wait!" In the stone-walled hall, Delbec's voice

was deafening.

Abaddon swiveled his fury on the golden giant as if he were surprised he'd turned his back on him in the first place.

"Let me have him," Delbec demanded, meeting Abaddon's cold stare. "Champion versus champion. Like the days of old."

Abaddon paused in thought, cupping his furrowed brow, then swept towards the dais. "Very well then, Delbec. Trial by sword. Champion versus champion. Call it what you will just be quick about it."

"Not here. Tomorrow, in front of all who wish to see." Delbec raised a clenched fist. "I'll rip him limb from limb and drown the crowd in his blood. Such a brutal killing will quell any thoughts of another uprising for generations to come."

Abaddon paused halfway up the grand staircase and turned his head to the sky. "An unburied enemy is a threat. When you've lived as long as I have you care less about the means in which they pass. Just that they're dead. And the sooner that is the better." He shifted his watchful eyes from Leo to Delbec. "You have until noon tomorrow then I'll kill him myself. If you must make a spectacle of it do it outside our walls. I'll not jeopardize our security so you can play gladiator."

"Thank you my king." Delbec's grin threatened to break his face. It was short-lived though and right back to resting dick face.

"Lock him in a cell in the meantime." Abaddon continued assent, passing by his throne. "Your Anakim will stand guard. He's to have no contact with anyone else. If anything goes awry, you'll be held accountable." Abaddon swept out of sight. Lyle and the Light Priest in tow.

"Seize him," Delbec ordered.

The Anakim shuffled around the pit. One of them took the end of the chain in his fist and jerked it over his head. Leo pitched forward into the air. The flames licking at his boots until he crashed awkwardly on the other side. The giant spooled the chain 'round his fist, slung Leo over his back, and carried him away.

***

Kano shifted into the shadows on the east bank of Indigo Bridge. He'd 'ported back and forth a dozen or more times now on the outskirts of Chaucer and found no sign of Boyce, Page, or Trion. Their dragonglass bangles must have masked them along their way. As the night began to drag on, the gravity of having lost their trail began to tug at his stomach and worry wrinkled his brow.

A locust called into the night, its companions echoed the call. The bridge was eerily quiet. Too quiet. Kano shifted his gaze past the bend in the rippling Gorro to the bridge lit only by the moonlight.

He patted forward along the water's edge. A splash

froze him in place. The recoiling vegetation drew his eye and sent him on a silent tangent, cursing the frog and all its lineage.

The silence stretched on and Kano cursed again. What the hell was he doing there anyways? The trio obviously weren't there. From the sound and looks of it no one was. He set his jaw and scaled the bank. He was starborn after all.

"Hello there," Kano called. His voice carried on without a challenge. His hair stood on end as he trekked forward to the first body. Then a second, and a third.

"Shit," he breathed, scurrying over to the first corpse. A road guard with a melted mess of brain matter for a head. Kano scanned the scene and risked calling out their names. "Boyce! Page! Trion? Shit, shit, shit."

He interlaced his fingers and rested them atop his shaking head. Kano regarded the corpse in front of him once more. The cadaver's hand was outstretched pointing due east. Beside his hand an arrow painted in blood, also facing east.

"The vault!" he exclaimed snapping his fingers. He shifted and 'ported down the road. His first stop he found nothing but the night. His second stop he found a pile of twigs on the road. He ran to them. Another arrow, this time pointed off the trail. He shifted some branches out of his way and padded into the woods. He scanned the forest, his nose tinged with the reek of giants nearby.

A mound of rocks rested at the foot of a tree and Kano scurried towards it, turning stone over stone. A dragonglass bangle rested at the bottom and Kano clamped it around his wrist. Beside the displaced stones, another pile of twigs pointing through the bush. Kano wrapped his cloak tightly around him and carried on.

With his senses dulled, each sound of the forest tugged at his nerves. Crickets calling, a scampering hare. Despite his soft approach the forest floor crackled underfoot and Kano winced each time it did. He carried on masked only by the night. The canopy so thick the rays of the moon were blotted out.

Kano had never been a woodsman. Too many predators roamed in the night and cared little about whether he was human or starborn. A hungry animal will take on prey twice its size with no qualms about it. Even the docile ones will attack if you walk up and surprise them whether you meant to or not.

"And just how the hell are we going to sneak into that? There's soldiers everywhere," a feminine voice whispered nearby. Upon further inspection Kano observed three figures crouched beside one another peering at the impenetrable stronghold that sprawled out before them.

"Impossible from the main gate. Our only chance will be the supply gate on the east side." Trion motioned towards a cobble pathway that winded to the south and disappeared in an easterly direction between a slew of thatched-roofed roundhouses.

"Shh," an impatient Boyce muffled through clenched teeth. He held up a finger the way one does to improve their hearing.

Their familiar voices shifted a burdenous weight off Kano's shoulders. He inched to the nearest oak and put his back to the bark. It probably wouldn't be good for his health to catch them by surprise. Another scan and he found Boyce and Page lying prone beside one another, their hoods drawn back for a better view. Beside them Trion wore a red-belted tunic. He shifted his helm back to mop sweat from his forehead.

Kano regarded the forest floor for a twig or a rock of sufficient size to toss in their general direction. He knelt down and retrieved a twig equal to the task. He gauged the distance, aimed for their feet and drew it back...and then he saw it.

A giant prowling through the trees like a void in the night. It carried a shield in one hand, a club in the other, crouched like a cat ready to pounce.

Kano's heart skipped a beat at the sheer size of the thing. It stalked forward eyeing its prey. The giant lowered its center hiding behind his shield, club drawn up for the bludgeoning. Only a few strides away the giant pounced with a throaty growl. It leapt and landed at their feet.

Kano reared back to cast a fury of starfire at the giant's broad back. His hand motioned forward but nothing happened. "No," he breathed, regarding the bangle on his wrist. He clawed at it with heavy foreign fingers till it toppled to the ground. When he finally freed himself of it, it was too late. "Boyce!" he cried in desperation as the giant's club rained down.

There was a flash of light that sent Kano reeling backwards. He landed hard, rolling on the forest floor. When he clamored to a stop his shoulder tingled from the impact, numb with adrenaline coursing through his veins. In what felt like slow motion, Kano picked himself up with one hand.

"Your bangle," Boyce cried when he saw Kano. Boyce shifted his own back around his wrist. The giant sizzled torsolessly to the ground.

Kano scanned the ground frantically. Twig, rock, leaves, divot about shoulder-depth. And then he saw it, just a few strides away. He leapt for it like it had legs to scurry away. His good hand shot down to pick it up but a foul scent tinged his nose. Kano's head swiveled right towards the musk just in time to see another giant's club raining down towards him.

His first instinct was to run. His second was to brace for the blow. The giant's club rose and fell. Somewhere in between Kano had the good sense to 'port out of its path and it hammered into the ground. The Anakim circled 'round in disbelief. When it found Kano once again its face twisted in rage as it barreled forward.

Kano flooded his being with energy from the else and when he twinged his hand this time starfire lurched forward. It engulfed the giant just below the knees and toppled it end over end.

The giant landed awkwardly on its side. It took a quick inventory of the damage. Its legs were blown off below the knees and blood spurted out to the rhythm of his heartbeat. "Grrrr," it hissed in a shower of spittle. It clawed at the earth with one hand dragging itself forward. The giant swung its club in a wild arc and it crashed into the base of a tree. Wood splintered and bark showered the ground. Kano longed to back away but fear rooted him into the ground. The giant crawled forward, grunting in jagged breaths.

"Good God," Kano breathed, entranced by the thing that knew no fear. Knew no pain. That would stop at nothing to kill him now.

There was another flash. This time the moonlight reflected off Page's sword as she swept it through the giant's neck. The giant's head thudded on the ground and rolled a few times.

Page mouthed words at him, but Kano heard nothing. The second time sounded like "strangle" and Kano splayed his hands defensively. She stormed forward and Kano swallowed gravel. "Bangle." She shoved something into his chest. "Put on your fucking bangle."

"Right." Kano slid it onto his wrist and the world started to shift back into place around him. With it came an acute pain in his left shoulder like his bones were grating against one another. He sank to the ground, where his dead weight sent another flicker of pain up his tailbone.

"Water," Boyce ordered, no more than a clipped whisper. Trion clanked forward and handed the water skin to Kano.

Kano drank deeply, his head spun, mind racing to slow it down. "I. I...froze," he said at last.

Boyce put his palm on Kano's head. "Good God, you're burning up." He snatched the water skin and dumped it on Kano's head. Water sizzled and steamed.

"What's wrong with him?" Trion asked.

"He's burning out." Boyce drew back Kano's collar and dumped water down his back. "He probably spent much of his energy 'porting back and forth looking for us. I reckon he dumped the rest of his energy at that giant's legs."

"I'll be fine. Give me some air." Kano sucked in shallow breaths. "What the hell happened back there? The Indigo Bridge is strewn with dead."

"There's been a change of plans," Boyce answered. "Leo has been taken to the vault."

"Talk about two birds," Kano heaved.

"Not exactly. Instead of facing soldiers and a few Anakim, it looks like Abaddon, Lyle, Delbec, and all their minions are dug in waiting for us." Boyce regarded the outer wall where the night watch started to shift under torchlight. The outer gate creaked open and a dozen men filtered out. The iron gate creaked close behind them. "It appears our little skirmish hasn't gone unnoticed either."

"So why isn't the front door an option now?" Page asked. "If they're onto us we might as well take the most direct route."

"No. The front door is our last option," Boyce answered. "If that patrol is heading this way, we'll use it to sneak around to the back. After an hour or so of finding nothing, hopefully they'll call off the search."

***

Leo swayed against the giant's back as its heavy footfalls stomped their way down a dark corridor. It was eerily familiar to the journey into the dungeon in Bresdan. He'd been so ready to get out of the oubliette back then that the dungeon didn't bother him much. But now as the manacles dug into his wrists, his weight slung over the back of a giant like a pack, Leo didn't expect he'd have the same luck of breaking out.

They cinched a threadbare hood over his head. Darkness enveloped his vision aside from the other giant who stalked behind the first with a torch in one hand, a burlap bag slung over his shoulder in the other. It ducked low through the passageway as they clambered down a staircase, scowling at Leo's hood as they went.

He should have been keeping track of their descent, the number of left and right turns, but his arms were throbbing at the wrists and it was all he could do not to cry out. They stopped abruptly and the giant let Leo deadfall to the ground. He managed to land on his feet, but his legs were numb to the world and Leo sprawled out, breaking the rest of his fall with his chin.

A key slammed home, an iron gate creaked open, and an empty cell received him as the giant slung Leo inside by the chain with far too much loft than necessary. He landed on his back, air escaping his lungs for the second time in close succession. The iron bars slammed closed and the two giants gave their version of a laugh, which sounded more like two boars mating, as they walked away.

"Ahhh. Home sweet home." Leo didn't bother taking the bag off his head. Nor did he try and tug at his manacles like a novice prisoner would have done. He simply laid on his back, stretched out his legs, and took in the nothingness.

"Hey there."

Fuck around. Leo's hands shot up to shake off the mask; when they did the metal edges of his manacles clept the bridge of his nose. His eyes watered, he tensed but found no refuge from the flaring pain. Blinking tears away now, he put his back to the stone.

It was a typical cell. Four walls, three of which were iron bars, the inner wall solid concrete. He'd heard of the stone powder before but until he'd seen the vault, Leo would never have believed that with just a little water, the mixture could turn hard as any stone. There was an empty cell to his right. At least he thought it was empty. He couldn't see shit either way. On his left the voice called again.

"Sorry, didn't mean to startle you. It's been a while since I had a celly. Last one cried through the night so the guards buried their blades in him. That was before the giants took over though. Name's Jexler."

As Leo's vision adjusted, he took in the emaciated frame of his new neighbor. He had long, scraggly hair and sunken eyes. He leaned towards the iron bars for a better look at Leo, but kept a cautious distance.

Confident the man didn't pose an immediate threat, Leo relaxed. Imprisoned in the belly of the vault with a date with death on the horizon, Leo resigned to the fact that his options were limited and they were likely not going to improve anytime soon. Leo crept to the bars with a hushed voice. "Where do your loyalties lie, Jexler?"

"Down here, loyalty won't do you any good. Won't keep you fed or warm at night"—Jexler motioned to his cell door—"and sure as hell won't turn any locks."

"Listen, Jexler isn't it?" Leo regarded the candlelit hallway. "Have you seen any sta...." Leo peered at the man's hands, careful not to make the same mistake twice. Satisfied there were no star patterns, he went on. "Have you seen any starborn prisoners come in recently?" From the looks of Jexler he'd been down here quite a stint and their cells appeared to be closest to the entrance.

Jexler's face twisted in thought. He studied Leo

quizzically for a time then went on. "A man with questions ought to have a name."

Now it was Leo doing the pondering as the two men started their sizing-up of one another like prisoners do. "I'm Leo." He studied Jexler's reaction.

Jexler shuffled forward, pressing his head between the bars for a better look. His nose flexed as he sniffed and Leo leaned away. "Leo Rosewood huh? I thought you'd be taller."

Leo breathed a sigh of relief. "I get that a lot. Now tell me Jexler, have you seen any starborn prisoners down here?"

"You mean the sorcerers." Jexler motioned over his shoulder, down the length of the hall. "If you ask me, anyone dangerous enough to come in caged should have been put to the sword already. These Kimans like playing with fire. What interest you got in them anyways?"

"So they're down here then?" Leo peered once again down the hall. He imagined cells running its length but how far or how many he couldn't tell.

"Far as I know. 'Less there's another way out down the end of that hall." Jexler regarded the way Leo came in. "Only see the giants coming and going from there though."

"Good." Leo fingered the bolts and rivets on his manacles and scanned his cell only to find the usual suspects. A piss bucket, darkness, and silence. A burlap bag caught his eye. Looked like the same one that followed him in. "My weapons." Leo shuffled to the iron door and stretched his hands out through the bars. Even without the manacles limiting his reach, the bag was more than two arm-spans away. "Shit," he spat, slumping down to the floor.

Jexler padded over and sat down. The two men were shoulder to shoulder against the iron bars. "Maddening isn't it? A fighter like you must feel safe with his blades. Down here who wouldn't? And yet they're just beyond your reach. I can't imagine that was an accident. Surprised they didn't mount them on the wall for you. Little good your sword would do in a cell though. That should give you some peace."

Despite his best efforts, Leo resigned to muscling his manacles to no avail. Heaving from the effort, his throat scratched with a thirst that only compounded his problems.

"What were you wanting with the starborn anyways?" Jexler asked, ignoring Leo's futile attempt at escape. "They friends of yours?"

"Ha." Leo chuckled to himself. "Guys like me don't have friends. Just people who'd rather not get on my bad side." At least that's what Leo kept telling himself. Only way to truly test a friendship is to see who defends you when you're not around.

"Is that why you came here alone?"

Leo arched a knee and rested an elbow on it. To his right, Jexler did the same. "No. Poisoned my friends on the way here to spare them all this." Leo regarded their cells with his manacled hands. "It was a sleeping draught, you see. Didn't see any reason for them to get killed in all of this. All I needed to do was buy some time in Chaucer and I ended up down here."

"Buy some time for what?"

Leo was about to go on but something in Jexler's hand caught his eye. The candlelight angled just right and for the briefest of moments Leo thought he saw a blade in the man's hand. He shuffled away from the cage while Jexler hid his hand. "What was that?" No answer came. Jexler stood smiling. "In your hand. I saw something." Was it a blade, or was Leo's mind playing tricks on him?

Jexler held his empty palms up. "A blade? Don't be foolish."

On closer inspection, Jexler wasn't as rugged as Leo had first thought. Sure his hair was a matted mess but he wasn't near as dirty as one ought to be living in a dungeon. His clothes were tattered in places but weren't threadbare from hard use. Cotton and wool don't hold up very well against concrete and stone. Leo backed away trying to angle the light just right. "Let me see your hands."

Jexler advanced with a wry smile. He tapped the back of his right hand against the bars. A faint tapping sound ensued. *Tap, tap...tap, tap.* "Oh this?" He held up his hand so the light caught it. "This is hardly a blade. Just a harmless old ring."

Leo's mind swam to the front gates. Saul

Harrington's men nearly stripped him to flesh on his way in. No way they'd miss a ring on Jexler's hand. Harmless as it may be, metal rings weren't that common. It would also fetch more than a few good meals or strong drinks, which would be more than enough motive for the guards to take it.

"It's you isn't it?" Leo set his jaw. Jexler's wolfish grin widened. "Couldn't bare pocketing the Ring of Solomon for your little ruse, huh?"

"So you're in bed with the Zodans after all." Jexler whispered a word and the air shifted around him. Leo's vision blurred. When it returned, a perfect replica of Kano stood before him. "Was it Kano who sent you here?" The air shifted again and Nicolai appeared. "Or Nicolai?"

Leo sucked in a breath.

"What's wrong, Leo? Cat got your tongue?" He shifted into General Soberal. A spitting image in uniform, even his boots glistened in the candlelight.

"You bastard." Leo lunged for the shifter but his shoulders got caught in the bars.

"Careful now. You'll need the use of that shoulder and what little strength remains for Delbec tomorrow." Abaddon returned to his natural form. He flattened his crimson tunic and ran a hand through his greying hair. "Disguises work only as far as you can keep up with the lies. Which is why I prefer shifting into strangers. So tell me, Leo. What was your plan? To just stroll into my keep and free the Zodans?" Abaddon *tsk-tskd* as if scolding a child. "Whose bright idea was that?"

Before Leo could resort to cursing, a door creaked open and heavy feet started padding down the steps. Lyle was flanked by two giants, both of which carried oil lamps.

"There a problem, Master Lyle?" Abaddon asked, not breaking Leo's stare.

Sweat beaded on top of Lyle's glistening bald head. "The night watch say they heard something outside. Reported bursts of unnatural light and two of the Anakim are unaccounted for. They're scouring the area now but haven't found anything yet. I thought I sensed something earlier but it didn't last long. Thought it was you tapping into the else."

Abaddon twinged his fingers and his cell door clicked ajar and slammed open. "You've brought company after all," he said, passing out of his cell. "You two"—he pointed to the giants—"stay here and watch him. If he so much as sighs I want you to spear him through the bars. Don't you dare open his door. Understand?"

The giants snarled in unison as they took their posts. Abaddon swept up the steps with Lyle in toe. The door slammed shut behind them. One of the giants shuffled down the hall and returned with two spears. He handed one to the other and they regarded Leo with twin frowns.

CHAPTER

11

By the time they circled around the back side of the vault, Kano's legs throbbed from the effort and rooted in the ground when they stopped. He sucked in air like it were limited supply. He regarded the supply door Trion mentioned as their point of entry. It was an iron gate nestled in the stone just beyond the moat. Much like the front gate but built for business rather than to impress. A watchtower stood above the retracted drawbridge where guards shuffled in the lamplight. Kano pulled on Trion's gauntleted arm. "Would you look at that? Another guarded gate. I can't imagine how we'd ever have found it without you. And how do you propose we'll get in this side?"

Again Trion removed his helm and mopped his forehead with a steady hand. "I figured we could just try knocking."

"Silence." Boyce was in no mood. There were sentries running in packs all over the place now, behind the melodic baying of their hounds. "The time has come."

Something in Boyce's voice gave Kano pause. The thought of Liz and the others caged like animals in the armpit of the vault readied him for the task though.

Similar thoughts of Leo must have flooded Page's mind. Her face twisted into a snarl as she drew her sword and buried the tip in the dirt. "Time to lose these bangles." She twisted the band off her wrist and let it fall.

Kano followed suit. Before his bangle hit the ground, the else's energy flooded him with power. He felt a weightless vitality purge the pain from his veins and let out a gasp of ecstasy.

"Take these." Boyce handed his bangle to Trion. "We might need them again." Trion shook off his wristguard and replaced it with the three bangles. "How far is the dungeon from the back gate?"

"If we're talking left and right turns then you might get dizzy." Despite the jest, Trion didn't smile. On further inspection Kano realized Trion had the look of a man who'd seen his share of scrapes with death. He'd seen the same vacant stare on Leo just before the battle in Tamore.

A giant roared in the distance. An imaginary breeze sent a shiver up Kano's spine. Damn he hated giants. "Delbec," he seethed.

"Let's go." Boyce stepped off towards the moat. "Trion, stay behind me," he added over his shoulder.

Kano imagined they should be running at this point but Boyce ambled on methodically.

"We swimming?" Trion regarded the moat then his Kiman armor.

"Not quite." Boyce spread his arms and his eyes cast a blazing blue light. The minor stars on his left hand seemed to have multiplied since the last time Kano looked.

Ten, eleven, twelve... Kano wasn't done counting them when Boyce called his name.

"Kano, mind getting the gate?" Boyce asked. Kano nodded. "Page, take out the archers."

"Done and done." Page was already loosing starfire at the watchtower when the moat began to ripple and the water began to split.

Boyce ambled on leading the way down into the mushy bottom of the moat. The water parted into a turbulent wall on either side. "Ahem."

Kano shook himself into action with a ball of mystical matter in his right hand that grew larger and brighter as they went. The four minor stars on his left hand felt oddly exposed as Boyce sauntered on beside him. Before them, men screamed and the watchtower buckled as Page pelted it from below. A horn sounded three times from inside and Kano loosed his shot. The gate and the stonework beside it blasted away. "That should do it," he said, pleased with his work.

"And then some," Boyce clipped.

Kano's force was excessive. So much so that the stonework was still crumbling down into a nice pile of rubble which blocked their advance right where the gate used to be. "Ooops."

***

It didn't take long for the giant goalers to find a reason to start poking at Leo with their spears. What spurred them into action Leo couldn't say; must have been the way he carried on blinking and breathing.

One of the giants was missing a thumb on his right hand but he was deft enough with his spear. He snarled as he jabbed and his second thrust nearly hit pay dirt. Leo managed to limber around their killing instruments easily enough, hugging the back wall of his cell. The other giant narrowly avoided breaking the tip off his spear when he jabbed for Leo and struck the wall. He came to his senses after that and started working Leo towards the spear-tip of his thumbless companion.

Thumbless caught onto the plan quickly enough. When the two of them started timing their strikes together, Thumbless drew first blood, stabbing and twisting his way into Leo's right thigh. The tip pierced through his flesh and jarred his leg bones. Leo winced as the tip grated its way out of his leg. He parried the other spear with his hand and limped away.

A tremor ran through the walls and shook the ground at their feet. The giants ceased their attack and stared at each other. Leo took the opportunity to regard the ceiling and blessed it for not crashing down on him.

The giants exchanged words in their heathen tongue and Ten Fingers stomped up the stairs. Thumbless regarded Leo like a turd that wouldn't flush. He leaned against the cage and started jabbing once more.

The hurried thrusts came in bunches like Ole Thumbless had better things to do. Leo didn't much appreciate that. Or being stabbed in the damn thigh for that matter, which reminded him he was losing a lot of blood. Leo sidestepped the spear once more, latched onto it with both hands, and ran the length of his cell with it in hand. The shaft pried against the bars till it crackled and snapped in half.

Leo stomped on the wooden end and came away with a manageable-sized weapon of his own. "Come and get me."

Challenging a giant twice his size to mortal combat wasn't the brightest decision Leo had ever made. Desperate men usually have limited options. The keyring jingled in his hand then Thumbless set the key home, slung the door wide, and ducked to enter the cell. Leo instantly regretted it.

The cell shrank in size as Thumbless filled the room, blocking Leo's only chance of escape. The giant barreled forward and Leo did what any sensible woman would do. He drove the spear right between the giant's legs and rolled out from under his crushing weight. Thumbless wollered on the floor clutching his manhood and Leo left him to it, closing the cell door and taking the key with him.

He went straight for the burlap bag and dug out his weapons. There was no time to dawn his armor. Leo slung his sword over his back and took off down the hall with his hatchet and shield. "Michael...Nicolai." Nothing but empty cell after cell as he ran. He pressed on, "Nicolai!"

At the end of the hall Leo thought he heard a voice but couldn't see shit. He cursed himself for not bringing the giant's lantern.

"In here," the voice called again.

Dread washed over him when he realized the voice was coming from another floor. Whether above or below, he couldn't tell. "Shit." He sank to the ground in defeat.

"The cell on the right," a voice called again. This time from a woman.

Simple enough instructions but Leo wondered whose right she was talking about. Two cells sat vacant on opposite ends of the hall. Only one had the door locked. Leo observed it was also a great deal wider than all the others. He fished out his key. When it sank home he was rewarded with a click and the lock turned. At the back of the cell, Leo pulled open a wooden door. Were he given the chance to go back in time, he would never have opened that door.

**

A dim lamp burned at the back of the room. It wasn't the light that first caught Leo's attention but the torturous screams of child-bearing women. Their cries pierced and jostled his soul. Along both ends of the room, naked women squirmed in soil-stained beds, bound at the wrists and chained to the walls.

The girl closest to the door clenched her eyes shut when Leo met her gaze. She glistened with sweat. Open wounds oozed where her belly stretched beyond its breaking point.

When his shield and hatchet hit the ground, Leo realized he was staring with his mouth agape. He set his eyes on the floor and backed away.

"Leo," Nicolai called again. He pressed himself against the front of his cage but there was no urgency in his voice. Beside him, Liz, Ambrose, and Brielle sat in matching cages of their own. They looked on more expectantly. "They're the giant concubines," Nicolai explained. "Surrogate mothers if you will."

"There's no cure for the wicked," came a distant

voice yet she was caged right next to Nicolai. "Every last one of the giants needs to be purged from the earth." Her frosty glare met Leo. "Get me the fuck out of here and I'll kill them all. But not Abaddon. Oh, not right away at least. I'm going to take my time with him. Might even build him a cage of his own. Cut his arms and legs off so he'll have plenty of room." When Leo didn't move she continued. "Forgive me. Where are my manners? I'm Liz. You already know Nicolai. That's Brielle over there and Ambrose there." She tilted her head. "Now about this cage," she added, patting the bars.

Leo moved to Nicolai's cage and ran his sweaty hands along the dragonglass bars. "How do I get you out?"

"I've given that a lot of thought." Nicolai ran his hand across the glass-inlaid iron bars. At the top of each cage, just out of hands' reach from its occupant, rested a round piece of dragonglass the size of a human head. "I can see only one flaw in Borin's design. His handiwork was meant to keep us in, not others out. Otherwise we'd be hanging on display in Abaddon's throne room."

The concubines continued to squirm and squeal in their beds. The rattling of their chains, their pain-laden cries made Leo's skin crawl. "What are you suggesting?"

"Brute force might do. I'm glad you brought your hatchet."

Leo retrieved his hatchet and readied himself for

the work. The cries continued to echo in his head. The visions of their distress wouldn't go away even when he closed his eyes.

Nicolai pointed above his head. "Start with the...."

The round glass cracked on impact. Leo's third blow shattered it into a thousand tiny pieces but those cries continued to pry at his ears and scrape in his head. His hatchet showered Nicolai in a fountain of sparks when the blade bit into the metal bars. His mind wandered back to the concubines. Their wailing like a whistling teakettle in his ears.

"No!" Nicolai cried.

"Oh my God. Stop him," Brielle said with her hands to her chest.

The screaming shrilled in his ears. Leo hacked and hacked till sweat started to blur his vision. When he paused to wipe his brow, the back of his hand came away crimson. The world shifted into place and bloody beds filled his vision.

Again Leo dropped his hatchet, this time backing away from a headless concubine. His heel caught on something and rolled underfoot. When he looked down, a mangled arm reached out to him. He remembered cutting it off now. One of the concubines had held it up to block a blow.

Behind him something stirred and Leo spun on it. Nicolai must have managed to get out of his cage during the carnage. The starborn dressed Leo down like a demon stood before him.

Leo waited for the flash of light. Welcomed it. "Do it," he rasped. Nicolai held his gaze thoughtfully. Leo spread his arms. "Do it goddamnit!" he roared, spittle flying. It would only take a mere flick of the starborn's wrist and Leo had never been more ready to die.

Nicolai pointed a scolding finger at Leo. "I imagine your brother wouldn't approve of you using the Lord's name in vain. I'll not tolerate it in my presence either." He flicked his wrist and behind him dragonglass shattered. He turned, ripping at the air, and one by one the metal bars peeled back like the skin of a banana until the other starborn were freed. "Pick up your shield, Leo."

The shield vibrated when Leo strapped it on his arm. The gentle humming of a sorrow-filled song.

"So it's true." Ambrose regarded Leo quizzically. "He's a Bright Eye. That hatchet burned like a blade in the forge when he started hacking with it."

"Nothing gets past you." Brielle regarded Leo like she was about to ask a question then her eyes went wide.

"Get out of his mind, Brielle. He just saved your life, after all." Liz wiped the hatchet off with a bedsheet then stretched it out to Leo. "You might need this again."

Leo drew his sword instead. Something about the hatchet repulsed him now, a gift from old friends or not. "No. Leave it."

Liz and Nicolai exchanged looks. "Here,

Ambrose." Liz handed it out to Kano's former protégé. "Carry this. Careful not to fall on it, huh."

Ambrose latched onto it with finger in thumb, dangling it before him like it was venomous. He patted his cloak till he found a suitable pocket.

There was another collapse of stone on the floor above them and dust clouded the room.

Leo tensed. "That must be Page and the others. We have to go."

"Your sister's here?" Nicolai asked behind him. They were running now.

"Yes. She's starborn. With any luck Boyce and Kano should be with her. And a man named Trion."

Leo felt a tug on his shoulder. "Wait. What? Kano's here?" Liz bristled then wrinkled her brow. "You guys planned this?"

"Yes. It's a long story." The burlap sack caught his eye as they ran down the corridor. Leo halted to dig out his armor. "I was supposed to act as a decoy in Chaucer while they broke in here to free you. It didn't quite work out the way...."

There was a crash against the cage beside him. A giant arm wrapped around Leo's neck and drew him in against the iron bars. "Harrrr," Thumbless roared in his ear.

Leo felt the air escape his lungs. The veins in his neck bulged against the giant's muscled arm. There was a sound like a watermelon exploding and the arm around his neck went limp and fell away.

"Holy shit." Leo rasped for air on both knees.

"One down." Liz blew at her hand then wiped her nails clean with her cloak.

Leo sucked in a lungful of air and swallowed hard. "I forgot about that one."

"You're welcome. Guess that makes you and I square." Liz didn't smile. It was a matter of fact not a debate. She turned to Nicolai. "So what's the plan now?"

"Do you trust the Water Bearer?" Nicolai asked.

"Who?"

"Boyce."

"With my life." Leo's blood was still up. His hands fumbled with the straps and buckles of his armor. Ambrose moved in to lend a helping hand. "Why do you ask?"

"You say you were supposed to act as a decoy, did you not?" Leo nodded and Nicolai went on. "Why didn't Abaddon kill you on sight? I can think of no reason why he'd keep you alive."

"Yeah, well you'll have to excuse me but we don't have time to go over the fine details. In hindsight it might have been bat-shit crazy anyways but here we are." Leo cut into the burlap bag, dressed the wound on his thigh then headed for the stairs and stopped when there was no patter of feet behind him. "Look. Boyce has a book Abaddon's been looking for. He said it would be all the leverage I needed to get Abaddon to leave his nest."

Nicolai's eyes widened. "The Book of Baraqiel?"

"That's the one. Now can we go already?"

Liz moved to follow but Nicolai steadied her with his hand. "What?" Liz asked.

Nicolai dressed Leo with a suspicious gaze. "Where's the book, Leo?"

"Boyce has it."

Nicolai brushed his beard. The walls shook once more and the battle cries of men and giants echoed down the staircase.

"What is it, Nicolai?" Liz looked on the verge of leaving him behind. "We don't have time for this. Kano's up there fighting a whole damn army."

"The Ring of Solomon isn't just a ring. It's a key," Nicolai confessed. "A key to the Book of Baraqiel. The book holds forbidden knowledge. If Abaddon were to get his hands on it he could seize the power of the else for himself. He could strip our access and grant it to whomever he sees fit. His abilities would be limitless. He'd be"—Nicolai faltered—"like a god on earth."

Nicolai turned to Leo once more. "The book was locked long ago. A bright eye like you might have the ability to unlock the encryption runes long enough to read a few passages. Tell me Leo, has Boyce read any of the book?"

Leo hesitated. He suddenly felt like used meat. Not only had Boyce read the book, but he used Leo to do it while he slept in the dungeon. Then followed him around till the book's light burned out. But Boyce didn't stop there. The bastard recruited Page to win Leo's trust, and masterminded the whole scheme to break into the vault.

"You see what I'm getting at?" Nicolai added. "Boyce may be stronger than all of us put together now. And if he gets hold of the ring...."

Leo and Liz shared a look of horror. If Nicolai's suspicions were on target, Boyce was using all of them to get Abaddon's ring. He wanted to believe it weren't true, but the truth was he could only count the people he truly trusted on one hand, and Boyce wasn't one of them.

"Let's go. I've got to find my sister."

***

Strewn rubble blocked their path where the outer barbican collapsed. It wasn't Kano's finest hour. He was supposed to take the gate out, not the wall with it. The archers on what remained of the wall seemed to multiply and he heard a thundering charge of armored men at his back.

"Kano." Boyce was killing archers with one hand, his right a trembling fist held to his chest.

"What?" he clipped. Kano turned his back on the wall to slow the charging attack from behind. One of the hounds was first on scene, chewing up ground with reckless abandon. Ivory fangs salivating for the kill. Kano dispatched it with a flick of the wrist but took no pride in its last whimper. A hound like that lives only to please its master. It probably would have died a million deaths, each more agonizing than the last, to do so. "I'm kind of busy," Kano continued both hands at work now.

Boyce nodded. "When they get in the middle of that moat let me know."

Kano heard a loud clank just behind him. It sounded too much like an arrow on shield for his liking. He risked a glance over his shoulder and found Trion making himself useful. Kano was too busy to thank the man at the present though. "You really think that will work? After the Red Sea and all?"

"When their blood gets running, men have a way of forgetting history lessons," Boyce replied.

"We can't wait much longer." The urgency in Page's voice was rather discerning. When Kano regarded the wall his initial suspicions were correct. Their attackers were multiplying after all. "There must be a walkway up there that circles around to the front," she continued as more Kiman helms were closing in.

"Do it now." Were it daylight, Kano had no doubt he'd be able to see the whites of their eyes as the Kimans crossed the moat to wedge them against the rubble.

Boyce gasped. His shaking fist relaxed and the water closed in on itself.

Soldiers splashed and kicked in its depths. Clawing at one another for floatation. Those attackers who hadn't fallen victim to the drink readied their bows and

Kano took off running.

Boyce led the way blazing a trail through the rubble. Another moat lay on the other side of the outer wall. Its water black as oil. Placidly defiant against the gently breeze. Again the drawbridge was pulled up, and the arrows continued to rain down. Page sucked in a lungful of air and got back to work.

"Clever." Boyce knelt down to run a finger through the water.

Kano shouldered up to Page and went back to work. "What's the problem?"

"Oil." Boyce regarded the inner wall, where ground troops guarded the drawbridge. Many of them leaned on their swords in a mocking display of satisfaction like they owned the board and had twice as many pieces.

"Oil's got water in it, doesn't it?" This time it was Trion asking the questions. It was really all he could do besides hide under his shield.

"It's also flammable." Boyce regarded the drawbridge across from him. A wooden affair, drawn tight by pulley and chain. "They'll wait till we try and cross it then set it on fire. Once it starts burning I'll have little control of it."

"Lovely," Trion mocked. "You know what? I'm starting to wish I'd taken a few pulls from Leo's bottle last night." Another arrow twisted off his shield.

"What I'm about to do, might crack the else," Boyce said.

"Break it, crack it. Hell, grind it up and fertilize a

garden with it," Trion said. An arrow thudded into his shield and he raked away the shaft. "I ever tell you how much I hate archers?"

Kano didn't know what Boyce was going on about. Cracking the else? He'd never heard of such a thing. In fact, quite the opposite. When a starborn got too carried away, he burned out. "Do your worst," he said.

Boyce regarded the moat with silent contempt. "Lord help us all," he whispered. A shower of sparks whisked off his hands like he'd struck flint and steel. The oil caught and flames spread full circle around the keep. The instant inferno sucked the air right from Kano's lungs. His back felt like he was dipped in fire.

The archers paused to watch the show. Many of them clutching their chests in a fit of coughing as the smoke began an assault on their lungs. When Kano turned around, Boyce raised his arms. All around them the fiery oil leapt into the air, submerging the keep on all sides. Men cried out as the burning oil washed over them.

Kano cringed. Starache brought him to both knees and Page cried out beside him.

The moat smoldered on but Boyce wasn't finished. Another flick of his wrist and a cold wind blew. The Water Bearer's cloak billowed in the wind. The flames receded and the oil turned to sludge, then froze into black ice.

Kano watched Boyce stagger back; Trion caught him before he fell. "You definitely cracked something," the Guardian captain said. "I've got one question though. Why the hell am I dressed in red when you can do shit like that?" Trion steadied Boyce on his feet and tore off his Kiman tunic.

"Let's go." When Boyce regained his bearings he shuffled over to the moat, testing the surface with the tip of his boot. "The ice won't last long." He hurried across and they followed.

CHAPTER

12

Ten Fingers must have left the door ajar in his haste to check on the noise. Leo broke the threshold at full speed, tucked and rolled into a fighting stance expecting to meet a slew of attackers. There were none. In fact the only noise that greeted them were the frantic voices of Kiman soldiers running like hell had two feet and an appetite for man.

One of them favored his right arm. A dark liquid covered his torso, soiling his crimson tunic. He ran with his eyes clenched shut, knocking wall decorum from the hall as he went. By the time he shuffled blindly within striking distance, Leo shoulder-checked him to the ground. The soldier went down hard.

Leo stooped over him, and the man cried out for mercy. His face burned to the bone like he'd been tar and feathered. Upon further inspection Leo noticed the man's eyelids were cauterized in the closed position.

"Where are they?" Leo hissed. More soldiers fled past sharing similar afflictions. None of whom itched to challenge them.

The burned man tried to shuffle away using his better arm. Leo kicked it out from under him and the man wailed. "Please, please let me go," he cried. "He's coming!"

"Who's coming?"

"The angel of death. He wields fire and ice. He's come to kill us all." The soldier's voice trembled and once more he tried to shuffle away. Leo let him go.

"What do you make of it?" Leo asked the others.

"If the man's never seen a pissed-off starborn until now, I can see how he'd get the two confused," Liz said.

"No. It's Boyce the man speaks of." Nicolai stared past them. "His intentions are what unsettles me. We must get to the ring before he does."

"Didn't you possess the ring before?" Leo asked. "If it's so powerful, why did you end up caged with the others?"

Nicolai didn't flinch at the stabbing questions. "Abaddon and I have known each other a long time,

Leo. Would you be so quick to raise your hand against Juan had he turned astray?"

When Leo didn't answer Nicolai continued. "I'm afraid the next time we meet will be our last. The thought gives me no peace but there's no avoiding it any longer."

Leo didn't like all this talking when he had so much killing to do. Better it he that reaches Abaddon and his Giant army before his sister does. "C'mon. There's only one room in this keep big enough for Delbec to protect Abaddon."

The maze of halls had a dizzying effect. So much so that Leo started looking for a prisoner of his own to show him the way. He eyed his prize in a massive dining hall on the right. Tables and chairs where pushed to the side of the walls and a group of soldiers awaited them with spears at the ready.

"Leave one of them alive," Leo barked as he shouldered on.

There were flashes of light before Leo parried the first spear and his sword jarred off a shining helm. A shrill cry rang out from somewhere behind him. It sounded a lot like Brielle. He had no time to look back with steel flashing all around him. A spear thrust forward, Leo parried then slashed and his sword came away bloody.

"Giant!" Nicolai yelled.

There was a lack of men to kill at the end of Leo's blade. When he turned 'round, a double door he hadn't noticed before was wide open and more soldiers filled the hall. Ten Fingers led the charge. Something about the giant made the wound in Leo's thigh flare up again.

It struck Leo odd that the giant was without a weapon. His next observation through the fog of war was Liz stooping over something with a spear jutting out. It was Brielle.

Nicolai glowed like he'd been dipped in the sun. A very angry sun. Light radiated from the Zodan leader so bright and white that it blotched Leo's vision. The giant exploded like he were a glass jar that fell from a table. Ten Fingers was no more but Nicolai had only just begun.

More men started to fall and Leo took the opportunity to hit the deck so he wouldn't be one of them. After a time, he brushed himself off and walked over to the others. Liz held Brielle's lifeless body in her arms. Ambrose bent over the other side holding onto her hand. Tears streaming down his face.

A quick inventory and Leo found none of the soldiers living. Probably wasn't the best time to point fingers though. Instead, Leo busied himself taking a tour of the room starting with the double door the giant used to make entry. If Leo were a guessing man, that was the path that led to Abaddon's throne room.

The distraction of finding the right path didn't last long enough. When Leo joined the others, Nicolai was finishing the last lines of a prayer. Leo didn't know the girl. Up until a few minutes ago, he'd never seen Brielle before. And for that at least he was glad, otherwise he'd be just as stricken as Liz and Ambrose.

A part of Leo envied Brielle as her star started to call her home. She was leaving all the suffering of this world behind and onto a better place. Leo knew his heart had hardened. He'd cried so many tears of blood he felt hollowed-out inside. Then the concubines started reappearing in his head. Visions of them reaching out for mercy as he hacked them to pieces.

"We have to go." Leo shook himself back to reality and headed through the double doors. He didn't care whether or not they followed.

The double door spilled out into another hallway. This one lined with a red carpet. The vaulted passageway wide enough to give even Delbec room to swing a sword. He heard the starborn following close behind. Before them a massive door swung wide to receive them.

The Anakim where clad in dragonglass armor. They traded their clubs for swords. Their shields looked especially menacing as they reflected the firelight from the smoldering pit. Delbec towered behind them. The King of Giants also clad in armor, his golden clasped beard jutted beneath his helm.

"Welcome back, Leo." Abaddon remained seated on his throne. Lyle at his side. "I see you've brought company this time."

***

"It's over here. Just down this staircase." Trion paused when he saw the door ajar.

"What is it?" Page asked.

"The door's open. It's never open." He eased down the steps behind his sword.

"No. Allow me." Page pushed past Trion, taking the steps two at a time. She reached the bottom quick enough then snagged a lamp from the wall and started checking each of the cells. "They're all empty."

"This one's not. That shaft there belongs to a spear. And the pointy end's missing." Boyce entered the cell and knelt down to swipe a wet spot on the ground. His fingers came away bloody. "There was a struggle here." He continued to scan in the dark and found a pile of ash. "A giant fell."

Kano hurried down the hall. "Trion. Where would our friends be kept down here?"

"I don't know exactly. I've never been this far down."

"In here," Page called at the end of the hall, then disappeared into another room.

Kano limbered down the hall, Trion and Boyce close behind. By the time they made it into the cell, Kano heard Page gasp. They spilled into the chamber and for a time none of them said a word. It was a grizzly sight. Kano heard a dripping sound next to him where a swollen-bellied woman lie butchered in a bed. Blood ran down her arm and pooled on the ground below. What was even more unsettling to Kano was the cages strewn about. They were wrecked from the outside in.

"Who could have done something like this?" Tears welled in Page's eyes. She reached for the hand of one of the dead concubines. When the dead girl's wrist ran out of chain, Page swore an oath, grabbed hold of it by the links, and ripped it out of the wall. She reached over the body and broke the other chain as well. Page crossed the girl's hands over her stomach. Mangled as she was, at least now she looked at peace.

"They were concubines," Boyce declared. "I doubt any of them would have been able to survive birthing a giant." Boyce squatted to inspect the cages, rotating something in his hand.

"What have you got there?" Kano squatted next to him. "What do you make of it?"

"I'm not entirely sure." Boyce handed Kano a piece of dragonglass then ran his hand across the riveted metal bars. "I've no doubt this is where the other Zodans were kept. It looks as if a giant came in and wrecked the place."

Trion backed to the doorway. "This is the Bloody Rose's work."

Page crossed the room in a flash and Kano heard a slap that sent Trion reeling. "Mind your tongue or I'll cut it out of your foolish mouth. My brother would never do such a thing. Never."

Boyce took Page in his arms. "Easy now," he said.

"I'm sure Trion meant no ill of it."

Trion met Kano's gaze and they shared a knowing look. "It doesn't matter," Kano said. "What matters is that Liz and Nicolai, Brielle and Ambrose have been freed, and they can't be far. They're probably looking for us now."

"Either that, or they're headed for Abaddon." Boyce detached himself from Page and pushed past the door. "If that's the case, they're going to need a lot of help. Come now. Let's finish this."

***

Leo watched Nicolai walk to the forefront of the star-patterned platform where the flames thirsted for flesh. While the enemy eyed Nicolai, Leo took the opportunity to gauge the distance. If he ran and jumped he might be able to catch one of the giants unaware but he'd have to strike fast. His only other option was to take the stairs to his right that would lead him along the wall to the giants. That was a lot more distance to cover but he'd avoid being cooked to death should he not make the leap across.

"You've risked a lot for nothing, Abaddon. Your blasphemy is too great to escape now," Nicolai said. "For many years I wished you'd find the folly of your ways. Yet you didn't and here we are. Let neither of us hold any punches this time."

"Ha!" Abaddon shifted in his seat. "You dare to

come into my halls and cast judgment on me? Enough talk. King Delbec, if you would please."

Leo felt the flames heat his boots when he leapt, his sword raised high. His golden shield hummed as he crossed the distance yet he felt like he was floating in slow motion. At the apex of his jump, he was eye to eye with an Anakim. He saw the whites of the giant's eyes widen. The giant's shield slowly rising up to push Leo into the flames. Leo's strike was well timed and well placed. His sword's only resistance was the giant's muscled neck yet even it wavered under the blow until his sword jarred against the links of its spine.

The Bloody Rose crashed into the giant and they both fell. Leo at least had the peace of mind to roll aside and avoid being crushed or pinned to the ground. When he rolled away a sword flashed past him and stuck the ground in a shower of sparks that tremored into his boot and up his feet. As the other giants closed in his plan felt suddenly half-baked. Their swords flashed as they clamored over one another trying to cleave Leo's head off. He tucked and rolled again, this time between the legs of a stomping giant, then ran like hell.

A hand clasped him on the shoulder and Leo's boots were churning in midair without purchase. Out of options, he sank his teeth into the meaty hand that bound him. There was a groan in his ear as the hand recoiled. Leo staggered back to his feet just in time to meet the wall. His grace had left him long ago and he splatted against it like a blind man running.

He bounced off the wall and his feet kept moving; the great hall shifted back into place around him. Delbec towered like the chamber was built around him. He swung his great sword towards Nicolai with reckless abandon. Even the Anakim shuffled out of his wrath. Nicolai's hands twinged and Delbec staggered from an invisible blow. The golden giant crashed onto the winding staircase with his shield raised before him.

Ambrose ran to Nicolai's side. Together they held back the Anakim with a hailstorm of starfire.

Leo saw a mighty fist swing towards him. He raised his shield just in time to blunt the impact yet he was hurled through the air nonetheless. When he landed, Liz hovered over him. There was stillness in her eyes like clouds rolling in before the storm. And it did.

"Al-Tarf," she whispered, baring her teeth. If Leo hadn't landed at her feet, he wouldn't have heard it more than two feet away. But as she spoke a funnel of air bellowed around her. Her cold eyes regarded Leo and he thought of playing dead for a moment. "Get up," she called to him. By no power of his own, Leo rose in the air and landed gently on his feet.

"Got any fight left in you?" Liz asked. Her divine voice echoed in Leo's ears like a rushing wind.

He felt her strength surround him, rejuvenating. "I'm still alive aren't I?"

"Good," she replied. "I need you to slay the golden giant. Do it now."

Leo regarded Delbec who rose back to his feet, shuffling up the staircase. His mighty shield marred by the starborn assault but holding true.

"And just how..." Somewhere along the line, doubt crept into his bones and he wondered when it had happened. He shook himself back to the present cursing his wandering mind. "Fuck it. Guess that's what I came for, isn't it?" He rotated his head, rewarded by the familiar sound of his neck shifting back into place.

Liz nodded with a wink. She seemed to tower over him now as the wind circled around her.

Nicolai and Ambrose were dug-in on the platform so Leo sprinted along the wall. His movement didn't go unnoticed and he was met by a giant before he could round the firepit headed for the staircase.

The giant ran to meet him with his sword reared back. Leo raised his shield to deflect the blow. Experience had taught him not to take his eyes off the incoming sword. How else would he know where to shift his shield? As the blade came down Leo readied himself for the jarring impact. To his surprise the sword was swept from the giant's grip like an invisible hand twisted the giant's arm beyond the breaking point.

The giant wailed, wrought with pain. Leo took the opportunity to stab the fucker right in the nuts. The giant dropped to both knees clutching his manhood. Leo wasted no time booting the bastard into the firepit.

It wasn't until Leo hit the first of the steps that he realized there was a funnel whisking around him.

Delbec's sword came down like Thor's hammer and Leo knew it would splinter his bones, shield or not.

Liz's swirling cloud of armor held true and Delbec's blow was thrust aside and lodged into the flaming rail. Leo's sword swept down stabbing through the arch of Delbec's right foot. When the giant roared, the chamber shook. Leo tugged to free his blade but it wouldn't give.

Liz's guardian wind started to fade. At the front of the hall, she trembled onto a knee. Her face paled, neck straining to hold her head upright.

Delbec swiped at Leo, wrapping his hands around the golden shield to tear it away but Leo's arm was fastened within. Delbec lifted him up by the shield and cast him high into the air. Leo's armor crunched into the ceiling then he landed on the second-floor balcony where he stirred no more.

Nicolai's blinding white shadow returned and he loosed a magic that left him greyed like a withering plant. Delbec didn't have time to reach for his shield. He roared one last time and the hall shook when he fell.

Only two Anakim remained. Side by side they backed up the staircase.

"That was impressive, Nicolai." Abaddon rose from his seat for the first time. Lyle stood at his side, a glowing orb in his hand. "And Liz, that thing you did with your wind." Abaddon descended one slow step at a time. His hand seethed against the flaming rail yet he showed no sign of burning. "What's wrong, Nicolai?

You look a little pale." He laughed; Lyle chuckled along at his side.

"To hell with you." Ambrose's hands twinged with bad intentions. Abaddon countered it with a scowl and a flick of the wrist that sent Ambrose reeling into the air. He smashed and planted against the back wall like he were pinned on a dart board. The back of his head cracked and his limbs went limp.

Abaddon twinged his fingers and Ambrose's lifeless body moved to the rhythm like a hand puppet.

"No!" Nicolai cried. Scraping the bottom of the well, he loosed all the magic he could muster towards Abaddon.

Lyle's mystical orb radiated with light in his hand. From it a bubble shield developed and enveloped Abaddon and Lyle safely within. Nicolai's attack was absorbed by the wall like a ripple in the water.

"That should about do it," Abaddon said, closing his hand and cutting Ambrose's strings. Ambrose fell to the ground with a bone-breaking crunch.

Blood streamed from Nicolai's nose. Burned-out, he doubled over wilting to the ground.

Only Liz remained, her legs trembling to carry her weight. She limped forward onto the platform, chin high in defiance. "I've no words that might curse the two of you and do any justice." She spat into the fire at her feet.

"I have a few." Boyce strode through the doorway twisting the bangle from his wrist. Page, Kano, and

Trion at his heels. Kano ran to Liz and wrapped an arm around her waist, shuffling her out of the way. "Trion, get Nicolai," Kano ordered. Trion threw his head under the Zodan leader's arm, wrapped a hand around his waist, and carried him off.

"Would you look at this, Lyle. All the starborn under one roof." Abaddon clasped his hands and smiled. "Ah, Master Kano. I was beginning to wonder when you'd show up. And you there"—he nodded towards Page—"you must be Leo's sister." He regarded Trion unimpressed and then moved to Boyce. "And the mighty Water Bearer returned at last." His face hardened. "Tell me, Boyce, have you reconsidered my offer, or have you cast your fate with this pitiful lot?"

On the balcony overlooking the hall, Leo stirred to life. He opened his eyes and the cold concrete floor greeted him. A sharp pain writhed in his swollen forearm where the straps of his shield latched on. He freed himself from the shield with an effort and rolled onto his back. He tried to flex his left hand but it didn't respond. If it hadn't hurt so damn much he could easily imagine it had been hacked off at the elbow for all the use it was to him now.

"What's he talking about, Boyce?" Page craned her head, clutching her sword with bad intentions. "And where's Leo?"

"Nothing." Boyce regarded the bubble shield 'round Lyle and Abaddon. "Now's not the time to play catch-up."

"Now, now Boyce. There's always time to build alliances." Abaddon descended two more steps and paused where the railing had been smashed by Delbec's sword. The golden giant looked almost at peace where he'd slid to rest at the bottom of the staircase. "I'm afraid your brother has been slain by the King of the Giants. It was an epic battle yet it like all who've fallen here tonight will be forgotten. There need not be any more death in this room. Pledge your allegiance to my rule and we shall have peace. Otherwise all of you will die."

Leo dragged himself to the rail. He saw Page and Boyce in a whispered exchange. Abaddon and Lyle were surrounded by some sort of mystical dome near the foot of the left staircase. Two Anakim remained hovering over Delbec's lifeless form. Ambrose lie crumpled on the ground, his legs folded unnaturally under him in a pool of what looked to be his own blood. Beside him, Kano held Liz in his arms.

Leo saw Trion shielding Nicolai's lifeless form in a corner. Like a fly on the wall, the Guardian captain peered over his shield, locked eyes with Leo then diverted his knowing gaze.

The silence lasted only as long as it took Kano to 'port over to Ambrose's crumpled form, grab hold of the hatchet beside him, then 'port up the stairs to do some cleaving. Kano's blood was up but he hadn't lost all his wits. He stopped just shy of the shield-wall, reared back and crow-hopped through the wall, and sent the hatchet flying. Had Kano done any training at all with the Antucha-whahs it would have been a killing blow. As it was, the hatchet missed Lyle by an arm's length and clattered out of view.

Leo learned two things in the blink of an eye. The shield-wall repelled sorcery and appeared to be passable on foot. Otherwise Kano would have 'ported right next to Lyle and chopped off his head. Lyle and his bubble shield had to be taken out if they had any hope of getting to Abaddon.

Kano stepped out of the bubble and 'ported away, narrowly avoiding Abaddon's reign of terror that scourged the steps behind him. Page lunged into the Anakim and once again the sound of steel on steel echoed through the hall. Boyce regarded Leo for the first time with a subtle nod. Leo felt a tingling sense of urgency ripple through his veins as he pushed himself upright with one arm.

An invisible force sent him reeling back to the ground when Boyce and Abaddon squared off.

Leo patted his hip where his hatchet should have been. Only an empty scabbard crossed his back. "Shit," he fumed, searching in a panic. Even if his shield were able to pass Lyle's defensive wall, it would do little good in killing the Conjurer.

Boyce staggered back; his urgent eyes found Leo once more. Leo froze, rooted in helplessness. Only then did he remember the dragonglass dagger tucked into his boot.

"Oh thank God," he mouthed, wrapping his hand around the bone handle. He staggered off at a lame-footed pace. Below him one of the last two Anakim fell. The other hacked into Page and she backpedaled away. Leo picked up his pace rounding the square balcony. The throne just a few steps away now. His Kotian target thirty feet below that. Leo rounded the throne clutching at the handrail for support. When the flaming rail scourged his right hand he nearly flung the dagger away.

There was a patter of footsteps behind him. Before Leo could turn, cold metal dug into his back and twisted into his kidney. "Gah," he gasped, reaching for the rail once more. This time his arm couldn't hold his weight and he collapsed onto the burning rail.

Berinon lost the handle of his dagger and backed away empty-handed. By the bewildered look on his face, Leo gathered the Light Priest must not have been accustomed to sharp work or he would have had the common sense to retain his own blade.

The Bloody Rose took a haggard step forward. With a grimace he bit down on the dragonglass blade, reached 'round and dug Berinon's dagger from his back. There was a sucking sound when the blade pulled free. Leo regarded the bloody blade then pointed it at his assailant. "You'll die for that." Leo meant every word but they wrenched his stomach on the way out.

"Dear God." Berinon splayed his hands then tripped over the length of his robe as he backed away.

The Bloody Rose wasted no time driving the blade into Berinon's head. Once, twice, the third time he left it there and the Light Priest died looking at the hilt buried between his eyes.

Blood poured from his wounded back; the scent doubled his heartbeat. Warm and sticky as it filled his trousers. It hadn't let up much in his thigh either and he was running short of supply. Used up like a broken blade, Leo rasped for air but his lungs spasmed and he choked like he were submerged in water. He clutched the dragonglass dagger then labored down the staircase. His eyes fixed on the back of Lyle's glistening head as he passed through the bubble shield.

Leo's breathing shallowed but the Bloody Rose had work to do. He lurched forward wheezing and bleeding. Abaddon's attention rested on Boyce as the two starborn locked horns, Lyle on the other hand, turned just in time to catch the point of the dagger right where his Adam's apple swallowed in fear. Lyle's orb bounced down the staircase and he clutched the hole in his neck on the way to the ground. The Bloody Rose was a veteran at red work and this time was no different. He pulled the dagger from Lyle's neck and inspected the blade. When it came away in one piece he broke it off in Abaddon's back.

The last thing Leo remembered as he fell was a flash of steel and the sound of something rolling down the steps. Then Page leaning over him, tears streaming down her cheeks. Her hands felt warm on his.

"No! Leo don't go!" she cried, burying her head into his chest.

"It's okay, sister. I'm ready as I'll ever be." Leo shivered. Smiling weakly, he squeezed Page's hand one last time. "I'll see you on the other side." He closed his heavy eyes. A gentle breeze carried him away.

***

They stayed in the broken hall until Nicolai and Ambrose were called home by their stars. Liz felt hollow inside as she stood there next to Kano watching their companions rise into the light. Kano was rigid trying to hold it together beside her; Liz had no words to console him. She turned away but the fallen were strewn all around the hall. Page hadn't left Leo's side—she snarled like a feral cat when Trion attempted to pay his condolences.

"Bar the door," Liz barked to Trion. "This isn't over yet. We still have to find a way out."

She knelt down on the other side of Leo. "Kano, get his shield. We'll carry him out on it. We owe him that much. And fetch his weapons too." Kano nodded and started his search. Liz spied Boyce hovering over the stains Abaddon and Lyle had left behind. The Water Bearer had the Ring of Solomon and the Book of Baraqiel now and Liz was too weak to challenge him.

Page brushed a hand through Leo's hair, planted a gentle kiss on his forehead. "I keep hoping he'll wake up." Her trembled the words out, there was a glint of iron in her eyes like she'd already started building a wall around the pain.

Liz regarded Leo's stricken form. "People like your brother can live a thousand years and yet their deaths always come too soon."

Kano returned with Leo's shield, hatchet, and sword. He set them down carefully and darted off. He returned with two Kiman standards in his hands, ripped off the banners, and tossed them into the smoldering pit. "We can make a stretcher to carry him out." He started fingering the buttons of his tattered cloak.

"No. We'll use mine." Boyce shrugged his cloak off and Liz noticed the leather satchel still slung over his shoulder. She also noticed the ring on his left hand. His knees cracked and popped when he bent over the poles to tie the knots. Liz noticed his hair had faded from grey to white. The lines and wrinkles had stretched and eroded deeper into his face.

"They're coming," Trion called from the door. Liz shook Boyce's aging presence from her head and heard a commotion on the other side of the door. The cries of men drew closer and the door bowed on impact, rattling at the hinges.

"Let's get him up." Boyce grabbed hold of Leo's shoulders and Kano took him by the ankles. Page lay the shield down then they situated her brother on top of it, his sword and hatchet across his chest. Kano shook off his cloak and fastened it over top the warrior king.

"Liz." The sound of her name drew her alarm from the door. Boyce had the Book of Baraqiel stretched out towards her in his hand. "Take this," he said, waving it once more until she did. He twisted the ring from his hand and pressed it into Page's. "And you take this." He pointed up and over the double staircase that led to Abaddon's throne. "There's a door up there. It has to lead out somewhere. Go now." The Water Bearer squared off on the door.

Page made a fist around the ring then drew her sword. "No. I won't leave you."

"Damnit woman, I said get out of here. All of you. Now!" Boyce shoved Page along. Kano grabbed one end of the stretcher and Trion hurried over to gather up the other end.

Liz wrapped an arm around Page, trying to pull her along. "C'mon, we have to get Leo and the mortal instruments out of here." Liz tugged at Page once more but made no progress. It was a hopeless task and she knew it. Like a dog who'd rather starve on watch than leave his fallen companion. Liz turned to Boyce. "I was wrong about you, Water Bearer. Thought you might take the ring and run." She flattened her cloak then brushed a strand of hair behind her ear. "If she's staying with you, I am too."

"Well that makes, three of us." Kano set down his end of the stretcher.

"Four." Trion drew his sword.

"Ha!" Page rested her blade on top of her fallen

brother then drew his hatchet and sword. "I pity the man behind that door."

The door rattled once more but showed no signs of giving. "Let's give them a hand, shall we?" Boyce flicked his hand and the double doors broke away at the hinges.

Liz took a deep breath to steady her nerves. The door clattered into oblivion and a bear of a man appeared on the other side with the biggest sword she'd ever seen. Something fleshy dangled from a length of leather around his neck. Liz bit back bile when she realized it was a human tongue. Page was the first to greet him and their swords rung together. Trion leapt forward with his sword raised then halted in front of a baldheaded brute wearing an eyepatch.

"Friendlies!" Kano shouted.

Page and the brute's swords crossed again, neither giving ground. Another flurry of strikes and their blades pressed against the other chest to chest.

"Juan?" Page exclaimed, pressing the hatchet into the meaty part of the man's neck.

The brute craned down at her. "Page?"

"Where's Leo?" a hard-bodied blade of a woman asked, swaying forward spattered in blood. She pushed past Boyce and Liz. "I'm going to castrate that sonof...." Natalie's short sword clattered to the ground. She followed it. "It can't be. No. It can't be." She drew back Kano's cloak then buried her head in Leo's chest. "No!"

A second sword clattered to the ground. Juan

staggered then clanked to his knees like he'd suffered a wound. "Leo," he breathed, barely a whisper. He settled his trembling palm on Leo's forehead. "We were supposed to shoulder through the last door together."

***

Juan, Mandy, Bruce, and Natalie carried Leo from the vault. The fallen King of Veronia's head rested upon his battered golden shield. His weapons crossed at his chest.

Behind them followed Trion and all that remained of the twelve. Page maintained a distant look in her eyes and wouldn't or couldn't speak of the loss of her brother. Boyce padded along beside her, his hand resting on the Book of Baraqiel just recently returned to his satchel. Page had given him the Ring of Solomon too. Said she wanted nothing to do with magic anymore. In the end Liz took the ring. She followed behind them next to Kano who carried the conjuring orb.

Leo's kingsguard had not been idle after they woke. Betrayed as though they might have felt, they spurred forth to Indigo rousing a formidable militia along the way to save their king. The Kiman soldiers who had not been slain tore off their red cloaks and pledged allegiance once again to Veronia. None of them could have foreseen that three kings had died before the sun rose.

As the procession passed over the Indigo Bridge, men and women on both sides paused to watch it go like a wrinkle in time. A farmer offered a cart and two of his best horses to carry forth their beloved king but Juan wouldn't have it. The kingsguard would carry their king all the way to Tamore, where the High Priest could say the final words. "It's what Leo would have wanted," Juan said.

What Juan hadn't expected was that by the time they made it to Tamore their procession had grown more than two miles long and in their wake all of Veronia wept. Abigail, the widowed mayor of Tamore, rode out to meet them. In the distance Juan met her gaze and her smile twisted into sorrow. She was the first to dismount and bend the knee as they passed but not the last. By the time they made it to Tamore's village square, only the High Priest was left standing.

Page rushed into Jewel's arms and the two held each other. The kingsguard set Leo down carefully and stepped aside.

"Our king returns victorious for the last time." Juan had prepared his words for days and yet he barely managed to croak them out. "He lived well and died well."

Jewel leaned heavily on his staff. He bent over top Leo and kissed his forehead.

"Suffer no longer, my brother. May your restless soul find peace at last. Know that your heart is the legacy you've left behind, not your sword. And with it

Veronia will rebuild. Stronger than ever before."

FROM THE AUTHOR

I'd like to express my sincerest appreciation for taking the time out of your busy lives to delve into *The Veronian Archives* with me. As an avid reader myself, I know just how tricky finding interesting books can be. Taking the time to read one cover-to-cover is an investment of what precious little time we have and because we are all racing against the clock, our reading lists are usually longer than we'll ever be able to complete. This poses a huge hurdle for relatively new authors, specifically those with enough respect for the craft and the reader to get their books professionally edited, which is quite expensive.

For me, writing is a labor of love but it doesn't pay the bills. Not yet anyway. By the time this book is published, I will have spent well over seven hundred hours writing it alone. Not to mention the time and costs of editing, marketing, and/or targeting an audience to get the book in your hands.

My plea to you is this: if you enjoyed this or any of my other books, if it was worth your time in reading it, please take a few more moments to let it be known. The easiest way to do so is by reviewing it on Amazon. Reviews are the lifeblood of a book's success. Without them it is hard to justify the immense amount of time and effort it takes to write and publish this not-so-profitable endeavor of writing fiction/fantasy.

ABOUT THE AUTHOR

Daniel L Welch is a fantasy/fiction author. For the past decade he's supported his reading and writing habits by working full-time as a Criminal Investigator. Daniel lives in the hills of Green Country Oklahoma where he divides his time between boyfriending, splitting wood, fishing, reading, writing, working, and taking care of his fourteen-year-old Chihuahua, Taco (co-author).